D.C. Ode

Beloved Villain – You c

D.C. ODESZA

beloved villain

You can't run from me

Novel

Translation by S. Marshall

everlove by PIPER

More about our authors and books:
www.everlove-verlag.de

ISBN 978-3-492-06603-7

Title of the original German edition:
»Beloved Villain – You can't run from me«, 2024 by everlove,
an imprint of Piper Verlag GmbH, Munich

Georgenstraße 4, 80799 München
For direct contact and questions about the
product, please contact: *info@piper.de*
Editor: Sarah Rimmington
Typesetting based on a CSS layout
by digital publishing competence (Munich)
with abavo vlow (Buchloe)
Printed by ScandBook in Lithuania
Printed in the EU

Dear Readers,

This dark romance is not a novel for minors. The story is not intended to be read by people who are not able to tell fiction from reality.

Violence is not glamorised in this novel, but there are scenes that contain violence.

The story is unfailingly dark, illicit, exciting, and seriously spicy. Anyone who is after a nice escapist love story should look elsewhere.

Every line will challenge you. Every scene will give you goosebumps and shock you.

Even if it doesn't seem like it at first, a love story unfolds over the course of the two books in this series.

I hope you read this letter carefully, to make sure you don't misunderstand anything, and I'd ask you to please decide for yourselves whether this book is right for you.

I'd now like to wish you an unforgettable read. Take care of yourselves and keep your wits about you, because some scenes will put you to the test.

Except for a few places, I don't use contraception in my novels – but this does not mean it isn't important in real life! Unfortunately, readers confuse fiction with reality more often than I had expected.

Cordialement!

♥

Odesza

Dear Readers,

This book contains potentially triggering content. To ensure you have the best possible reading experience, you will find a content warning on page 281.

Your *everlove*-Team

For my demon,
who showed me the dark,
but also the way to the light.

Everyone should have a demon by their side.

CHAPTER 1

Nuria

"Run! Run faster!"
Pure determination to kill
glints in his jet-black eyes.
If I don't run, I know
he'll kill me!

As cool fingers caress my throat, and lips leave a tingling breath on my neck, I stand, frozen, in the middle of the crowd.

He is here.

I turn around abruptly, but there is no one behind me. No dark figure standing behind me, face hidden under a hood, lips curled into a withering smile.

Yet my heart is racing as if I've been running from something. I seem to hear it beating, although I'm in the middle of the Crystal Passion nightclub dancefloor, with strobe lights overloading my retina, drunken people all around me, laughing, screaming, dancing, and smoke drifting among the clubbers.

Having turned, I reach under my ponytail to the place on my neck where I felt his fingers. It's still throbbing.

"Nuria," Rhea calls, and is then swallowed by a veil of smoke. I can just make out her fleeting silhouette in the bright strobing light. But before I can reach out my hand to her, someone grabs my arm and pulls me deeper into the crowd.

I blink repeatedly, trying to see through the fog, then collide with a firm chest and have to crane my neck to look the person in the face. But there is no face to be seen. I can only see white runes glowing against pure darkness.

Confused, I push myself away. The techno beat hammers loudly in my ears.

Although I choke out a "no", the person won't release my hand. Clothed entirely in black, like a demon who has entered the club through the gates of Hell, he looms tall and powerful before me, his hair concealed by a hood, his eyes barely visible.

This could be my moment, my chance to unmask him. To find out who it is that has been shadowing me for weeks, like a ghost. Or is he just a normal clubber? It's Halloween, so almost everyone is in costume or wearing a mask.

I jerk myself free from his grip and lurch backwards, crashing into the guy behind me, practically falling into his arms, and getting drenched in his Guinness. Shit!

The alcohol soaks my whole back – some is absorbed by my black corset and some trickles down my spine to my miniskirt, underneath which I'm wearing tights patterned with black roses and rhinestones.

"Sorry," I say, before the guy, who's daubed with fake blood, even has a chance to size me up. As his drunken eyes bury themselves in my cleavage, a dark hand encircles the throat of the stranger in front of me. Another encircles my waist.

The figure behind me shoves the guy in front of me, hard, into the dancing crowd. *It really is him. Demon. My stalker.*

"Shit, dammit. What... What... are you doing here?" I ask, trying to loosen the fingers around my stomach. But they drill themselves possessively ever deeper into my midriff.

"Do you want to go to him?" he murmurs into my ear. "Or disappear into the darkness with me?"

What darkness? There's no way I'm going with him. Alone, I would be completely at his mercy. That would be virtual suicide.

Suddenly the lights go out. The music falls silent, and the world briefly stands still. A power cut. *What the hell...?*

"Tell me." His breath caresses my ear.

"I don't want either of those things."

A dark laugh surges into my ears. "Then I will decide for you."

Before I can work out what he intends to do, he lifts me up, carrying me in his arms, and cleaves a path through the crowd as though he can see in the dark like a wolf.

"Dammit, put me down. I can walk for myself."

"And end up in someone else's hands? No."

"The last thing I want is to be in your hands." Although I have heard his voice a few times before and know how sonorous and deep it is, it still gives me goosebumps. I writhe and call out for Rhea. But panic has broken out among the clubbers, who are blind and jumpy, and all shouting out names, and my screams are lost in the noise.

"You don't get to decide for me. Let me go. Leave me alone, Demon!"

I notice him deflect a heavy blow, preventing it from landing on me. Without warning, he releases me, letting me go, and the soles of my thigh-high boots touch solid ground.

Since when did he start following my instructions? A strange feeling spreads through my chest. I am confused and somehow disappointed when he does what I ask. I had somehow assumed he wouldn't make it so easy for me and would tease me like he usually does.

I turn to him in surprise. The only thing I can make out in the suffocating darkness are the glowing runes painted on his face, which is otherwise shrouded in darkness.

"Run!" he orders.

"What?" I ask, confused.

"Run, because when I catch you next time I won't be so merciful and you'll belong to me."

There won't be a next time because I will – no, I must – be free of him. I'm leaving Barcelona tomorrow. For a very long time. I need distance from him, from my family, from this life.

"RUN!" he yells, his threatening command piercing me to the core and startling other clubbers. Then they follow his instruction and run. As though a fire had broken out.

His command makes me jump, and then I turn and run, too. Holding my arms out in front of me to avoid bumping into other people and careering blindly through the crowd. Towards the exit on my right, by the bar. I am carried along by the current of agitated people.

"This is the way out!"

"The exit's over there!"

"I have to get out of here!"

"Help!"

"Switch the bloody lights back on!"

I hear different voices all around me. I move further into the crowd, and like the others get my smartphone out of my bag and use the light from the torch to try to make out which way to go. A vast crowd has gathered by the black doors, over which a red exit sign is glowing. I scan the panicked faces of witches, devils, and pumpkin monsters, but I can't see Rhea. She's wearing a striking white wig and a crown of bones on her head. Her face is painted white, with pitch-black eye sockets, as though she were crying black tears. She ought to stand out in the crowd. Where is she?

"Rhea!" I call her name again and look around. Someone bangs my upper arm with their elbow, someone else treads on my foot. My back is still sticky from the Guinness. I didn't think my last night would be like this.

I can't leave the nightclub without my friend.

Run! – my stalker's command pursues me. No, dammit. Right now, this isn't any kind of game. He has never yet seriously hurt me or injured me. If I don't follow his instructions he probably won't punish me. I hope. If he does... but I can't think about that now. I have to find Rhea. I'm not leaving the club without her.

So I decide to turn back, pushing past all the people thronging towards the exit.

"Rhea!" I call her name over and over and keep looking for her. For her, and for Demon, too, who has been toying with me for months. The light runes should be easy to spot in the dark. But all I can see are strange faces and masks.

"RHEA! Dammit, where are you?"

"Everyone stay calm!" someone shouts over the crowd. "Don't panic! It's just a power cut! Everything's under control!"

You've got to wonder why there's been a power cut. I've never experienced anything like this in a club. I can't help suspecting that Demon might be behind it. Demon, who is somewhere in the darkness and will definitely be watching me. He'll be enjoying this game, for sure. My stalker is sick!

I snake past more people, and the beam of my phone torch catches a flash of bright white hair in the corner below the DJ booth. As I get closer I can see my friend making out with a guy in an alcove. She can't be serious!

While most people are losing it and I am worrying about her, she's taking advantage of the opportunity and getting it on with some random guy. Anger rises in me as I approach. I don't want to know where her hands are under the guy's costume. When I am only a few metres away from her, the lights and music snap back on. I look up at the booth in surprise. Behind it is a screen showing a 3D animation of Lilith dancing with the devil.

"The party's back on!" announces the DJ. The clubbers stream back onto the dance floor as though nothing has happened. Fog drifts eerily between the costumed figures.

I slowly lower my phone torch, and just then it vibrates. A message from an unknown number flickers on the display.

You didn't even try, little rose.

As I finish reading I feel a hand on my left shoulder. I look behind me and see Demon. *Fuck*!

Thousands of emotions flood through my body at his mere touch. Fear at the words he has written, a thrill and curiosity at the sight of his face shrouded in shadow and illuminated by pulsing red and blue lights.

If there's one thing I've learnt in the last few weeks, it's that he never makes empty threats.

I clench my hand into a fist, then twist skilfully out of his grip and aim a powerful blow at him. He needs to leave me alone. Or tell me who he is. What he wants from me.

He knocks my arm out of the air before my fist connects with his face. His reflexes are unbelievably, frighteningly quick. He doesn't manage to grab my arm, so I turn around quickly and flee into the crowd. At that same moment I hear Rhea calling my name. Has she seen me now?

"Nuria! Where are you going?"

I look sideways at her briefly as I channel my way through the crowd, colliding with people repeatedly, apologising hastily, and keeping on running. *I want to shake Demon off. I must.* Because my shadow is gradually gaining more control over my life. So far he hasn't hurt me. But I know from news reports that stalkers usually murder their victims in the end. Especially when they don't get what they want: the person they're obsessed with.

I manoeuvre my way nimbly through the crowd. My weekly runs and gym sessions are paying off: they have been for a long time. I check behind me repeatedly; I can't see Demon now. But I can still sense a dark, glowering presence nearby.

In my panicked state, the first place I think of seeking refuge in is the women's toilets. There are always people there. He's hardly going to follow me into the Ladies in public, or climb over the walls between the cubicles.

Leaving the dance floor and running past the huge, illuminated bar, I turn right into the mirrored corridor where the toilets are. As most clubbers headed for the exit during the power cut there is, as I expected, no long queue. Even if there had been women standing here I would have pushed past them and barricaded myself in a cubicle.

I see my face in the mirror beside me, painted with black and white make-up to look like a Mexican death mask. And fuck! I can also see a black figure behind me. I can't get through the door to the toilets on my right because there is a hand holding my ponytail. Shit!

The skin on my head is pulled taut as my head is yanked back. Instinctively I reach behind me with my right hand to free myself from his grip.

"Wait...," I beg.

"What for?"

He has pushed up the sleeve of his hoodie and my fingers encircle his bare forearm. My nails rake his skin. But that doesn't seem to bother him.

"Not here. People might see us." I try to throw Demon off with my words. He must know people could witness this power game, and possibly report it.

In response, he lets out a sharp laugh that sounds louder and more powerful than when we were on the dance floor.

"Do you think I care?"

Think of something better, Nuria. Something to get rid of him... But is that what I really want?

Every muscle in my body is strung to breaking point, poised to flee, but at the same time I feel this inexplicable curiosity when he is near.

Step by step he steers me away from the ladies' toilets to the end of the corridor. He propels me ahead of him like a sacrificial offering without arousing the suspicions of those around us. I see our reflections in the mirrors out of the corner of my eye. The only source of light in the corridor is purple LEDs, and nobody behind us can see that I am being held captive.

"If I am so important to you then you should care about what I want."

"I already know what you want, my rose." *My rose?* "But say it aloud. Tell me what you really want."

A shudder that alternates between fear and tension runs down my spine. I am always asking myself how far he will go this time and what will happen next.

He pushes me on towards a door at the end of the corridor, on the left, my ponytail tightly wound around his wrist and his left hand below my corset.

"I want you to go. Get out of my life for good," I answer. I wish my words sounded more assertive, louder, more forceful. But they don't.

He lowers his face to my ear, his teeth bite into my earlobe and are then replaced by his warm tongue. His touch makes my neck tingle and a nervous fluttering starts up between my ribs. "Tell me how much you want me gone."

I writhe in his grip. As we arrive at the door he has been steering me towards, he shoves it open.

At first, the room behind the door is in complete darkness. But the door has barely closed before a movement sensor switches on the lights. We're in a lounge with slot machines and neon lettering on the walls. The walls are adorned with framed portraits of famous musicians. Black sofas and armchairs are grouped around an angular coffee table next to an inviting modern bar, with an array of spirits. We are alone. I hear a click. He's locked the door. Fuck!

Panic spreads through my stomach immediately. What if this is it? What if he kills me because I won't give him what he wants? What if clubbers or the cleaners find me in the morning, in a pool of blood?

"Go on, tell me how much you want me to go," he orders again.

But I won't say what he wants to hear: that I want him to stay. I would rather die than give up without a fight.

"Leave me alone, dammit!" I say loudly.

He gives an ominous murmur, one that makes me shudder every time I hear it.

"We'll see about that. You haven't quite convinced me yet."

He jolts me forward, pushing me towards the black corner

couch. I stumble to a halt in front of it, so as not to topple onto the seat.

"I want...," I begin, and am about to turn around to him when he grabs hold of me again. He takes my shoulder and shoves me towards the football table and then forces me down onto it, face first. I brace myself quickly against the metal bars with the plastic football players attached to them, ready to resist.

But he moves bloody fast, taking up a wide-legged stance behind me and grabbing my hips. "Carry on. Weren't you going to say something?" he mocks.

"I want you to leave me alone." I try to get the sentence out again, even though there's so much more I want to know about him. Even though, strangely, I want to know what he's going to do with me. Even though the feeling of his body behind me doesn't actually leave me cold. Which I won't tell him. That would mean I was enjoying his little game and would prove him right: it would mean I want more. But my voice is shaking, partly from fear, partly from pent-up excitement, because he has never gone this far before. The colour rises in my face as, without warning, he reaches under my short skirt and rips at my tights with an impatient tug.

"Shit. What's going on?"

"What does it look like?"

I cling to the metal bars of the football table and try to straighten up, but am stopped by his hand on the back of my neck. The next moment, he holds out his gloved right hand to me.

"Take off my glove."

"Fuck you."

He gives another amused laugh. "Do you want me to fuck you with my gloves? Okay."

Okay what?

"Okay, then my anticipation of feeling your pussy properly will be delayed even longer."

I inhale sharply. He has stood outside my window numerous times, tailed me, followed and watched me, sent me messages, phoned, and left presents outside my door. But never, not a single time, has he taken what he has referred to in his messages.

"Demon," I gasp, to bring him to his senses.

But at that moment his fingers glide between my legs, wander over my knickers. "Shame I won't find out today how wet you are. How silky and warm your pussy feels."

Surprisingly, he's not rough. He caresses my knickers almost playfully.

"What are you doing?" I ask, unable to keep the tremor of excitement out of my voice.

"We're just getting to know each other," he replies teasingly. "I'm not fucking you, not tonight."

I raise my eyebrows in astonishment as he lets go of my neck and replaces his hand with a noose around my throat. I raise my right hand quickly to feel for the leather belt he's using and immediately lose my balance. Slightly drunk and exhausted from dancing, I can't support myself with my left hand on the bar of the football table for more than a few seconds. And my will to fight him is increasingly being eroded by my curiosity to find out what he will do to me.

"Shut your eyes, open up to me, and enjoy what I give you." I clutch both bars of the football table again and let myself sink against it, realising that Demon isn't pulling the belt too tightly, although he is using it to control me. In that moment he pushes my knickers aside, and two gloved fingers circle around my clit. He has located it in spite of the gloves, which... which is almost impossible.

And instead of pushing inside me, fucking me with his fingers, he is circling my pearl, more firmly and with more and more pressure. A crazy desire spreads through my pelvis instantly, my nipples tingle under my corset, my clit pulses. And although I should defend myself, biting, scratching, and hitting him, I succumb for a moment to the insane feeling his fingers are creating and push my pelvis towards him. His bulging hard-on presses against my backside. I feel him rubbing against me as he chokes me harder and gives me an unexpected thrill by controlling my breathing.

I've no idea how this can have happened, but it's as if all my fears have been blown away. He isn't fucking me, and yet, and yet, that's exactly what I want right now. I want so much more, even though this game is sick, forbidden, and completely insane.

"Still sure you want me out of your life?" he asks, his voice rough and excited. His sharp, smoky scent, unique to him, surrounds me, as he spreads my wetness between my labia, then continues to circle my clit. And he does it so devilishly well that a few seconds later my legs are trembling and I am gasping for air and whimpering. A strangled noise leaves my throat as he increases the pressure from the belt around my neck and drives me even more obsessively towards orgasm. I blink, intoxicated by the feeling of being completely at his mercy and not hating it.

Fuck! This can't happen. I can't come with him. Although right now I want to so much. God! He's like a drug – I'm addicted, even though I know it makes me ill.

Don't weaken, Nuria.

Whimpering and quietly groaning, I am so damn close to climaxing.

"Yes," I bring myself to say, so as not to let him win, although I know that in this moment it is a lie. He has already won. "Get out," I lie, because my mind is continuing to resist him, though my body wants to go further.

My body is briefly flooded by an overwhelming wave of pleasure, the heat mixes with pure desire, only to end abruptly. Demon steps back from me, undoes the belt, and leaves me standing at the football table with my skirt hiked up and my tights torn.

What the hell?

I look back over my shoulder and see him standing there with his arms folded. This has got to be the most uncomfortable moment of my life. He did what I said? But... but I wanted the orgasm, the thing that no man has yet ever given me.

"Do you think I'm some terrible rapist?"

"I didn't say that," I counter. No, that wasn't what I felt. He is dominant, unapproachable, terrifying, but he hasn't attacked me like a wild animal. It was important to him that I got my money's worth.

"You're right, you haven't earned it." His words are so dismissive, they hit me like a bucket of cold water.

Holding the belt at both ends, he slaps it against his hand and lowers his rune-covered face. He shakes his head slowly, giving the impression he regrets what he has done. But not like someone who regrets a bad deed, more like he regrets almost bringing me to orgasm. As if I didn't deserve it. As if I didn't deserve Demon's attention, his hands on me, and his closeness.

"I didn't say that..." Hurriedly I push my skirt down and pull up the shreds of my tights before I turn around to face him. But he has disappeared. Has just gone, without bringing me to climax, because now, of all times, he has done what I asked and gone.

And now? Is he gone forever? If so, why don't I feel relieved?

It's a puzzle. A fucking sinister puzzle.

CHAPTER 2

Nuria

When one door closes,
a new one opens.
What if your shadow slips
through the new door too?

My hair is being blown off my face by a powerful wind. As I tilt my head back, the dark blanket of cloud above me threatens to break. No sooner do I have this thought than the first raindrops land on my face.

The engine of the Uber that brought me from the airport to the Monairs' estate roars to life behind me. I watch as the old, silver vehicle makes its way back to the gentle slope down to the coast.

At the same time, an uneasy feeling unfurls in my stomach. The feeling of regretting my decision.

There is nothing more anxiety-inducing than a new beginning. When I decided to start again in a strange land, on a foreign continent, with new people, it had somehow felt right in my head. But now, it feels like I've made the wrong decision. But hey, I wanted this, and now here I stand, in front of the Monair estate.

The wind whips under my light blazer, inflates it, and even makes the tall trees all around creak. The storm is getting fiercer and the rain is falling ever harder.

To avoid entering the house with my white pleated skirt, light blue blouse, and camel-coloured blazer completely soaked, I take a deep breath, grip the handles of my suitcases, and pull them towards the imposing gate. I see a doorbell to my left, with a video camera directly above it that will certainly be notifying the residents of my arrival.

"Just ring. It's easy." *But you could still turn around.* The thought flashes through my head.

"No, you can't. You've already signed the au pair contract, stupid," I murmur to myself.

Contracts can be cancelled.

"Damn," I curse, under my breath.

Why do I suddenly want to change my mind? The night before last I couldn't get out of Spain fast enough. And why? Because my personal demon was getting more and more insistent. A bloody lunatic, tracking me like a shadow.

But now, the sight of the impressive, four-storey manor house in dark-coloured sandstone, towering into the stormy sky, is making me uneasy, too. The house has countless rows of windows, like a government building, but only the lights in the top storey are lit. It is almost eight in the evening, the sun hasn't set yet, and the property looks stately, powerful, and magnificent, yet at the same time somehow cold, dark, and menacing, like a lurking monster.

"The sun will be out tomorrow, and you'll laugh at yourself for having these thoughts. How could this place be threatening?" Children live here, for heaven's sake.

A bright flash streaks across the sky, followed by an angry clap of thunder. I gasp in fear. *Mierda!* A sign that I should actually ring the bell.

I'm no coward, but I hate storms.

I turn to the doorbell, take another deep breath, and then push the golden button, letting my gaze travel over the house one last time. Then I see a pair of child's eyes looking at me through the twisted iron gate. A flash of lightning illuminates the girl's face in the garden like a horror film. My heart sinks.

"Where did you come from all of a sudden?" I ask. The girl has damp strands of ash-blonde hair sticking to her cheeks.

She's wearing a dress with purple flowers, white sandals, and a little light-coloured jacket.

The girl doesn't answer, but continues to regard me with a keen gaze.

"Yes, hello?" A voice comes through the intercom.

"Erm, hello, it's Miss Endrinal here. I'm the new au pair."

"Oh, Miss Endrinal, how lovely, you're here."

"Unfortunately, my flight landed an hour later than scheduled. I'm sorry," I explain to the friendly female voice and look up at the camera. She can definitely see me.

When I turn back to the gate, the little girl has disappeared. She must be one of the children I've been engaged to look after. Although the girls on the photos I was emailed looked less stiff and sad.

"No problem at all. Please come through. I'll be waiting at the entrance."

The buzzer sounds. I open the door, grab my luggage, and enter the Monairs' extensive grounds.

Dragging my suitcases, I fight my way through the pouring rain to the building entrance. The wheels keep getting stuck on the smartly paved driveway, which is lined with low boxwood bushes. Although the rain is hammering down and I know I'm going to meet the family looking like a wet dog, I take the opportunity to look at the well-kept garden.

A thick, flowering hedge runs alongside the high wall. The lawn is neatly mown, and a few palm and acacia trees, several metres high, are dotted around the immaculate plot. The most beautiful areas are the flower beds by the entrance, where shrubs of all colours are in bloom.

But however hard I look, I can't see the little girl. Where has she got to? Is she hiding in the hedge by the wall? A child of that age – no older than six – shouldn't be running around on her own in the pouring rain.

Just as I reach the entrance steps, a brunette woman wearing a smart suit and angular black glasses rushes out to meet me.

"Wait, let me help you." She descends the steps in high-heeled shoes, which looks pretty dangerous. "This should really be Jack's job. But he's phoned in sick today."

"Jack?" I ask. I recognize her voice – she must be Mrs Warner. The housekeeper I've already discussed my arrival with on the phone.

"Yes, our chauffeur, porter, caretaker, spider-catcher. A jack of all trades, if you know what I mean." She gives me a broad smile, then grasps the handle of my mint-green suitcase.

"Oh, don't worry, I can manage," I say, worried she might fall down the stairs in her heels and break her neck.

"You've been standing in the rain long enough. Let me help." Her words clearly convey that she will not be deterred.

"Okay." I shrug my shoulders, then grab the white suitcase, which weighs over twenty-five kilos, and carry it up the steps.

Behind me, Mrs Warner curses and sniffs. "I'll have something to say about this tomorrow, Jack!"

It seems as though Mrs Warner will have a lot to say about everything, if this is how she talks about Jack.

Arriving at the covered stairhead, I gasp for breath, then catch a glimpse of the inside of the house through the open double doors. And I already love what I see. I can't believe that just moments ago I was worried about moving into a haunted house wreathed in shadows.

The interior is brightly lit. A gleaming dark marble floor extends throughout the entrance hall. In the centre of the foyer stands a round table with a glorious bouquet of flowers on it, and directly behind that I can see double glass doors flanked by two curving staircases. Resplendent above the entrance hall is a magnificent, contemporary crystal chandelier.

"Done!" I hear Mrs Warner proclaim. "I've broken a nail, but that doesn't matter."

I turn to face her. As she inspects her broken nail, chewing at it unabashedly, I take the opportunity to ask about the girl in the garden. "Was that Maily I saw just now?" I ask. Mrs

Warner continues to work on the nail with her teeth. She looks at me questioningly. "Where?"

"Outside, by the gate," I reply.

Mrs Warner shakes her head. "It can't have been. The twins are both in their room. I saw them playing in there myself, just now."

How strange. What if it was a different child?

"Oh, really? I'm sure I saw someone standing in the rain there before." I don't like the thought of a girl hiding in the garden during a storm. Perhaps she's afraid. Perhaps she's shy and doesn't dare approach us.

But Mrs Warner must be right when she says the twins I'll be looking after really are in the house. That reassures me. Only... it bothers me, the thought of leaving a strange child out there to fend for themselves.

"Your eyes can play tricks in the storm and this rain." Mrs Warner closes the front door behind me with a bang, shutting out the weather and immediately enveloping me in cosy warmth. I breathe in the scent of vanilla and listen to the calm sounds of a piano. Either someone is playing an instrument somewhere or the music is coming from hidden speakers.

"I'd better show you your room. It's on the second floor. You can freshen up there for a minute. The family have delayed dinner for you and would like to see you at 8:30 in the dining room."

I glance at the pendulum clock next to the double doors. It is already 8:10 p.m.

"Of course. I'll get a move on."

"The dining room is on your right." Mrs Warner indicates a corridor with multiple dark wooden doors leading off it. The floor is again laid with black marble, the walls are dark green with contrasting features in gold stucco. It is reminiscent of an old manor house with an added dash of modern flair. A golden-brown dog with floppy ears lopes out of the corridor towards us. He approaches me, tail wagging, and sniffs excitedly at my wet skirt.

"Hello, who are you then?"
"This is Henry. The family's labradoodle."
I crouch down slowly, letting Henry sniff me and scratching his ears.
"Would you like to follow me?" It gradually dawns on me that, since closing the door behind us, Mrs Warner has adopted a more formal demeanour.
I nod, stand up, grab a suitcase, and follow Mrs Warner up the black-carpeted staircase to the first floor.
Henry pads along behind us. I arrive on the second floor, out of breath, and look around curiously. My progress towards my room is watched over by embittered, grim-looking nineteenth-century men in tailcoats, with high foreheads and sporting greying goatees.
"Are these the Monair family ancestors?" I ask, looking at the dates in the corners of the last two portraits.
1843 and 1879.
"That's right. Those are the Monair brothers; they emigrated from England to Australia in search of gold."
I give the portraits another interested glance and then follow Mrs Warner down a corridor with a dark floor and lined with crimson wallpaper. Above us hang a number of small lamps with bell-shaped glass shades.
"And did they find gold?" I ask.
"No."
"How did they get so rich then?"
"They started mining iron ore. Iron ore is now Australia's biggest export."
Iron ore. Somehow I had imagined something different. "Sounds very exciting."
"Yes, it is. Are you interested in history?"
"Yes, a little." Mrs Warner stops by a door beside a portrait of a pale, dark-blonde woman in a ruched white dress.
"Here are your rooms. Right next to the twins, Maily and Hailey."
As she opens the door I stop, open-mouthed. I never expected such a spacious room. Beyond a small hallway with

built-in cupboards is a living room-cum-bedroom panelled in dark walnut.

I see an expansive sofa that extends around a low table in front of a fireplace and a TV. As I follow Mrs Warner into the elegant room, not knowing where to look first, I see a large four-poster bed, its dark blue curtains drawn back. The bed is to my left, in front of two tall windows with views onto part of the garden. Instead of the cool, dark marble flooring in the other parts of the house, there is warm, dark parquet, with soft, patterned rugs here and there. The bed looks as though it belongs to a princess.

Only when Mrs Warner looks at me do I shut my mouth.

"What do you think?"

"Beautiful. Is this all mine?"

"Yes, of course. The dressing room is right here." Mrs Warner goes around the corner from the bed and motions to a sliding glass door. "And the bathroom is next door."

She walks down a passageway lined with empty shelves in dark wood and opens another sliding door at the end. Behind the door is the bathroom, with a wide washbasin, a large circular mirror, a shower with glass doors, and a toilet.

"Unfortunately, you don't have a great deal of time to look at everything properly. I'd ask you to present yourself in the dining room in ten minutes, please. Do you remember where it is?"

"Yes, I do," I reply, looking away from the reed diffuser and the precisely folded towels. "Could I meet Maily and Hailey quickly first?"

Mrs Warner turns to me and furrows her brows over the rim of her glasses. "You'll see the girls downstairs in a moment." Then she shrugs her shoulders. "But I'm sure we can manage a quick introduction."

Relieved not to have been rebuffed, I take a deep breath and follow her out of my rooms. Mrs Warner opens the door to a large, brightly lit playroom, where two girls are kneeling on the floor amongst mountains of soft toys, dolls, games, and a teepee tent. Both are painting their fingers, feet, and arms with nail varnish, causing Mrs Warner to let out a horrified gasp.

"My goodness! Where did you find that nail polish?"

The dark-blonde girl applies the varnish generously to all her toes.

"Not telling," she replies cheekily, before painting lines on her arm using her index finger. "Don't say, Hailey," she whispers to her sister, who is wearing red dungarees and a blue and white striped T-shirt.

"You both need to get changed." Somewhat overwhelmed, Mrs Warner intervenes and grabs the two open bottles of polish, hurrying with them into an adjacent room. "If your father sees this, he won't be happy," she grumbles, although the girls are unconcerned.

I look at the two of them more carefully. They look like the photos I saw before I arrived, and neither of them looks anything like the child in the garden. Hailey and Maily are identical twins, and I can only tell them apart by their clothes. Both are wearing their long, dark-blonde hair in plaits. They have dark eyes, freckles, and sweet snub noses. Exactly the way I remember them from the photos.

I introduce myself. "Hello you two. I'm Nuria."

The girls stare at me, neither pleased to see me nor remotely interested. "Okay, we'll get changed." Maily, who is apparently the one who does the talking, stands up.

"Come into the bathroom, both of you! I have to get the nail varnish off your hands and feet first. Hurry!"

"Can I help at all?" I call to Mrs Warner, who can't see me.

"I'll see you downstairs, Miss Endrinal," she replies, looking at me around the door.

Okay, clearly she doesn't need my help.

Back in my room, I open my white suitcase and take out fresh clothes, then grab a hand towel from the bathroom. Changing in record time, and hanging up my soaking wet clothes on the drying rail in the bathroom, I rub my hair dry and stare out of the window. The storm continues to rage;

leaves are dancing through the air and falling into the pool at the end of the garden.

However hard I scrutinise the garden, I can't see a child. I could have sworn I wasn't mistaken.

CHAPTER 3

Nuria

Love is a sick game,
In which there is usually always
a loser.

Arriving in the dining room, I am given a heartfelt welcome by the family. While Mr Monair is chiefly focused on the smartphone next to his plate, his wife bombards me with all the information she wants me to know about the household.

"... unfortunately we have had more than one au pair in the past who has been more interested in partying and going out than looking after our children. Of course you have the weekends free, Nuria. Please don't take this the wrong way, but in our house we do have rules that must be followed."

So there have already been several au pairs before me. In my mind I can't help imagining them inviting guests round and having wild pool parties while the family were away.

"Of course," I reply and look from the slim, brown-haired woman with green cats' eyes and heavy gold hoop earrings to her husband.

Mr Monair continues to look at messages on his phone. He has a bald head and tanned skin, wears a white open-necked shirt, and looks in good shape for what I'm guessing are his late forties. In any case, the family has style and class. They know how to wear their wealth.

Just like the somewhat bored guy, also glued to his phone, with thick black hair and features that are too perfect for my taste. He has striking dark brows, appealingly curved lips, and a straight nose, as well as slightly pronounced cheekbones and a small dimple in his chin.

Nothing against good-looking people, but they're usually too self-assured and arrogant, they think the world revolves around them. I've had enough to do with that sort of people to know to steer clear of them. I prefer people with flaws who are beautiful on the inside, and not in love with their own reflection.

"And you know the core working hours, Nuria? It's all set out in the contract, which I'm sure you'll have read."

"I have," I reassure Mrs Monair, who has told me to call her Jacky. Her real name is Jacqueline, but she insists I use her nickname because she finds Jacqueline dreadfully old-fashioned. I suspect she would like people to think she is younger than she is.

She's in her early forties, but dresses like she's in her late twenties. She came into the room after I had already sat down at the table, wearing a light-coloured embroidered top, a long, dark blue pleated skirt with a gold belt, and wedge sandals. Accompanied by an overpoweringly sweet haze of perfume, she circled the table and planted a kiss on her eldest son's temple. He seemed more annoyed than pleased by the gesture. Since then he's clearly been constantly messaging with friends, or women, and not listening to his mother's instructions.

More than half my view of him is blocked by a candlestick and a white floral arrangement, so I can't sneak a peek at his phone screen. But he types something every minute or so, so he must be messaging.

Maily and Hailey are sitting right next to me. They scarcely glance at me, dunking their chips in ketchup and mayonnaise while asking every five minutes whether they can leave the table.

Why is everyone at the table annoyed by everyone else? Apart from Jacky, they all seem completely disinterested, as though they always had a stranger at their dining table.

I'll admit I expected something different. Perhaps a family

with strict rules and religious views, but who were respectful of each other. Or maybe a modern family who had relaxed conversation around the dinner table, but not this.

If I'm honest, I'm disappointed. I really hope I've got the wrong first impression, or I won't be able to stand a month here and I'll be desperate to get back to Barcelona.

"The staff are responsible for cleaning your rooms and doing your washing. You don't have to worry about that, Nuria," Jacky explains, as she spears the salad leaves on her plate. "But tidiness is very important to us. We once had an au pair who piled up pizza boxes in her wardrobe until they attracted cockroaches. That was an experience I don't want to repeat." Jacky shudders in disgust. "The vermin got everywhere in the end. It took six months before the pest control..."

"Can we get down?" Hailey interrupts. "We're bored."

Like everyone else here, probably, I think, looking down. I toy with my mashed potato and then stab two beans and put them in my mouth. The two girls were served different meals, fast food, because according to Jacky they don't eat adult food, hate vegetables, and make a scene if they don't get their chips, nuggets, pasta, and pizza. That's something I'll need to tackle, when I get the opportunity.

"Just wait five minutes. Nuria hasn't finished eating."

Mr Monair and the eldest son, Zain, both look up from their phones towards me. I feel awkward. Apart from Jacky, everyone else has finished.

"I'm done," I declare, because I don't want to be a trouble with my slow eating.

"Really?" asks Jacky, blinking her fake eyelashes at me and giving me a mild smile. "You haven't finished your plate."

"I'm full to bursting, honestly," I reassure her. This seems to act as a signal for the girls, who immediately push back their chairs and jump up.

"Hey!" Jacky complains. "I didn't say you could get down."

"She's finished. Everyone's finished. Come on, Hailey." Maily takes her sister's hand and pulls her out of the dining room, past a member of staff carrying a tray with dessert glasses on it. The door closes loudly behind them, making the glass in the doors rattle gently.

"I have to go too," Zain adds, placing his napkin next to his plate and standing up. He's wearing a black polo shirt and dark jeans.

I've no idea how old he is. Could be mid-twenties. His gaze wanders over to the window behind his seat; he seems to be looking for something. Then he walks around the table without so much as looking at me.

I don't like you either, you smug bastard, I think, grimly watching him leave.

"Should I put the girls to bed from now on?"

"No," Jacky explains. "Mrs Warner will see to that." She puts her napkin down too, before looking over to Mrs Warner, who is already standing in the doorway behind me.

"Of course, Jacky."

"You rest today after your long journey, Nuria. Relax and settle in. Have a look around, if you like. You'll find the gym and the sauna in the cellar. There's a library on the ground floor, if you like reading. My husband's and my private rooms are always locked. Otherwise, feel free to explore."

With these words, she leaves the table, whereupon her husband and I stand up. Mr Monair gives me a brief forced smile, as though sympathising with a stray cat that has hidden itself, trembling, behind a rubbish bin.

What's going on here? Something isn't right. I had been looking forward to meeting a friendly host family, not these aloof people who might have been carved out of ice. But who knows, perhaps something has happened today. Maybe an argument or they've had bad news. I shouldn't jump to conclusions.

Around 10pm, after taking myself on an extensive tour of the house for nearly an hour, I decide to go back to my room and unpack.

The people who live here aside, this place is utterly amazing. I was expecting a tiny gym with a couple of machines and a little sauna in the corner, but instead there is a dedicated fitness suite and spa area, like a hotel.

The private library is housed in two large rooms lined with floor-to-ceiling shelves. There's even a ladder if you want to reach the upper shelves. I relax in the garden for a while, on the rattan furniture under the canopy of the spacious terrace, looking at the pool and the pavilion in the distance. Half of the property is surrounded by dense eucalyptus forest, behind a two-metre wall.

I wonder why the Monairs live in such a remote spot between the forest and the cliffs. Is it the seclusion? Did they inherit this historic property? Possibly both. The whole place is an adventure for me – it's a stark contrast to the turbulence of Barcelona.

Arriving at my room, I let myself fall back onto the soft four-poster bed. I can hear the twins protesting through the wall – Mrs Warner's instructions are evidently not to their liking. I hear children's footsteps stamping repeatedly over the floor, sometimes even banging in the corridor, and doors being slammed.

It seems the girls are highly strung. Tomorrow certainly promises to be interesting.

I grew up with two siblings and know how hectic things can be at home. While I am wondering whether to look in and ask Mrs Warner if she needs any help, my mobile rings in the pocket of my shorts. I reach back and take it out.

The thought briefly flashes through my head that the call might be from my sick stalker. But that's impossible. We are thousands of kilometres away. We are oceans apart – there is no way he could have found out my new number so quickly. On the other hand, I've changed my number repeatedly in recent weeks, to no avail. He found my number every time. Just thinking about my stalker causes the back of my neck to tingle. On the one hand, I want to be rid of him, and on the other I am desperate to know what he looks like. Will he find me? And if he does, will we pick up where we left off in the night club? Whenever I think of that night in the Crystal Passion I feel this nervous fluttering in my breast. I am lost, doomed.

But when I see the name Anston on the screen, I breathe a sigh of relief. Anston has been a best friend of mine for over a year. He's even come to Australia with me. I first met Anston at university when I dropped a tray in the canteen. While everyone else just stared, Anston jumped up to help, and we got talking. Since then, we have met regularly for meals in the canteen, and a great friendship has developed out of an embarrassing moment.

After we landed he checked into a hotel in Brisbane, around thirty kilometres from the Monairs' estate.

"Ans?" I answer. "What's up?" I roll onto my stomach and pick at the silky bed covers.

"Hey Nuria. I thought I'd call because you didn't get in touch like we agreed. Forgotten about me already?"

"Oops," I say, with studied remorse, propping myself on my elbows. I comb my fingers through my chestnut-brown hair with its lightly curling ends. "I was just about to message you."

"Come on, don't lie. No, you weren't. What's your host family like?"

"So far so good." Which is something of an exaggeration. Anston can probably hear the children's shrieks through my door. Pensively, I twirl a strand of hair around my index finger.

"So it's not as great as you thought it would be."

There's a brief silence. Then I sigh and inhale noisily. "No, to be honest the people here are a bit strange. So different and, no idea how to describe it... disinterested."

"Are they unfriendly?"

"No, not exactly. But, I don't know, I was hoping for something different. Let's see how it goes over the next few days. I could just be completely exhausted after the long flight and feel like going home."

"Oh man." As he speaks I hear people talking in the background, followed by a doorbell, as though Anston is going into a busy bar. The voices get louder and I can hear jazz. "You don't want to go back right now, do you? Think of that lunatic who's after you. He'll have no idea you've sublet your apartment in Barcelona." He gives an amused laugh. "I bet he's filming a strange woman through your window right now, thinking it's you."

I don't find this thought at all funny, because the woman – Amber – doesn't know what she's let herself in for. I repeatedly stressed that there was someone who stood on the street, took photos, and blatantly stared through the window. That he would continue to check out the apartment, leave presents by the door, and ring the doorbell in the middle of the night. But it didn't put the student off renting the apartment for six months – the rental market was tough and she hadn't found anything better.

"Very funny, Ans. What if he hurts her?" The thought is not at all far-fetched. From what I know of him, Demon will be furious when he realises I have given him the slip, and will probably take out his anger on my tenant.

"Why her? It's you he's obsessed with."

I chew my lower lip. "Let's hope he stays in Spain and forgets about me at last." That was the plan I had made, when I realised my shadow had been following me for over four months.

It had all been pretty unremarkable to begin with. One night, when I was leaving the bar I worked at, I was followed by someone dressed in black. I didn't notice him immediately. Unfortunately, guests at *Luna Ilena* frequently offered to buy me a drink at the end of my shift, wanted to get to know me better, or wanted to escort me home.

Many of them were very insistent, or drunk, and they sometimes got rough. That's why for the first three evenings I assumed that it was different drunken guests. But I soon realised that the tall man, always in black trousers, heavy boots and a dark hoodie, was one and the same person. He started to follow me more and more.

Once a week became twice a week, and at some point it became every day. Regardless of how often I turned round to the person twenty metres behind me, calling to them to leave me in peace or tell me what they wanted from me, I never got an answer. The guy frightened me; he didn't say a word. I kept thinking he would pull a knife and attack me. But he never did.

He tolerated my insults, threats and questions without responding. When I approached him, he withdrew and disappeared. Only to continue following me when I went on my way. The stalking drove me to the edge of madness and tormented me. I gradually came to understand that although he was following me, he didn't want to engage with me. But that was unsettling in itself.

That's how the nightmare began. He never once answered my questions. For a long time he didn't speak at all. Until the phone calls began. Calls where all I could hear was his regular breathing. After around a month the doorbell rang and I started receiving strange black envelopes containing sick declarations of love, or threats. Things like:

You'll never be rid of me, my rose.
We are inseparable.

Those were the nicer messages. If I did something that apparently displeased him, the messages got much nastier.

Do I really have to tell you,
not to smile at another man,
when he hasn't earned it?!
Do you want to make me jealous?

Soon the messages didn't just arrive in the form of letters left outside my door; I began to receive texts from an unknown number. No matter where I went or who I met, he knew about it. Always.

I repeatedly restored my phone to the default factory settings, to make sure no spy app had been installed. But nothing helped.

A little while later I heard his dark, quivering voice on the other end of the phone for the first time. He didn't just breathe into the receiver, he gave a furtive laugh and asked how I was doing. My bloody stalker was asking me how I was doing? He knew better than I did, because he'd definitely been watching me. The thought that I was continually being observed gave me the creeps. For the first few days I shut all the doors and windows, kept the curtains closed, and barricaded myself in. But it didn't help. I continued to receive letters, calls, and messages.

That's why I suspect he's here. That he has travelled to Australia, too, or he will come out here if his obsession with me continues. Although a small part of me hopes he'll lose interest if I flee halfway around the world.

He must have family and friends he can't drop just like that, a job he can't just quit. Or maybe he hasn't?

What if he's a loner? No, everyone has family and friends. And that's why I chose Australia, to put the greatest possible distance between us, to make him give up. To stop his pursuit of me and forget his obsession.

"Let's not talk about it. He won't be here." Not yet, at least.

"Then make the most of your freedom. Let's go and explore Brisbane." Glasses clink in the background. "Or are you looking after the children today?"

"No, I start tomorrow."

"Perfect."

"Perfect?" I ask. "Perfect how?"

Suddenly the connection is lost. "Hello? Ans?"

CHAPTER 4

Demon

The rose is the queen of all the flowers.
And that is what you are for me, my flower,
my dark queen.

Relaxing music plays through my headphones as I take a swig of my whisky. It's bloody cramped in economy, but this way I have a perfect view of my flower.

She is asleep four rows ahead of me in the aisle seat, leaning her head back, with a mask over her eyes and her mouth open. One day I will sit next to her on a flight, and she can rest her head on my shoulder while she sleeps. One day I will lie next to her while she sleeps, pull her towards me, and watch her undisturbed for hours, count every single eyelash, bury my face in her hair, and slide my fingers between her legs.

There's a warning signal, and the seatbelt sign above me starts to flash. A crew member makes a tense announcement about turbulence ahead, and my flower wakes up. Damn.

She pulls off her mask, rubs her neck and looks around sleepily.

Fuck, can you see me? I'm sitting really close to you.

"Can I take your glass?" the stewardess asks, her serving trolley obscuring my view of Nuria.

Quest is dozing next to me in spite of the turbulence, and doesn't wake up when the stewardess speaks.

"No," I reply irritably, hoping she will move on quickly.

When she pushes the trolley out of the way and I can get a clear view of my flower again, her seat is empty.

Fuck! Where has she gone? Although there are only three places she can be, losing sight of her makes me feel really bad. As though I had lost her – forever.

She could have gone to the toilet. The most likely reason for standing up.

She could have got up to stretch her legs and walk around the plane.

But she could also have been intercepted and approached by someone, or even dragged into a hiding place.

Total bullshit! Not on a plane.

A Boeing 777 has pretty much no hiding places. Someone would notice straightaway if a woman was being kidnapped. But the uneasy feeling in the pit of my stomach expands. *Where are you, my flower? Where?*

I scan the aisle frantically. I can't see her. I'd better go and look.

Just as I am about to get up and walk down the aisles between the rows of seats, Nuria appears. She was in the toilet.

Obviously.

I sink back into my seat, unnoticed. Dammit, this woman is driving me out of my mind. I am lurking on a plane, just to be close to her. Travelling halfway around the world so as not to lose her. Sitting in shitty economy class so I can watch her the whole time.

But I still love spending time near her. In my whole life, I've never felt so alive as I have in the past few months, since I first met her.

I grin involuntarily as I watch her.

Want to run from me? I'll catch you.

Think you're safe? I will persuade you otherwise.

Think you're free of me forever? Hell, no, our relationship is only just beginning.

Then my gaze falls on Nuria's friend Anston, who is eyeballing her periodically from across the aisle. It has not escaped me that he is also interested in her. I hate this guy.

He's been pulling the best-mate-number for months now, so he can fuck her soon. Slimeballs like him should crawl back where they came from, under the ground.

If he touches her, tries to force himself on her or shag her, he'll be the next person I get a grave dug for. There's something not quite right about this guy. I've hardly been able to find out anything about him.

"What is it?" Quest asks suddenly. Reluctantly, I take my eyes off Anston and his blond party-boy haircut, and look at my friend.

"Nothing. The shitting turbulence woke me up, but you went on snoring like a tramp on a park bench."

"Fuck you. I don't snore." Miffed, he straightens up in the narrow seat, stretches his arms in the air, and then glances at the Rolex on his right wrist.

"Shit, another hour. I want to get out of this crappy little plane."

I feel the same. I would also have preferred to travel business class, like I usually do. But then I couldn't have shadowed Nuria. She can't afford a business class ticket, she doesn't have the money. I could have given her some, but that would have given the game away and she'd have known I was hot on her heels. No, I need this kick. Right now, she thinks she's left me thousands of miles behind her, in Spain.

I can't help smiling at the thought.

"Why are you grinning like that?" Quest wants to know, studying me sideways. "You look even worse than me. It's a miracle you even fit in that seat."

I roll my eyes. Quest doesn't know I'm tailing Nuria. He thinks we're going to Sydney because of a new contract.

"I'm looking forward to the lovely Australian weather."

"You're taking the piss," he replies. "You hate Australia, you hate the heat, the sun, the good mood, all the people."

He's spot on there. But I love being anywhere Nuria is.

Still, Quest is right. He knows me well, that's why I brought him along in the first place. I don't need him, we both know *that.* He is a long-time associate, loyal to the death, and the person I trust most implicitly. But I can get my jobs done without him. It's me that calls the shots, not him.

"If we stay longer in Australia, that's fine by me. Unlike you I love the summer: the sea, the hot chicks in the clubs." He grins provocatively. "And the change of scene won't do you any harm either. A bit of a holiday, partying, flirting, fit girls, blow-jobs..."

"No," I interrupt.

"No? When was the last time I saw you really having fun or hooking up with a woman? Two years ago."

The thing is, I make sure he doesn't know or see anything. If he knew I was out on the prowl as Demon at Crystal Passion the night before last, keeping an eye on my flower, he'd want to know more. I don't talk about my private life. Especially not about Nuria. No one can know I only took the contract in Australia in order to follow Nuria. I don't want anyone to be able to use this knowledge against me. For one of my enemies – and there are plenty of them running around the planet – to kidnap, torture or kill her to get even with me.

That's why I have to keep my obsession a secret. It's the same reason I won't tell Nuria who I am or how I earn my money.

The contract in Australia – we have been hired by the parents of a missing daughter – might only take a week to complete. Sometimes these missing persons cases can be more difficult to solve than they seem at first, though. In most cases, the missing girls or runaways are found with friends, hiding from their families. Sometimes this is justified because the families have put them under pressure, or they've been having arguments or, in the worst cases, they've been sexually assaulted or victims of domestic violence. Many of those who have gone missing do not want to be found, they want to start a new life.

But sometimes we come across intriguing cases that are almost impossible to solve. Where people disappear without trace and all the signs are that they were victims of organised crime. These cases are usually very serious.

But Nuria was not such a case. The clients wanted to find her at all costs, and it had been easy to track her down. Every now and then, depending on the status of my investigation, I decide not to pass all the information on to my clients. If children or teenagers are justified in having escaped from a chaotic home and are leading a better life without their family, I tell the clients I had to close the investigation because there were no leads.

I'm still holding out on Nuria's client because I can't figure out the intentions of the man who is looking for her. Why is he looking for Nuria? While I don't know, I won't give the client any information about my rose.

"I asked you a question," Quest interrupts my musings.

"What?"

"Why you haven't hooked up with a woman for so long?" He looks at me expectantly, as though he is actually hoping for an answer. I grimace, grab the collar of his shirt, and pull him closer to me.

"None of your business, Quest. I don't randomly fuck women just for a bit of fun."

Quest grabs my wrist and twists it expertly, so that I feel a crack, then a nasty sting. *Fuck, he's good.* I hiss in pain.

"What about something serious? A steady girlfriend?"

"Who'll wait at home for me whenever I'm abroad, for weeks at a time?" I raise my eyebrows mockingly. "Or will be anxiously glued to her phone because the next call she might get could be from the police, telling her I've been shot or ended up in jail?"

I've fucked plenty of women, but fucking a woman for one night only in every conceivable position just doesn't do it for me.

"Whatever. You're making excuses."

"How so?" I ask.

Quest laughs. "You'll change your mind when you meet the right girl."

My eyes involuntarily seek out Nuria, who has drawn her knees up against the seat in front of her and settled into the confined space, in her jogging bottoms and white crop top, and her hair tied back.

I've already found the right girl. Even if she doesn't know it yet. Because nobody knows and nobody can ever know.

And tonight I will visit her, taste her, feel her, touch her. Wait, little flower, I am closer than you think. You can feel it too.

CHAPTER 5

Nuria

If he wants me,
he must know
all the shadows of my heart.
Know that evil lives within me.

"Are you a total idiot?" I shout angrily into the phone, catching sight of him as I stand at the window. He can't be serious. How did he get here? What on earth is this blockhead thinking?

"Come on out. I'm waiting."

"No, Anston. I'm not going out tonight."

"Don't leave me hanging, Nuri."

I am completely done in after this exhausting day. I have to be ready for work early tomorrow morning. Besides, I have just reassured Jacky I'm not obsessed with partying like her other au pairs were. What would she think if I left the house on my very first evening to go out and have fun?

"Another time."

"Today!" He won't give up. He walks back and forth in front of the gate as he speaks. It's now just after midnight. I'd be asleep if I wasn't tormented by jet lag. Wearing my dark blue silk pyjamas, I watch his silhouette from the window. He's standing in the glare of a car's headlights.

"Did you come by taxi?"

"I've rented a car. I won't drink a thing and I'll bring you home safely. Anston's honour. Don't make me keep asking." He waves at me, trying to change my mind, and in the same moment the light begins to flicker. The lamp next to me, the only source of light in the room, flashes as though there's a loose connection. I immediately think of the power cut at Crystal Passion the night before last.

Is he here? Goosebumps creep along my forearms. The hairs on the back of my neck stand up at the thought that Demon could actually have come here. Impossible.

"It can't be," I whisper.

"What did you say?" Anston yells through the phone, making me flinch and close my left eye.

"I'm staying here. You can't change my mind, Ans. Have a lovely evening. I'm going to bed."

I hang up before he makes another attempt to persuade me, which he would be bound to do eventually. Suddenly the lamp stops flickering and goes out completely.

"Fuck. *Coño!*" I don't believe in coincidences.

But what if it is just a power cut, after all? I let my hand drop, still holding the mobile phone, glance quickly at Anston, who is walking towards his car in the beam of the headlights, shoulders drooping, and then turn away from the window. Then, out of the corner of my eye, I see a shadow outside. I blink furiously, uncertain of what I've glimpsed. The lights are so bright that I can hardly make out anything in the darkness behind them.

Presumably Ans has just opened the door and that was the movement I saw.

My mind is playing tricks on me. I'm sure of it. When the car reverses and makes a U-turn about a minute later, I breathe a sigh of relief.

But what's going on with the lamp? I turn on the torch on my phone and make my way through the lounge area to the light switch.

When I press the main switch for the ceiling lights, all the lights come on.

There was absolutely no need to worry. "He's not here." The plug socket probably tripped, or maybe the old lamp with its fabric-covered shade, which looks like a relic from the last century, has simply given up the ghost.

I dart over to the bedside table and turn on the spherical lamp, then switch the ceiling lights off. The best thing to do would be to go to bed and finally try to get some sleep. I want to get up at 6 a.m. tomorrow and go for a jog in the forest, then be ready for the twins at 7 a.m. They need to be taken to pre-school at 7:30 each morning, and then I have to pick them up again at 3 p.m. I am excited to start work, and to find out which of the cool cars they're going to let me drive.

I sit on the bed and plait my hair, then slide my feet under the covers and switch off the light. It is strange spending the night in a new bed.

The pale moonlight falls through two narrow gaps in the curtains, which I haven't fully closed. Otherwise the bedroom and the open-plan living area are in complete darkness. I am not used to the quiet ticking of the clock on the mantelpiece. It sounds almost like quiet, subdued footsteps. *Tick-tock. Tick-tock.*

I could take the battery out and put a stop to the annoying sound. But tiredness overwhelms me before I can get out of bed. My first night without Demon staring through the ground floor window.

The thought is so liberating. And unaccustomed, as in the last few months he has become a part of my life. A burdensome part.

You are free of him. Hopefully for ever.

The wind tugs at my skirt. It inflates like a balloon as I back towards the abyss, training the gun on the person in front of me.

"Stay where you are, Nuria!"

I grip the gun with both hands, sniff, cry, and shake my head. A tall figure approaches step by step, like a sinister black ghost. The person is male, or at least his voice sounds male. A man with no contours and no face.

"If you come any closer I'll shoot," I say shakily. Why is my voice trembling so much? As much as my arms are?

"You won't shoot me."

"I will." Which is a lie. For some reason I can't pull the trigger. I want to, but I can't.

"Prove it. I know when you're lying, darling." Tears are rolling constantly down my cheeks and I continue to move backwards.

My lips tremble. I narrow my eyes briefly. Push through it! Shoot him! Do it!

When I open my eyes I can't move the gun any more. Someone has hold of it.

"Just shoot! Kill me!"

The muzzle of the pistol is pressing into the dark, shadowy figure's chest. "What are you waiting for?"

I shake my head. I don't feel well – I'm dizzy and freezing cold. My hair is in my eyes. It's so windy on this barren, rocky outcrop.

"Shoot!"

"No," I gasp and release the weapon. He has won, again. I let my hands fall limply to my sides. Before his free hand can reach my throat I recoil in horror, turn around, and run the last two metres to the abyss. I'd rather die than go back with him!

And then I fall. Into unfathomable, all-consuming depths that envelop me in pure darkness. Before I feel the hard, deadly impact of the water, which must come at any moment, I jerk upright, breathing frantically.

Shaken, but relieved it was only a dream, I sit in the strange bed, breathing heavily. My heart is racing as if I've been sprinting, and the blood is rushing in my ears. I hate it. I hate this dream so much.

Cold sweat beads on my forehead, and I wipe it away with the back of my hand. So as not to be trapped in the merciless darkness a second longer, I lean over to the bedside lamp and switch it on. The darkness is instantly banished.

I hate these senseless nightmares. The ice-cold shudder

that runs down my spine every time. The oppressive, paralysing fear that creeps into my guts. Instinctively, I touch the scar on my neck.

I'm sure I'm just imagining it, but whenever I wake up from these nightmares, it feels like the scar is itching.

I go to the bathroom to wash the sweat from my face. The clock radio on the shelf next to the washbasin reads 03:27. Just two and a half hours and then I can get up and escape the fear and torture of nightmares.

"I hate them. So much." Because I don't know what they mean. It's always the same. I jump off the cliff over and over again. No matter what I do. I've been having these nightmares for three years.

I turn on the tap, wash my face, and brush the strands of brown hair from my forehead. When I've dried my face, I go to the toilet, wash my hands, and go back to bed.

CHAPTER 6

Nuria

Is it the darkness that draws me,
or is it the depths of my heart,
that will eventually, inevitably,
lead me to my demon?

Minute after minute passes, and I stare up at the canopy over my bed, unable to find sleep. My eyes have got used to the darkness, so I can make out the outline of the cupboard diagonally across from me in the small vestibule, and also the fireplace, bookshelves, sofa, and armchair further off in the living room.

I roll restlessly onto my side, shut my eyes, and try to banish the dreadful thoughts. Without success. As I turn to the bedside table again to grab my phone and watch something on YouTube to calm me down, my fingers find empty space.

But... I put it down just there. I feel for the bedside lamp, to switch it on, but however I press the switch, it won't turn on. Is there something the matter with the plug?

"Bloody hell!" I grumble, and get out of bed, but then freeze in my tracks as I hear footsteps on the parquet floor on the other side of the bed. My heart instantly turns to ice.

The back of my neck tingles hot and cold at the same time.

"I love the way you swear."

Impossible. It can't be.

I look slowly over my shoulder. He is here. And he is standing in my rooms. So far he has never broken into my private rooms when I have been there.

Is he here for revenge because I left Spain? Especially after our last meeting... Is he more unpredictable than usual when he's angry?

"Why so still suddenly, little flower? Have you forgotten how to speak, or are you disappointed that I found you so quickly?"

Jerkily, I turn to him. His tall, shadowy outline is picked out by the moonlight against the tiny gap in the curtains.

"You should be in Spain," I whisper.

"I am wherever you are." Scared and confused, I furrow my brow and move slowly around the bed. I have to get out of here. As quickly as possible. I'm sure there won't be a power cut in the hallway.

"You're messed up."

"Tell me something I don't know," he demands, in a throaty and damn arrogant tone, before moving towards me, crouched like a tiger in the dark. Fear constricts my stomach, but I keep moving towards the vestibule. I don't even have a weapon or anything to defend myself with.

"Fuck you! I'll be rid of you. Soon. You've gone too far."

"Are you threatening me?"

"No, I'm warning you," I hiss, running barefoot over the soft rug and then the wooden parquet.

I'm almost there. I'll be at the door any moment and I'll get away from him.

He approaches with an even, fluid stride and snorts mockingly. "Warning me?"

"I'll tell the Monairs you've broken in." I've no idea how he managed it – I'm certain this huge estate has an alarm system.

His snort gives way to arrogant laughter, and my warning seems like a mouse trying to bite a tiger's paw.

"Don't be stupid, *corazón mío!"* he replies, using the Spanish term of endearment for the first time, which makes me even angrier. "If you woke the family, they'd never find me and they'd think you'd gone mad. Besides, I'd come back."

"I'll take that risk, you bastard!" I spit, turning on my heels and running to the door. When I try to pull it open, it won't budge. *Coño! Shit, fuck!* Why not?

I push down on the handle repeatedly, tugging at the door, and feel Demon's presence looming just behind me.

"Listen, you can't escape me. Not if I don't want you to." My heart races like a cornered chick, hypnotised by the deadly gaze of a snake. I turn abruptly to face him. I have nowhere to go.

"Go away! I'm serious! If the stalking doesn't stop I'll report you to the police. Then you'll be behind bars and all you'll be staking out will be the maggots in your mouldy food."

Although it is bloody dark and I can only just make out his tall form, I stick out my chin, feeling for the key in the lock at the same time. I am a thousand percent certain there was a key in the lock when I closed the door behind me after my tour of the house.

Once again, my words seem to amuse rather than impress him.

"I love your smart mouth. I'm sure it can do other things besides threaten me."

"I love that you're going to hell!" When I feel his breath on my face I gather all my courage and push him away from me with both hands. Although I am no weakling, and use plenty of force, he doesn't even flinch. Instead, he seizes my wrists and pulls me to him, so that I involuntarily collide with him. I snarl angrily.

"You belong to me. Even after you die that won't change." He is seriously messed up! Completely crazy!

"I don't belong to anyone," I reply proudly, noticing too late that my hands, which had previously been on his chest, have slid down to his stomach. At this touch, images from our last meeting flash through my mind. How I lay bent over the football table in front of him as he thrust his fingers under my skirt, brought me to the brink of climax.

The door presses against my shoulder blades as he seizes my right wrist and brings it to his hip.

"And I belong to you," he murmurs. Suddenly I feel his hard, powerful erection. To my surprise I don't free myself from his grip. "I belong to you every night, every fucking hour, every moment that you dream of me."

"You are sick," I retort, my voice shaking.

"Then heal me." His grin is unashamed.

I look at him, although he is melded with the darkness and I am practically blind. When I lift my free hand to his face, which I have never seen or felt before now, he backs away a few centimetres from my fingertips, as if my touch causes him pain. Finally, however, he tolerates my fingers. Rough, even stubble runs down his right cheek and tense lower jaw to his chin. Warm, soft lips, whose contours I can feel. In the next moment, teeth bite into my index and middle fingers.

Fuck. This is dangerous, foolhardy, and bloody stupid, but it's exciting, too. He is tall and obviously in good shape and very fit. My nose detects a fine scent of cedar with a hint of mint, as his cock gets harder and harder under my left hand. How is he feeling?

I haven't had sex in a long time. *And sex with a stranger who is stalking you is the answer? No way!*

"Find a psychiatrist. Seriously, there's something wrong with you." Answering his question, I pull my hand back. The next moment, I hear a dark, threatening laugh in my right ear. How this laugh turns me on. It sounds confident, powerful, endlessly captivating, and it vibrates through my body.

"And clearly with you too, given that you kept a hold of my cock." Fuck. He's mocking me.

"Fuck you."

"No, I will fuck you. In every position that will make you scream. In every hole, to mark you as mine. Everywhere, when you least expect it." His words give me goosebumps. But not out of fear.

I have never had an orgasm during sex before. Not with either of the two men I've slept with. Only when I have brought myself to it. And now he's claiming he can make me climax, although he hardly knows me?

"Remember those words. Keep fantasising, because it'll never happen!"

Then I kick his shin hard, squeeze past him, and try to escape to the bathroom. The bathroom is the only place I can hide until dawn.

Demon is a ghost. He disappears as soon as dawn breaks. It's always been like that.

Unfortunately, I don't get far because he grabs my arm, twists it back like we're dancing a tango, and pins me against the door again. This time, however, I have my back to him.

"Dammit! Let me go."

"Absolutely not. I have waited a fucking long time to be able to smell, taste, and feel you again." I breathe unevenly, my breath fogging up the wooden door in front of my face. "Tell me something, Nuria, how often have you thought about me in the last few hours?"

Very often. But not in the way he would like. "I have cursed you every damn hour in my thoughts," I reply confidently.

"You've been begging to see me again since the night before last." If I claimed I didn't enjoy what happened that night, I'd be lying.

"And you want it again, want to feel me deep inside you and you want to come this time. To scream my name and give your body to me."

I shake my head. "You'll kill me when you're done."

"Why would I do that?" He seems genuinely surprised by what I've said.

"Stalkers always kill their victims once they've got what they want," I tell him, aware of his warm hands on my stomach and the back of my neck. He's holding me like a kitten, gripping the back of my neck. He must be hellishly big and strong. I feel the hardness of him against my bottom, feel how he is slowly rubbing himself against me. My memory replays the night before last in every detail, when I was just about to come and then he let me go.

"I don't have to kill you, because you're giving me what I want of your own free will."

I shake my head instinctively, although I know deep inside he's right. His fingers wander over my stomach, sliding down lower to the waistband of my pyjamas. When I hold his wrist, feeling his watch and leather wristbands, he doesn't stop; he grabs my hand and takes it along with his under my pyjama shorts.

"Show me how you want it."

"What?"

My heart is racing, and although I want to stay strong, my body is shaking with anticipation. "Do it to yourself, stick your fingers in your wet pussy. If you come, I'll leave."

"You are..."

"Sick, I know," he murmurs close to my cheek. He bites my ear, and then directs my fingers to my pussy. "Be a good girl and finger yourself."

Gasping, I try to pull my hand away from his, but I can't. He has me trapped against the door with his massive body, pressing his hardness against me, sliding my index and middle fingers against my labia. He rubs and circles my pearl as if they were his own fingers, dipping inside me briefly to spread the wetness around my clit. No, no, no. If he carries on like this, I won't last long.

"Fuck, I can smell your wet pussy. Are you ready for me?"

I immediately freeze, tense up, and beg my body not to give in to his seductive scent. Not to react to his rough, sonorous, and oh-so-expressive voice. Not to continue, even though he keeps on tempting me on.

"Demon."

"I know you have never come with any man before me. That you have kept yourself for me. And I would fuck you hard here and now, make you scream so loud, until you couldn't walk tomorrow. But you have tried to get away from me, repeatedly, even though I gave you so much the night before last. I could fuck you in the arse as a punishment, without making you orgasm." Gasping, I struggle for air. He wouldn't do that. "But I think a much worse punishment would be for you to do it to yourself right in front of me, until you can no longer stand. Begin."

This guy is even more of a sadist and a psychopath than I thought. He continues to circle my clit, applying more pressure. As he goes on, I feel a tingling sensation in my pelvis and my nipples stiffen under my thin top.

"I'm not going to come," I tell him.

"I think you are." How can he be so certain of everything he does? He pulls my hand out of my pants, lifts up my arm, and then licks delightedly at the fingers that have just been touching my pussy. A deep groan leaves his lips as he sucks them. "You taste unbelievably good. It will be a feast for me when I lick you into climaxing."

None of the men before him have ever tried that, because I didn't want it, I couldn't be persuaded to try it, I was somehow too inhibited.

"Never."

I wriggle in his grip again, as he leads my fingers back to my pussy and hungrily pulls at my shorts, which slide down my legs. Before I can resist, my wet fingertips are resting on my clit, which he massages, rubs, and circles until an incredible heat surges through my body and my legs start to tremble.

"That's good. Give me your orgasm."

My clit feels swollen, and soon he doesn't have to direct my hand anymore, because I take over myself. I've reached a point where I don't want to stop anymore, I follow his instruction, let myself fall and finger myself.

"Fuck yourself with your fingers," he orders me. Instinctively I swallow hard, shake my head and close my eyes. "No, if I stop, then..."

Ignoring my objection that I'm going to come soon, he seizes me around the waist and lifts me up effortlessly.

"I make the rules." I utter a disappointed cry.

"This is so ridiculous. Put me down and go away."

"You think what I'm doing is ridiculous?" he asks fiercely,

carrying me to my bed and throwing me face-down on the mattress. Before I can crawl away from him, he grabs the back of my neck and pushes my upper body down deep into the sheets, so that he is standing between my spreadeagled knees. Gripping my neck with one hand, he slaps my right buttock with the other.

"Shit! What are you doing?!"

"Yes, shit. Carry on, or I'll come on you without you having your fun."

"You wouldn't do that, you bastard," I curse. He gives an evil laugh, then gives my buttock a second stinging slap. More powerful than the one before, and the heat burns my skin.

"Finger yourself for me. I want to know how good you are at pleasuring yourself, little flower."

I grind my teeth, then he grabs my right hand and moves it down below my stomach to my pussy. I suddenly feel his breath close behind me, moving over my bum and my labia. Before I realise how near he is to my ass, he licks my buttock, pushes the other one to the side, and sinks his teeth into my skin. God! He has never been this close to me before.

My pussy reacts immediately to his warm, tender breath, and I can feel myself getting wetter.

"Believe me, I know what I'm doing," I assure him.

"Show me." He is not here to take what he wants. He's not trying to fuck me against my will, he wants me to touch myself and pleasure myself?

He leads my fingers more firmly to my opening, until I give in and push a finger inside myself. "Very good. Fuck yourself faster."

And I do exactly that, although just putting my fingers inside myself isn't enough for me. Then he grabs me round the waist and flips me onto my back. "You need my big cock," he jokes.

"I need peace and quiet when I do it. I don't need spectators, you bastard."

"So uptight, little flower?" He laughs darkly before leaning over me and pushing his finger into me with the same rhythm, pressing on my most sensitive spot with his thumb at the same time. This time he doesn't hold me tight.

I gasp for air as his finger goes right inside me, really deep.

"Fuck, you feel even tighter than I imagined. No gloves this time."

He bends down over my throat, bites into my neck, and circles my clit faster.

God! He's better than me. It's as though he knows every detail of my body. The next time he pushes his finger inside me, he puts a second one in too. He fucks me faster, stretches me, makes my body tremble. Without warning he sucks and kisses my neck, exactly where the scar is that I loathe. As his soft lips and the rough stubble of his beard move down towards my collarbone, he tears open my top. I dig my heels into the sheets, wanting to squirm out from under him, but this time I want to orgasm.

"Please..."

"Say my name." And as he increases the speed, I can feel how wet I am, I'm dripping, I shake my head and shut my eyes. His teeth bite painfully into my right nipple, and at the same time he rubs my clit so hard I see stars flashing in the darkness before he pulls me into a never-ending vortex of lust and desire.

I have been gripping the sheets with both hands but now I lift my hands up to hold onto his hoodie. My groans give way to whimpering. Shit, no. No, no, how could I let this happen?

But why does it feel so hellishly good? So good that I want him to be inside me, fucking me hard, like he promised before.

He twists my nipples firmly and in that moment my pussy contracts, while his face moves downwards and he licks my clit. He fucks me so quickly with his fingers that I entwine myself in the sheets, then cry out loudly, "Fuck, Demon!" So bloody loudly that someone will definitely have heard us.

His rough tongue moves firmly over my pearl, which

twitches and feels so tender. Without thinking I screw up my eyes and enjoy what he is doing, tilting my pelvis readily towards him and gripping his hood tightly. I've no idea who he is. No idea what his real name is. No idea what he wants from me.

But damn, what he's doing to me is sooo good.

After what feels like an eternity in which I have completely relinquished control to him and come for a second time so deeply, I beg him to stop.

"Fuck! Please... PLEASE!" I cry ecstatically, arching my spine. My legs are shaking, I breathe jerkily as my pussy tightens around his fingers. "DEMON! Come... on!" He carries on relentlessly, partly to show me how well he knows what my body wants, partly to punish me.

As his fingers move more slowly inside me, the orgasm ebbs away and leaves behind a hot surging feeling in my body. He straightens himself up between my legs. I squint at him, my breathing laboured. A man with no face. A hidden face that he may never reveal to me.

His hand moves possessively over my pussy. "I hope I don't have to spell out to you that from now on she belongs only to me." He pushes his finger inside me again, making me inhale sharply. An unstoppable wave of heat courses through my body. I have never felt so damn happy and satisfied, or so strangely light and weightless.

But I am still determined to take back control from him, and I push myself up on my hands and laugh. "No, we're not together. She doesn't belong to you."

"Oh, really? I don't think you have ever come on another man's hand as hard as you just did on mine." His fingers move provocatively over me. "She belongs to me. Only me."

I move his hand off me immediately, so he can't manipulate me with his touch any longer. I hold the ripped pyjama top over my breasts as he moves his hand up to his completely dark face and demonstratively licks his fingers again.

"We'll meet again soon." He's going?

"Yes, piss off! I'll make sure you don't get anything else from me."

"Have you still not learned that you can't lock me out or hide from me? The game will continue. But do try harder."

"Bastard." Where else can I escape to if not the other side of the globe? To the rainforest? The Antarctic?

"*Your* bastard from now on, little flower," he repeats self-righteously. "Before I forget." His silhouette stops at the corner by the hallway. "What was the dream that made you so afraid?"

My stomach sinks.

What? How long has he been here? I switched the light on in the bathroom. I would have noticed if he'd been in there when I got out of bed after the nightmare.

"Tell me."

"I don't know," I answer truthfully. "About you, perhaps." The figure in my dreams is just as dark and swathed in shadow as him.

He gives a thoughtful "Hmm," then disappears into the hallway. "We'll get to the bottom of it. I'll be seeing you. Everywhere." With these words, he leaves my room. I hear the click of the lock. But...!

He had the key the whole time? Immediately I scrabble over the bed – where I can feel a wet patch – to the bedside table. My shaking fingers make contact with my phone, which had previously disappeared. He must have taken it so I couldn't use the light from the screen to see him by. *Devious, and bloody clever.*

As I switch on the bedside lamp and the light snaps on, I find myself in bed with no pyjama bottoms and a torn pyjama top, bite marks on my breasts and dishevelled hair.

Immediately, I rush to the bathroom, grab the light grey dressing gown, push my arms hurriedly into the sleeves as I go, and tie the belt. I have to follow him. He can't just stroll through the Monairs' house without being seen. There are cameras in practically every corridor as well as on the walls outside. I saw them all yesterday. There are well over twenty cameras, one of which must have spotted this man.

I want to see a picture. After all this time I want to know what he looks like and who he is.

CHAPTER 7

Nuria

I shouldn't enjoy this game of hide-and-seek,
I should bow to reason and shake off my demon.
But how can I,
when I am so enthralled by him?

I pull the door open in a hurry, and am about to rush out into the hallway when Henry, the Monairs' dog, bounds towards me, tail wagging, a white rose in his collar. I ruffle his head in passing, then resume my pursuit. Demon must have fled downstairs to the ground floor. I reach the banisters and look over. The rooms are in semi-darkness. Moonlight shines through the mullioned windows into the luxurious reception area. There is no sign of Demon.

Great. He has got away from me, as he usually does whenever I try to follow him for a change. He lives up to his name – he actually does move like a demon. Noiseless, fast, discreet. "Who are you?" I whisper to myself.

"Awake already?" someone asks behind me, causing me to give a loud shriek. Henry's paws tap over the floor, followed closely by footsteps. I turn around to find Zain, who has appeared in the hallway behind me, his tie undone, his shirt unbuttoned and his hair dishevelled.

"I just woke up and heard a noise."

"Probably me. I got back ten minutes ago and was about to go to the kitchen to get something to eat. Are you coming?"

Zain is obviously drunk. A faint smell of alcohol wafts towards me with every word he says.

As I'm not going to get back to sleep now anyway and this is the first time Zain has shown any interest in speaking to me, I shrug my shoulders. "Sure."

His brown, slightly glassy eyes glide over my body.

Mierda! I had completely forgotten that I'm not wearing pants or shorts under the dressing gown. Somewhat embarrassed, I cross my legs. Zain raises his eyebrows, then looks at Henry, who has sat down next to me. It's only now I realise that Henry didn't make a sound when Demon was here. Surely the family dog would growl or bark, wouldn't he, if a stranger entered the house?

"Where did you get that flower from?" Zain frowns, bending down to Henry, who is pushing his snout against his hand, asking for a tickle. But Zain pulls the rose out of his collar, twists it in his fingers and squints at it.

"Did you put the flower on him?"

"Do I look like I would know where to find roses here?"

He stands up to his full height, and I have to crane my head back because he is at least a head taller than me. He must be around 1.85m tall, not as tall as Demon, but at 1.67m I am definitely small by comparison.

"D'you know what's weird?" he slurs, looking at the flower for a moment and then beckoning me closer with two fingers.

"What's weird?" I ask, going over to him. He lowers his face towards me.

"There are no white roses anywhere in this house. My mother hates white flowers. It's not from here." Carelessly, as though the flower were an empty coke can, he tosses it over the banister.

If Demon sees that, he won't be happy. The rose is definitely from him – he sent me white roses before, in Spain.

"You smell kind of like...," Zain says, unexpectedly sniffing me, grabbing a strand of my tangled hair and studying my face. "Men's aftershave."

"You're imagining it," I reply and hastily step backwards towards the banisters.

"Am I? I saw a guy in a car earlier parked right by the entrance to the house. Coincidence?" He raises his right eyebrow questioningly. I know immediately what he is trying to imply.

I quickly take another step back; his manner is too intrusive for my liking. "What guy?" There's no way he can have seen Demon. "What did he look like?"

"Normal. He was asleep in the driver's seat, blonde hair. That's all I saw." *Blonde hair?*

Suddenly he turns away and walks down the staircase. Henry follows at a trot, wagging his tail.

"Was he in a Mustang by any chance?"

"Yes, that's right."

Damn, that was Anston. Why on earth had Anston parked by the Monairs' drive and gone to sleep? He wanted to go out partying, find some girls, have fun. Or was he hoping I would come with him after all?

"Have you changed your mind or are you coming to the kitchen?" Zain asks. The next moment, looking over at me, he misses a step. He stumbles and curses. "Bloody stairs!"

"I'm coming."

"Not so loud, please," he teases, grinning suggestively and carrying on down.

"Idiot."

Might he have heard me earlier? The heat rises instantly to my cheeks. Shit, please no.

On the one hand, I want to ignore his remark, on the other, I have to know whether he heard me when Demon was there.

I follow him and consider what to say.

"Do you really think I would smuggle a guy into the house on my first night?"

Arriving at the bottom of the stairs, he turns around and looks penetratingly at me, until his gaze becomes too much and I look away. "Well, did you smuggle a man into the house?"

I hate rude counter-questions. "No," I answer truthfully.

Ultimately it's nothing to do with me how Demon managed to gain access.

"Then you don't need to worry about being thrown out. Because believe me, Nurisa..."

"Nuria!" I correct him.

"Nuria, then. A few girls before you tried that and were caught."

He pats Henry's head, grinning broadly.

"You mean, Henry would attack them?"

"That, and the building is alarmed and has video surveillance. It's practically impossible to get in through a window without setting the alarm off. Or to enter the grounds without being caught on film. The recordings are viewed by staff every morning. So if someone had broken into the house and made you moan so loudly that I thought for a moment I had forgotten to pause my porn playlist before I went out, then yes, you'd be found out very quickly."

A semi-provocative, almost angry grin darkens his face. I feel a pain in my stomach. Did he really just say that out loud?

But now I know for sure. He heard me.

"You don't need to feel embarrassed, Nurilla," he teases, laughing mockingly and continuing on his way.

"Do you know what, fuck you. My name's still Nuria, get it, in case your ant brain hasn't grasped it yet!"

"Ants don't have brains," he says, luring me on. "Anyway, I care less about your name than your nocturnal activities. In a few days, you'll be one of the many who have left because they've been kicked out or can't stand it here. So why should I remember what you're called?"

Such an arrogant idiot.

At the beginning of our encounter he was friendly enough, but now he's just having a go at me. He can forget it. I'm not one of those women who let themselves be bullied and humiliated because a guy is rich and self-important. "We'll see whether you end up remembering my name. Because I'm planning on sticking around." I'm definitely not throwing in the towel this fast!

"I'll bet you $10,000 that you don't make it through two months." He must be pretty confident.

"Fine." I walk confidently towards him, hold out my hand and give him a dark look. "I bet..." Shit! What can I bet on? What have I got that's worth $10,000? I don't have that kind of money. Even if he does, he's just blagging and showing off. There's no way he would give me $10,000 if he lost the bet. What a hypocrite.

"What do you bet? Do tell, slut."

"I'm not a slut. I can fuck who I want, when I want and where I want. There's no rule against it."

An unspeakable rage rises in me. But I still can't think what I could stake. He smiles at my hand, moves towards me, puts his arms around my shoulders, and lowers his head, not looking at me.

"There isn't, you're right. But there are rules against letting strangers you do it with into the house."

I didn't let him in.

"You don't have any proof." I jerk free from his grip and push him off me. He veers back, laughing. There's no way my push would have had any impact on him if he weren't drunk. He stinks of gin, cigarette smoke, and weed. His pupils are so dilated, I'd bet my ass he's been taking pills too.

"Oh, I think I'll have some very soon."

"Don't be so sure." If there's one thing I can be absolutely certain of, it's that Demon won't be caught. I've no idea how he manages it, but he's clever. So clever, it scares me. I can feel his presence even now, as though he were listening to the conversation between me and Zain.

"All right, let's wait and see. In the meantime, I've come up with a nice wager, Nutella." *Wanker!*

He takes my hand, only to put it in his other one the next moment. I tug at it. "If you lose, I want you."

"Me?" I frown angrily.

He grins wryly. "You," he confirms, though he'll certainly

regret that decision in a few hours. He has no idea what he's let himself in for. One night with me would mean death. Demon was clear that he sees me as his property.

"Do I have to spell out what I mean by that?"

"You arse!" I hiss. He knows I understand exactly what he means. Sex.

"Do you accept, or are you backing out?" His dark brown irises glint at me.

I swallow hard. "Why do you want me?" It's obvious he doesn't take me seriously, or even like me.

"That's not relevant," he says, unimpressed. It is for me. "You're backing out. I understand, you're all talk." He's extremely good at provoking me.

"I accept, you arrogant arsehole. But only because I'll win. You can be sure I won't be going anywhere in the next two months."

"Wonderful. It's a deal."

I face him resolutely and he lowers his gaze, then looks past me to the banisters. "Father."

"I see you two are getting to know one another." *If only he knew!*

I quickly pull my hand away from Zain. "When did you get back, Zain?" Mr Monair asks, coming down the stairs dressed in a black satin dressing gown and slippers. "Good morning, Nuria."

"A while ago. I went to bed ages ago but then I heard a funny noise in the house and got up to see what was going on." He glances sneeringly at me.

That rotten...!

I smile as if I have no idea what he means. Then I walk towards the rose lying on the marble floor a few metres away and pick it up. "Good morning, Mr Monair. I don't want to disturb you. I'll just get a quick coffee." I hold the flower carefully in my hand as though it were something precious, closing my fingers around it.

Before Zain can get another word in, I head down the corridor that leads to the kitchen.

"Why are you up so early? Couldn't you sleep?" Mr Monair calls after me. Before Zain has the chance to say anything, I stop, turn around and reply, "The jet lag messed me up. I'm going to go for a quick run and then I'll be ready for my first day with the girls."

"That's what I call discipline," Mr Monair says. "You should try it, Zain."

Zain rolls his eyes as Mr Monair looks at me. I carry on walking, and hear subdued conversation between father and son. It sounds less friendly than it did a few seconds earlier.

"Where have you been?" his father says to Zain. "Have you looked in the mirror?"

I don't want to eavesdrop, so I hurry through the door into the kitchen and bury my face in my hands. What a crazy morning.

CHAPTER 8

Nuria

Only the light can drive demons away.
Yet during the day, every demon
seems like your best friend.
Who is really wearing a mask?

Drenched in sweat and breathing heavily from my run, I knock on the driver's side window. Anston is asleep on the seat, though it's already light. "Ans! Hey! Wake up!"

He doesn't move at first, and it flashes through my mind that he might be dead. I am not completely certain my shadow is capable of killing people, although he has more than once given me to understand that he would dispatch anyone who might represent competition.

Demon is welcome to take care of Zain the Arsehole. After this morning's conversation, I'd even approve.

After a minute or so of me drumming against the window, Anston pulls a face, blinks, and stares at me sleepily. *Thank God, he's still alive.*

I gesture frantically for him to open the window. Instead, he opens the door, and I immediately pull it wide open.

"What the hell are you doing here? The family's son has seen you parked here. I thought you were going to drive back and go out for the evening," I grumble. He screws up his face as though he has the headache from hell.

"Can you talk more quietly, Nuri? My head is absolutely pounding."

"From what?" I ask. "Did you get drunk on your own in the car?"

"No, damn it. Don't talk such shit. Why would I drink here on my own? Where's the fun in that? I was waiting for you."

In my black leggings and dark purple sports bra, I straighten up by the open passenger door.

"I said I didn't want to go into Brisbane with you. Why didn't you drive back?"

"No idea... I was standing by the gate..." He nods at the closed wrought-iron gate to the property around twenty metres away and then looks at me with a confused expression. "Now I'm here... in the car."

"What does that mean?"

"No idea... I don't know what I'm doing here, that's what it means!" Yesterday evening I saw his car turn around. I watched him walk past the headlights to get into the car. What could have happened to make him forget why he parked up at the side of the road all night? It doesn't make any sense.

"Although," he stammers, running his hand over his forehead, then looking in the rear-view mirror. "When I got in, there was someone in the back seat."

"Someone was in the back seat?" I repeat, frowning and grimacing as though he's making it up or has seen too many horror films.

"That's what I said. They pushed something against my mouth and then... everything went black."

Does he mean he was drugged? Could it have been Demon, trying to get Anston out of the way? To stop him trying to persuade me to go out with him? I wouldn't put it past him.

"Okay. That sounds pretty weird." And creepy. At the thought of Anston being attacked and drugged, an ice-cold shudder runs down my back.

Somehow I have the uncomfortable feeling that everything has got much worse and much more dangerous since we arrived in Australia.

"Did you see what the person looked like?" I ask. But Anston shakes his head. "No. No, I didn't see anything. It was dark and it all happened much too quickly."

"Shit! You should report it to the police, Ans."

"I thought of that, too, but... what would I say? I don't know what the guy looks like. I couldn't give them anything to go on."

As messed up as this is, he is probably right.

Agitated, I run my hand over my face, sigh, and close my eyes.

"The best thing for you to do is to drive back to the hotel. I have to go into the house, shower, and then take care of the children. Do you think you'll be ok on your own?"

"I'd rather you were with me, but I don't suppose I can persuade you to come back with me?"

He looks bloody awful. But if I drive him back to Brisbane, there's no way I'll start work on time.

He gives me a pleading look, then hangs his head. "Did you go for a run?"

"Yes, in the woods." And I honestly never imagined Anston would still be here. I actually thought Zain was playing a trick on me.

"I can't, Ans. You'll have to drive yourself back."

He sighs in disappointment. "I didn't think the trip to Australia would be like this."

If I'm honest, neither did I. "I came because you didn't want to fly out here alone and because we wanted to spend time together, remember?"

"Of course I remember. But I have to do my job. When I have some free time, I'll drive over and make it up to you, okay?" Guilt stirs quietly in my stomach: he's feeling bad and I'm letting him down again.

"This evening. Let's do something this evening."

I bite my lower lip, thinking, then give him an encouraging smile. That usually placates him. "This evening. I promise. I've got to go." I stroke his left shoulder apologetically, by way of goodbye. He grabs my lower arm and runs his fingers over my skin.

"You really do promise?"

I grin, raise two fingers and say, "Nuria's word of honour. See you this evening."

I can see from the look in his chestnut-brown eyes that he's already looking forward to the evening. Before I remove my hand from his shoulder, he lifts it to his lips. He's never done that before. Then he releases my fingers.

It feels strange, him touching me like that. Was it deliberate? Did he mean anything by it?

So as not to continue staring at him, I step away from the black Mustang and wait until he starts the engine and shuts the passenger door. As he reverses and turns the car around, I run over to the gate. My Apple watch glows on my wrist and I see a message from an unknown number.

> Do I need to worry about my flower
> having two other admirers?

I snort and ignore Demon's message. It's starting again. He's tracking me, and he knows exactly where I am and who I am with.

By the time I am back in my room it is 6:40. I hurriedly shower, clean my teeth, dry my hair and tie it up. Then, as it looks like it's going to be a hot day, I put on some comfortable dark blue shorts and a loose-fitting sleeveless blouse.

Another message from Demon catches my attention as I'm threading my belt through the loops. I shouldn't read it. Just pretend I haven't seen it. It's followed by another. From its position on the bedside table, my phone keeps flashing.

I am far too curious to know what he's writing. And I also want to know whether it was him who attacked Anston. As soon as I've done my belt up, I grab my phone and read his messages.

Tell me. Do I have to start planning how to get rid of them?

There's no point in ignoring me, my flower.

You know I'll keep messaging until I get an answer. And I'll always get one.

I inhale deeply, then type a reply.

Why don't you tell me whether it was you who drugged Anston in his car? That wasn't funny!

I have hardly replied before he is back.

Why would I do that?

Did you or didn't you?

No.

No? Who was it then? Or is he lying to me? I look up from my phone irresolutely, and at that moment there's a knock at the door. Oh, shit! It's 7 o'clock.

Hastily, I shove the phone into my pocket, then run to the door, stepping into my slippers as I go.

Jacky is standing at the door. "Good morning, Nuria. Are you ready?"

She's wearing a pastel green suit and an expectant smile.

"Of course. Let's go."

"Very good. I'll show you the girls' morning routine." Which turns out to be highly chaotic.

Hailey fights tooth and nail to avoid going to preschool, while Maily looks on and runs away from Jacky.

In the dining room, the situation escalates to the point that Hailey knocks over her cereal bowl and milk runs all over the table.

"I'm not going to preschool! Not anymore!" she cries defiantly, crying tears of hysterical rage. Unsure whether to get involved, I look at Jacky, who is losing her last vestige of patience. She keeps looking at her phone. I know she has a meeting soon.

"This isn't how mornings normally go," she apologises, embarrassed by her children's behaviour.

"I can stay with the girls," I suggest. "And then we can really get to know each other today."

A member of staff wipes up the spilt milk, as Jacky jumps up quickly from her chair. "Are you sure that would be all right?"

I nod, smiling. "Of course it would."

Maily examines me closely. "I don't want to get to know her." Lovely. She's a real ray of sunshine.

"You'll like her, my darling," Jacky tells her, hugging her from behind her chair and kissing her dark-blonde hair.

Hailey throws her spoon down on the table, then pushes herself forcefully away from it, her chair scraping loudly across the floor. She slides off her seat.

"Where are you going?" asks Jacky.

"To my room. I'm packing my case and moving out."

What an announcement. Jacky inhales deeply, exhausted and overwhelmed by her spirited children. I get up too, passing my plate of half-eaten pancakes to the staff member, and Jacky asks me a second time whether I'm okay to look after both girls today.

"It's no problem, really," I reassure her.

She smiles thankfully at me, then disappears, her Louboutin heels tapping quickly through the double doors to the dining room. She inhales again and turns round. "Thank you, Nuria. If you need any help, just ask the staff. My husband is already at work. Zain will be upstairs in his room, asleep."

What would I want with Zain? To wake him up and save his life if the house was burning down? That'd be the last thing I'd think of doing.

I'm not malicious, but after this morning's encounter I can picture myself standing outside the burning house with both children, looking up at the third floor and knowing Zain's backside is about to get a good roasting.

Luckily, Jacky can't see my grin as my imagination runs away with me.

Maily runs off ahead of me, too, and I follow both girls up to the second floor. When I get to their door, it is locked. Not just closed, but blockaded somehow.

"Hey, can you open the door, please?" I call to the twins.

"You stay outside! We don't want you in our room." *Cheeky little squirts.*

"Well, I'm afraid you're out of luck, because I'm coming in whether you like it or not."

I put my shoulder against the door and push it open forcefully. I have no idea how two five-year-olds managed to push a chest of drawers across the door in such a short time, but it takes me a lot of effort to open it. When I look through the crack in the door, the chest of drawers has been pushed aside. Behind it, Maily, a sugar-sweet expression on her face, is standing on a chair, hiding something behind her back.

"Get out!" she orders, as if she could tell me what to do. As if I'd let a five-year-old girl boss me around.

"Why?" I ask, pushing the door further open and moving the chest of drawers back, so that neither the door nor the piece of furniture sustain any damage.

"Because we don't want you here. Just like we didn't want the others."

"Which others?" I ask, confused.

"The other women who were supposed to look after us," Hailey answers. She's dressed in red trousers and a white T-shirt, and she walks past the wobbly chair on which Maily is standing. Something floppy smashes into my right leg. I look at the floor in surprise as more shots are fired at me.

A lake of water forms around my feet. Are they serious? They're pelting me with water balloons.

"Hey, stop this nonsense!" The two of them giggle at my response. "That's not..." *Wham!*

A water balloon hits my right shoulder, bursts, and sprays water in my face. "... funny."

"Get out!" "Go away!" they both shout, over and over again. "We won't stop. We have loads of balloons here." Hailey runs around the corner of the bedroom wall and drags a large plastic box over to her sister's chair. Maily throws two more balloons that I quickly try to catch.

"I'm not going away." They can forget that idea.

I have every desire to get out of here and slam the door behind me, but I am definitely not giving in. If I give in once, they'll just carry on pushing the boundaries.

I manage to catch one of the balloons mid-flight and throw it back at Maily. But I aim it to burst on the seat of her chair. I don't want to hit her in the head and make her fall off the chair and hurt herself. Thanks to my volleyball training, I can throw pretty well. But how would I explain to Jacky that one of the girls had injured herself on her first day under my care, and we might have to go to hospital? No, better not.

"Don't throw them back," Maily grumbles.

"I will! If you're pelting me, I'm going to pelt you, too." I fight my way closer to them as Hailey chucks more water balloons in my direction and gives two to her sister. A lot of them miss, burst on the chest of drawers, or hit the walls. As Hailey runs to Maily again to pass her two balloons, she slips and bangs her arm on the back of her sister's chair. Shit!

Maily immediately stops her attack and I rush over to Hailey, who has landed on the floor and has started to cry loudly.

"Hailey, are you okay?" her sister asks, jumping off the chair and kneeling down next to her. "Get up. She's in the room. Get up."

But Hailey carries on crying, shakes her head, and pulls her hand away from her sister, who's trying to help her up.

"Where does it hurt?" I ask Hailey, crouching down next to her and coming to her aid. Cautiously, I get her to her feet. She points to her shoulder, large tears rolling down her cheeks. She tries to break free, but I hold her more tightly. "Wait a minute. The battle will resume later. First we must attend to the casualty," I tell them both. Maily glares at me angrily.

"We have won. You are the loser."

As if that was important now, but if it calms them down, I'm happy to agree. "Yes, you two are the victors. You have very good aims."

Maily folds her arms proudly and nods, while Hailey continues to whimper. I rub her shoulders gently. She pulls back the collar of her T-shirt. "I am broken."

"You're broken?"

"Yes, my shoulder." She taps her shoulder with her finger. But with every second that passes, her tears lessen. A red spot appears on her little shoulder, which I blow on. She looks at me as if I am from another planet. "What are you doing?"

"Blowing, then the injury heals faster. Everyone knows that."

"Does it help?" Maily asks, bending down next to me in her soaking wet purple trousers and canary yellow T-shirt, watching me.

"Can you feel the magic?" I ask Hailey. Carefully, I wipe her tears away with my knuckles.

"A little bit. It tickles."

"That means your shoulder is healing already," I reassure her.

Maily purses her lips. "When you're better, Hailey, we'll carry on with the battle." She rushes over to the box to fetch more water balloons.

The parquet floor is already slick with water. If the water damages the wood, I'm in trouble.

"I've got a better idea!" I say.

"What?" Hailey asks, looking over her shoulder. I straighten her T-shirt. It's lucky she isn't more seriously hurt.

"Let's carry on with the water fight outside, in the garden. We can run around out there and hide. It'll be much more fun than in the bedroom." Hailey looks at her sister, her cheeks flushed.

"We'll need more water balloons for that."

"Oh yes. A lot more," I agree, smiling. "Where's your supply?"

While the pair of them go in search of the balloons, I go into the children's bathroom to fetch towels to wipe the water from the floor, and then push the chest of drawers back into place against the wall. I have a sneaking suspicion the twins will be keeping me on my toes. This won't be their last attempt to get rid of me.

CHAPTER 9

Demon

Even her thorns can't
keep me from getting close to her.
The stabbing pain is nothing compared
to the emptiness
I feel when I'm not with her.

It's like an addiction. She's my personal drug, the habit I can't kick. Once I've started, I can sit in front of the monitors for hours, watching what my little rose does all day.

Quest has hacked the Monair estate's security system to allow me to see the camera footage from my laptop. Getting into the building undetected, without triggering the alarm, was a piece of cake.

My outstretched legs crossed loosely on the table, I stroke Odin's head and take a drag on my cigarette. The smoke rises to the panelled ceiling of the fireside lounge.

This is where I have set up my temporary work station. The Airbnb property exudes the classic charm of a stately home. Dark parquet flooring, elegant fireplaces of tile or polished stone, wood-panelled walls, paintings of polo players, and antlers above the solid wooden doors. The house has an English flair that makes a change from my modern loft in Barcelona, which I rented using false papers.

The leather of the Chesterfield couch creaks under my weight as I bend over to the ashtray on the broad armrest and stub out my cigarette. Odin winds his way across my chest to my shoulder as I watch Nuria playing with the twins in the garden. She's doing pretty well. I didn't think she'd be so good with children.

Especially not when the brats have locked her out of their room and drenched her in water. The girls are giving her a really hard time, but she won't back down. That's my flower. Fragile, but determined, and bloody strong-willed.

There is an unexpected knock on the door, just as I am watching Nuria's slim body running across the lawn, the outline of her breasts wonderfully clear as they bounce up and down under her damp blouse. What will her tits look like when she's riding me?

"Yes, come in," I mumble irritably, snapping the laptop shut. Quest and Lexton enter the room. While Quest is more of a classy guy with a heart, Lexton is a sly dog who takes everything he can get. Even if it's not his due.

"We've got news you'll probably want to hear. Or are we disturbing you?" *Yes, you fucking are disturbing me. I'm watching Nuria.*

"What news?" I lift Odin's head carefully off the back of the Chesterfield couch before he slides into the gap between the wall and the sofa and I have to move the furniture to get to him. He loves dark slits, just like me. Fuck. I can't help thinking about last night. I can still taste Nuria's pussy on my tongue, hear her loud, ecstatic moans in my head, and feel the soft skin of her nipples against my teeth.

Concealing my hard-on, I stand up and carry Odin over to his terrarium.

"Damn, that creature has grown," observes Lexton, his eyes wide. "He was a lot smaller two months ago."

"You're just imagining it. Before, you saw him coiled up in the terrarium. Can you hold him for a minute?" I know how scared Lex – who is otherwise pretty much afraid of nothing – is of snakes. Without giving him the chance to find an excuse, I hand him my pet, who is almost 1.5m long. He takes him rather awkwardly, while I open the lid of the terrarium and ensure the lamp is set to the correct temperature.

"Shit, he's heavy," he grumbles.

Before he can whine any more, I take the tiger python and place him in the terrarium.

"What news?" I repeat my question, because they're not getting to it.

Lexton, who is wearing a suit, clears his throat, exchanges a quick glance with Quest, and continues. "We've found two witnesses. The pair are allegedly the last to have seen the missing seventeen-year-old woman."

"She's more of a girl really," Quest interrupts.

"Girl then," Lexton replies irritably, rolling his eyes. "The two witnesses were the last to see Vendra before she disappeared."

"Where?" I ask, closing the terrarium and turning to face them.

"Near an abandoned church. St Michael's is now derelict and has been overgrown with bushes and trees in recent decades. Young people meet up there as a dare. They sleep overnight and do other dares because – brace yourselves – it's supposed to be haunted."

How funny. "And that's where the witnesses saw Vendra?"

"Right," Quest says. "According to the police reports, Vendra filled up her car at 11:47 p.m., and was caught on camera at the petrol station. These are the last video recordings of her, from two months ago." Quest shows me the footage from the petrol station, of a blonde woman getting into a Toyota. "Then, puff, she's gone. Her car, a silver Toyota Yaris, was found three days later around a mile away from this church. Empty. The doors were wide open, and the heavy rain and wind had destroyed any evidence in and around the vehicle. Do you think she was in the church?"

"I'm not making any assumptions until I have more evidence. Let's pay a visit to the church," I decide. "Tonight."

They both stare at me as though I've eaten an alien for breakfast. "Has one of you just shat yourselves because you're afraid of ghosts? I assure you, the only ghost we're going to meet will be me."

"As if I'd believe those stupid old wives' tales," Lexton

counters, with an artificial laugh. "Why don't you want to go there during the day?"

"Because I'm sure the church won't be empty at night."

There'll definitely be young people hanging around. And intimidating teenagers when they're drunk is far more entertaining than intercepting them at school and forcing them to talk to us there.

"What about the witnesses? Do you want to speak to them beforehand?" *Of course I do.* The faster we fulfil this missing person contract and find Vendra, the more time I can spend with my rose.

And I can hardly wait to watch her sleeping again tonight. Even if I'm bothered by the nightmares that make her mortally afraid night after night. I'm working on this too. On Nuria's past, which has to be at the root of her nightmares.

"Yes, I want to speak to them. Who are they?"

"Kai Wilson and Jenna Whittaker. Classmates of Vendra's, but not her best friends."

"Her enemies, perhaps?" I ask, grabbing my leather jacket from the couch and slipping it on over my grey shirt.

"No idea. So far it doesn't look as though Vendra had enemies. She was well-liked, full of energy, friendly. One of those classic high-school girls everyone likes."

Everyone has enemies, even if they don't know who they are. There's always some kind of envy lurking behind the façade of friendship.

"Okay, let's talk to them."

We enter a typical high school to meet Kai and Jenna, who wanted to talk to us somewhere safe.

No wonder. As a teenager, I would have panicked too, if I'd come across Lexton. Lexton has tattoos that extend from his neck all the way down to his knuckles, and he has this penetrating killer stare that a lot of people find off-putting. He only reveals his other, slightly friendlier side to those who are closest to him.

Kai swallows nervously as he regards Lexton from the bench in the school reception. Kai is a gangly boy who I assume usually has a big mouth. Right now, he looks as though he has swallowed a toad.

Quest is examining the sports trophies and student photos on display further into the reception area, and I sit down next to Jenna. Jenna – a red-haired girl with a side parting wearing a light-coloured skirt and a neckline that is too low for my taste – immediately moves away from me.

"You offered money in exchange for information," Kai begins. At this, I lean my head back and look up at the staircase of the large, newly renovated school. A few groups of pupils are coming down the stairs.

"There is a payment. But only if the information proves useful," I say to Kai. Jenna also turns to face Kai, who is sitting next to her on the long bench in front of the window, chewing nervously on his lower lip.

"Okay. Sure, bro, I understand. We're not lying. We're telling the truth."

"Then tell us again what you told me and the guy over there this morning." Lexton gestures behind him towards Quest, who is looking at each photo with studied indifference, as though we were on a visit to a museum.

"How much will we get, if the information is correct?" Jenna wants to know. She looks at me as if she thinks she can stand up to me. I give her a tired smile. "5,000 dollars."

Her neatly plucked brows twitch. "Okay. Do you want to start, Kai, or shall I?"

"You. You were the last person to speak to Vendra."

"Never mind who does the talking, just get on with it," Lexton urges them.

"Like we told you this morning, there is this hidden church in the woods, about ten miles from here. There are secret parties there, rituals, people make recordings, sick things. Stuff that's completely illegal. Not just smoking grass, more than that. I think it's haunted. And I'm not the only one who thinks so. Kai and I saw Vendra there for the second time one Friday two months ago. She isn't the kind of girl who goes to things like that, but she had a crush on some guy, so..."

"Jazeem Lender," Kai reveals. "The captain of the football team." What a cliché. "He and his mates go to the church nearly every weekend and kick off. That's probably why Vendra was there. She seemed different when we ran into her."

"Different how?" I enquire.

"Well, she seemed kind of jittery, sort of confused, a bit desperate, she was on the path that leads to the church. She was mumbling to herself, her hair was all messed-up, like she'd been pulling at it."

"Was she hurt?" Lexton asks. "Was she bleeding, or dirty, like she'd fallen over?"

Jenna and Kai look at one another. "Maybe. No idea. It was so dark that night. I just shone my phone torch at her quickly, because we wanted to know who she was."

Lexton narrows his eyes.

"And then?" I ask.

"Well then I asked if everything was ok. She said it was all good, she was fine. Which was obviously a lie. Anyone could see that. Perhaps she was embarrassed we'd seen her like that. She looked really awful." Jenna shrugs her shoulders. "I would've been embarrassed." Her mud-brown eyes shift from Lexton to me.

"And then you carried on?" I continue the questioning and make notes on my phone. Damn, Nuria still hasn't replied. Time for another punishment.

"Yes," Kai explains. "We went to the church, where the party was rocking."

"Around what time was that?" Lexton interrupts.

"Er, around half past midnight maybe? Or maybe quarter to one. I didn't look at the time. But I happened to look at the clock when I saw Jenna leaving the church with Vendra, around 2:20 a.m."

"You left the church with Vendra, Jenna, who you're not really friends with. Why?" I ask.

"Because she seemed really upset. Drunk and somehow..." She tries to think of the right words and gestures in the air with her right hand. "More."

"Somehow more?" Lexton takes a step towards her. "What do you mean by that?"

"Well, I know how someone behaves when they're drunk. She seemed like she might have taken something else."

"You mean drugs?" Lex asks. "Do they deal drugs in the church? Hash, coke, pills?"

Kai and Jenna exchange meaningful looks again and nod in a practised way. "You didn't hear it from us, okay? Or we'll be finished."

I rub my forehead and smile briefly. "Don't worry. So you went into the woods with Vendra because she wasn't feeling well, Jenna. And then?"

"I hoped someone would take her home. That she might get a lift with friends. I didn't want to let her drive by herself. She was drunk and completely out of it. But no matter how hard I tried to persuade her, she didn't want to leave the party, she wanted to sort something out. She kept saying that over and over again. 'I have to sort something out. I have to speak to him. '"

"Him?" Quest asks, having found his way back to us after his tour of the reception area.

"Yes, him," Jenna replies. "She definitely meant Jaz."

"Jazeem?" I ask.

"Yes, Jazeem. Most people call him Jaz. She can only have wanted to stay longer because of him." Unless Vendra said who she meant by *him*, I don't completely buy Jenna's interpretation.

"And then things got strange," Jenna continues. "I mean, really weird." The seventeen-year-old inhales deeply and then gives her head a brief shake, as though she can't quite grasp what she experienced. "She suddenly agreed after all that she'd go with my friend Layla, and she went over to her.

Kai rang me just at that moment, so I only caught a glimpse of Vendra as she walked down the path through the woods to Layla's car. She even spoke to her, Layla told me the next morning. But she never asked whether Layla could give her a lift."

"So what did she say?"

"She said Layla would be next" *Next?*

"Next what?" Lexton asks irritably. "Stop talking in riddles, just say."

"Layla didn't know either. She asked Vendra what she meant. But then Vendra carried on down the path and no-one saw her again. No-one I know, at least."

"Where could she have gone?" I ask.

"No idea," answers Jenna. "There's only forest, fields, and marsh for about five miles all around the church. The police think she ran away, had a fatal accident, or somehow took her own life in the woods or the marsh. Complete rubbish, if you ask me."

"Why's that?" Lexton asks curtly. I'm aware that the questioning is going too slowly for him, and that he's sick of having to drag each piece of information out of the two youngsters.

"Because although she did seem really upset that evening, she wanted to speak to someone. I bet she met that person and that the conversation didn't go well."

The question is, why she was so distressed an hour earlier. If she drove from the petrol station to the church in a normal state, something must have happened in the half hour before Jenna met Kai the first time. But what? What happened?

"You didn't tell them about the thing with Layla," Kai interjects.

"What thing with her?" I study the pair's expressions. I'm usually very good at reading people's faces and know when they're lying to me.

Kai licks his lips and looks me directly in the eyes. A sign that he wants to make a connection with me, make me believe him.

"Layla Newman went missing a week ago," Quest preempts him, holding a missing poster of her right under my nose. "This was on the notice board over there."

"Exactly. She went missing last Friday, after going back to the church."

Dammit, there seems to be a lot going on at this church, the place where young women mysteriously disappear. "Were you at the church last Friday?"

They both shake their heads vehemently. "No," Kai replies. "Definitely not."

"I'm never going there again in my life." Jenna shudders. "There are either evil spirits there, or someone is targeting schoolgirls. Both are horrendous. As far as I'm concerned, St Michael's Church is a bad place."

CHAPTER 10

Nuria

He poisons my mind,
yet it feels good.
He possesses my body,
yet I feel free.
He punishes my sins,
yet I feel drawn to him.

"Why don't you want to go to preschool anymore?" I ask Hailey, as we jump up and down on the trampoline in the garden, with her doing some daredevil twists and turns.

"Because Ranja always used to take us there. She's much nicer than Mama."

"Ranja?" I repeat, lowering my head and pushing myself up off the trampoline.

"Our sister," Hailey replies casually, not looking at me, as she falls and then pulls herself back to her feet using the fabric of the trampoline.

"You have a sister?" I stop moving, abruptly. "Where is she now?"

"Dead." Maily climbs through the opening in the net around the trampoline, shuffles over the edge on her bottom and jumps down onto the grass. "Dead. She's dead." What is she saying?

"No she isn't!" Hailey counters, giving her twin a poisonous look. "She's not dead."

"Where do you think she is, then?" I ask, dropping onto the undulating fabric so I can look Hailey in the eye.

"She's just out of town. Ranja would never leave us and not come back," she says, looking down.

"She can't come back if she's dead," Maily puts in.

"And how do you know she is dead?" I direct my question to Maily. I didn't plan to talk to five-year-old children about death, but how else am I supposed to respond? I'm also interested in finding out more about this sister I didn't know about before. If their sister was able to drive them to preschool, she must have been at least sixteen years old.

"Mama and Papa spoke to the police about it, secretly. We listened in." These girls are really smart. Maily puts on her trainers then moves away from us, her shoulders hunched. The loss of her older sister obviously troubles her a great deal.

"I can show you something, if you want," Hailey whispers to me unexpectedly, cupping both her hands around my ear.

"Show me what?" I whisper back, because it's probably top secret.

"I have a book of Ranja's."

"And that's what you'd like to show me?"

She nods. "I can't read very well. Only a teensy bit." She raises her delicate thumb and forefinger, indicating a tiny amount. "But you can read it to me. Do you like reading stories?"

A broad smile spreads over my lips. "I really like reading stories. My favourites are fairytales and fantasy stories with evil princes."

"I can't stand evil princes." Hailey wrinkles her little snub nose. That moment, I catch a movement out of the corner of my eye. I turn my head towards the terrace and see Zain. I haven't seen him since our encounter first thing this morning. It is now just after 4 p.m. Has he been asleep all this time?

But hey, why should I care what that pain in the arse has been doing? "I can't stand most evil princes either," I agree.

She giggles. "Come on, I'll show you the book."

Zain walks across the terrace to the lounge, bare-chested

in low-slung black tracksuit bottoms, a towel around his neck as though he's just come from the gym. I catch myself studying him closely. Although he is over 20m away, and the glittering pool lies between us and the terrace, I can see how toned his body is, even from this distance. His stomach is flat and he has well-defined chest and arm muscles. I can also see a tattoo on his side, although I can't make out the design.

I purse my lips as a blonde woman with a ponytail steps through the patio doors behind him, wearing close-fitting violet shorts and a sports bra. She is definitely not just his personal trainer. Zain drops nonchalantly onto the white cushions of the dark outdoor seating and a member of staff brings him a shake. He only turns his face in my direction when I have clambered off the trampoline and am looking for my shoes.

"Do you want to show me your book now?" I ask Hailey, in an attempt to get away from Zain's gaze as quickly as possible.

"Yes."

I hold out my hand and she places her hand in mine. Maily has retreated to the garden swing, and seems to be deep in thought, or sulking. I haven't really managed to connect with her yet. Though I've been able to gain Hailey's trust in just a few hours, Maily is still mostly shutting me out.

"Maily, come inside," I ask.

"No!"

Zain continues to observe us. Shit. I can't leave her out here on her own. If anything happens to her it'll be my fault. Her brother doesn't look like he'd be willing to watch her for a moment – he's more concerned with trying to feel up the blonde, who sits down next to him, hitching a leg over his. His fingers circle her knee absentmindedly, moving up towards her inner thigh.

Dammit, look away, Nuria. He's just winding you up.

"Come on, Maily, I'm going to show her the secret book," Hailey calls to her sister. "She can read it to us."

Maily jumps straight off the swing, streaks towards us like a bolt of lightning, and races past without comment.

What's up with her? I follow, holding Hailey's hand. As we reach the terrace, the blonde woman throws her arms around Zain's neck, buries her hands in his thick, dark hair, and tries to kiss him. Tries, because he turns his face away to stare at me.

"Everything hunky-dory, Nuria?"

If Hailey wasn't with me, I'd have given him the middle finger. No, shoved it up his arse.

"Perfect," I reply. "It looks a bit crowded over there."

He snorts, opens his mouth, and narrows his eyes.

"What did she say?" the blonde asks, put out, as I quickly disappear into the house with Hailey.

I suppress a laugh, and Hailey notices.

"What's so funny?" she asks as we walk, looking up at me.

"Oh, nothing," I reply, then crouch down in front of her and point to my back. "Okay, hop on." Her eyes light up as she grasps what I mean. She climbs carefully onto my back, and wraps her arms around my neck and her legs round my stomach. I give her a piggyback up to the second floor.

As we arrive in the children's room, she jumps off my back, laughing. "That was fun. You are the best horse, Nuria."

Maily greets us, standing by her bed with a closed expression on her face.

"She can't have the secret book," she protests.

"But she can read it. She'll tell us what's in it," Hailey says, walking towards her sister and taking her shoulders. Maily shakes her head obstinately, holding something behind her back. Probably the book in question. What's so interesting about it? Why's Maily decided not everyone can see it?

"It doesn't matter, Hailey. It's okay if your sister doesn't want to show it to me." Hailey turns to me.

"You have to read it to us. I want to know what's in it. The writing is too curly for us." Curly? So it's handwritten, not a regular book of fairytales. Hailey tussles with her sister for a while and gets the book off her.

"Don't give it to her!" Maily cries angrily. Hailey proudly presents me with a black notebook with *Daily Notes* written on it in golden lettering. I raise my eyebrows in surprise before leafing quickly through the book. It is clearly a diary. "Where did you get this?"

"It's Ranja's story. Her book. She wrote fairytales in it every day. That's what she always said to us. They are secret fairytales. You have to read them to us."

"We'll be able to read them ourselves soon," Maily interrupts, stepping towards me and holding out her hand for the book.

"Hailey, your sister is right. These are private stories, they're not meant to be read by anyone else," I tell her. I shut the book and return it to Maily, who immediately wraps her arms around the cover, as though she were protecting a precious treasure.

"I don't want to wait. Ranja's fairytales are in the book. She always read us stories. Nearly every evening." Hailey looks as though she's about to cry. She looks helplessly at Maily, who has a tight grip on the book. "Please, Maily..."

Maily looks at her sister, sticking resolutely to her position. "We'll get in trouble if Mummy and Daddy find out we have the book," Maily says to her sister. "They're already looking for it."

I hold back. This all seems very strange. A daughter in the family is declared dead – a fact no one has mentioned to me before. Police officers talking to their parents. A diary that has been hidden by the twins. Shouldn't their parents know about this? I have already toured the estate twice. I have never seen a young woman or a teenage girl in any of the pictures. If my daughter had gone away or died, there would be memories and pictures hanging on the walls.

"They won't look in Nuria's room, will they?" Hailey looks at me. "Mummy only looks in our cupboards for the book. If she finds it there she'll know we took it."

"Where have you been hiding it?" I ask them.

"Under the mattress," Hailey tells me.

“Shhhh.” Maily presses her index finger to her lips. “She might tell Mummy.”

“She won’t. You promise, don’t you?”

I nod and hold my fingers up. “Word of honour. I won’t say anything to anybody.”

It would be a fatal mistake to blow the whistle on them. That would destroy the little bit of trust I’ve built up over the last few hours, at one blow.

Maily comes up to me and puts the diary into my hands. “Read it aloud.”

I sit down on Hailey’s bed. To be honest, this whole thing is making me uncomfortable. This is a diary of the intimate experiences of a young woman I don’t even know. But what if there are secrets in there that might be important? To read or not to read? The girls sit down either side of me on the bed, and Maily speeds my decision by opening the book. “Read it out.”

CHAPTER 11

Demon

In most forests, wolves lurk
deep in the shadows,
waiting to quench their bloodlust
on innocent girls.
I stand over them and slay the wolves,
because I am the only one who can.

I switch off the headlights of my Cadillac Escalade. It is just before midnight and dammit, I'd rather be with Nuria than going to a silly teenage party. Especially when I know Nuria is off partying in Brisbane tonight with her pea-brained boyfriend, Anston. If that son of a bitch touches her, I'll rip his eyes out of his skull and shove them down his throat.

"Shall we?" asks Lexton, taking a last drag on his cigarette before flicking it out of the open window. "Or do you want to keep on looking at Instagram stories? Who is that, anyway?"

Without waiting for my permission, he grabs my phone from my hand and watches Nuria's Insta story. She's filming herself in a bar. My stomach clenches at the thought that other people besides Anston could be throwing themselves at her. She belongs to me. All of her.

"An assignment," I explain, removing my phone from his hands.

"Hot stuff." I turn slowly towards him and give him a murderous look. "What?"

"Shut your mouth and get out," I order gruffly.

"Uh oh," Quest chips in from the backseat. "Looks like our boss has a thing for that little piece."

"You're kidding," Lexton blurts out. "There's finally a woman you don't just want to fuck, you actually..."

"Get out! Move!" I tell him, before I give him a kick in the arse.

Quest inhales sharply and jumps out of the car first, followed by Lexton, who looks at me as though he is expecting an explanation. "We'll talk about this later."

No, we certainly won't, my friend. I stash my phone in the inside pocket of my leather jacket and get out of the Escalade. We can already hear the loud music, the raucous sounds of the party-goers, and drunken laughter.

Below St Michael's Church, a woodland path leads through the area of brush where most of the cars are parked. A steeper path, with overgrown steps covered in moss, leads to a stone church building which looks dilapidated and half caved in, like a ruin.

We are watched by curious pairs of eyes as we climb the path to the church. Our every step is observed by young men smoking cigarettes and giggling girls.

"I thought it would be creepier," says Quest, looking around. "It's pretty unremarkable."

Let's see. I want to talk to the drug sellers. I'm not after the revellers. When I'm done, I'll drive to Brisbane to watch my rose, and accompany her back to the Monairs' estate.

The massive doors have been lifted off their hinges. One door lies across the entrance like a bridge, and everyone has to walk across it to get into the church. In one corner is a JBL speaker playing a song by Drake. The walls of the church are partially covered in graffiti and there's rubbish all over the floor: empty Coke cans, crisp packets, and chocolate wrappers. The wooden pews are still in their original locations, and young people are sitting on the backrests, chatting, drinking, and smoking. We walk down the central aisle towards the altar.

That huge structure is intact, but the walls and stained-glass windows have been damaged. It looks like a godless rubbish dump. Even the crucifix has been torn off the wall and vandalised; it's leaning carelessly in a corner. There are spotlights throughout the church that must be battery-operated as the electricity can't still be switched on. The roof above us looks as though it is about to collapse. All in all, it's exactly what I expected.

"Hey," I say to a tall guy wearing a grey band T-shirt and jeans, as he's walking past with his mates.

"What do you want?"

"Where can I get some coke?" The guy, who can scarcely be eighteen, examines me for a moment, and then points to an alcove by the altar. His eyes linger on my temple.

"Stop staring," Lexton tells him. "Just answer him."

"From Cloudy. But I wouldn't bother him right now if I were you," he advises, grinning stupidly, without giving a reason.

I narrow my eyes. I don't care about bothering anyone. I stride towards the alcove, where I find a blond guy with his back to me, pressing a young woman against the wall.

I tap his shoulder.

"Piss off!" he barks.

"Wrong answer!" I reply angrily. I pull him back forcefully by the shoulder and he lets the woman go. He stumbles backwards several paces, then rights himself, and Lexton grabs him under the arms.

"Let go of me, you fuckers. What do you want from me?"

"You're the only wanker breathing my air around here. Put your cock away!" I turn to the young woman who is holding onto the old walls for balance, swaying gently from side to side and looking confused and unsettled.

"Did you want him to do what he was going to do?" I ask her insistently, aware that a woman would probably be better at this interview than a guy like me.

"Keep your mouth shut, Cassidy! Don't talk any shit!" the Cloudy threatens. I immediately turn towards him. Lexton keeps him in check as I swing my fist and punch him hard in the face. "Nobody asked you!"

His head flies violently to the side. Lexton straightens him up again.

"Don't go limp like your cock now," he laughs.

I turn back to Cassidy, who shakily smooths down her brown shoulder-length hair, then wipes a tear from under her eyes. Her lips tremble as she shakes her head and whispers, "No. He said, he... he wanted to have a quick word. And like... He said I shouldn't make a fuss. Or everyone would laugh..." She puts a hand to her head. "It's just... My head feels so empty."

"You've had too much, bitch, you begged me to fuck you, and now you're crying like you don't remember. You're beyond help. Get yourself sectioned, you slut!" This guy is seriously getting on my nerves. I turn to him again, grab his lower jaw and bore my fingers into his face.

"One more word, little boy, and I swear to you, I'll drop you off at the police station with two broken arms," I bark menacingly. I finally see a flash of fear in his eyes. "I'm deadly serious. Do you get it, you little prick?"

I see him staring at my face, seeing the scars that extend from my temple over my jaw and down to my neck. They burn hot under his gaze.

"Do you understand me?!" He nods, once. I turn back to the girl but she's not there. *Shit! Where has she gone?*

I let go of the wanker abruptly. "Take care of him," I say to Quest and Lexton, who need to get information out of this worm. I don't mind if they use violence. I'd bet my left arse cheek this guy knows something about Vendra's disappearance. Presumably he tried to force her to have sex, too, and dosed her up with some sort of shit beforehand.

Meanwhile, I start looking for Cassidy, who must have gone through the church's collapsed wall into the next room. There are no lights in the passageway, so I switch on my phone torch to light the way out, passing young people making out with each other.

Before long I find her, cowering by the trunk of an old tree. She is crying bitterly, her arms clasped around her body, and whispering to herself.

I can hear the noise and laughter of other revellers nearby, racing to drink themselves senseless.

I crouch down slowly by the young woman, who hasn't noticed me yet.

"That wasn't your fault," I tell her calmly. She looks up in shock and stares at me as though I were the devil himself. I hastily turn off the light on my phone, so my scars won't scare her.

"That guy in there is to blame and he will soon be punished. How are you doing?"

She doesn't say a word; she just sniffs, her lips trembling as her tears continue to fall.

"Not so good. I get it." I answer my own question. How could it be any different? "How did you get here?"

"With a friend... She's... she's... already gone and..."

Even if it's a crap idea and the last thing she'd want to do is get a lift with a strange, frightening, and much older guy, I offer to take her home.

"Come on, I'll take you back."

Pure fear flashes over her young face. She looks to the side, shakes her head, and frowns. Red lights illuminate her as someone turns car lights on in the forest and the other visitors to the church party behind us.

"Can I call someone to come and pick you up? A friend or maybe someone from your family?"

"No," she answers quickly. "No. They aren't at home."

"Okay. Should I call the police?"

Distraught, she runs her hands over her face and shakes her head. "No, I'll get back somehow."

If there's one thing I won't allow to happen, it's for her to fall victim to another pervert who might take advantage of her helplessness.

"Then I'll drive you. Come on, let's go. No discussion." I

stand up and hold out my hand to help her up, waiting for her answer.

She looks unsure. *Clever girl.* "I don't know..."

"I promise to get you home safely. I have two younger sisters who went missing, and I'll do anything to make sure that doesn't happen to any more women."

"Your sisters went missing? What happened?"

I nod, feeling the deep hole in my heart at the memory of Eden and Summer. "Someone broke into our house and kidnapped them. Believe me, from that day on I swore to track down and punish people like that guy in there." I jerk my thumb towards the ruined church behind me.

"They were kidnapped?" Her eyes grow bigger, although I still have the impression she's only getting about half of what I'm saying.

"Yes." It was a while ago now. Five years. "Don't think about it too long. I won't be giving you another chance."

Finally she puts her hand in mine and I help her up. Somewhat unsteady on her feet, she follows me up the steep path between the trees to my car. After a few metres she slips and falls, and I help her up again. "Wait..." She seems really out of it; she can barely put one foot in front of the other.

Without giving her any warning, I gather her up in my arms and carry her carefully along the last section of the path to my car. There are whistles as we pass a group of drunken lads.

"Cassidy, are you into older guys, or what?" I give the boy a dark look and he backs away a little. "Watch your mouth."

He looks briefly shocked, but then just gives a sleazy laugh.

Arriving at the Escalade, I put Cassidy down, open the rear door, and wait for her to get into the back seat. I am sure she would rather not sit next to me. That's something I know from my sisters, who never liked riding in the passenger seat with strangers.

Cassidy fumbles nervously with the seatbelt until I decide to help her, fasten the belt, and then shut the door.

I get a blanket out of the boot, slide into the driver's seat and pass it to her. "Take this."

"Thank you," she breathes quietly and spreads the blanket over herself. I ease my phone out of my jacket pocket to let Quest and Lexton know I'm driving the young woman home.

They are both old enough to find their way back to the house on the cliff, even if they'll curse me the whole way there.

I open Nuria's story quickly, and wish I hadn't. She and Anston have snapped themselves holding drinks at the bar, and she is kissing his cheek. Pure jealousy ignites in me immediately, eating away at my insides. When I click on Anston's profile and open his story, my anger makes me grip the steering wheel even more tightly. He has filmed Nuria dancing in the club with two complete strangers, who are holding her by the hips and gyrating in front of her.

Big mistake! I will take back what belongs to me. And before that I'll break every single one of their fingers.

"What is it?" Cassidy asks me anxiously. "Aren't we going?"

"Of course. Where should I take you?"

CHAPTER 12

Nuria

I will cut off each of her thorns one by one,
if my flower thinks my addiction to her
needs to be put to the test.
The blades are sharpened, my rose.
Ready to bleed?

"If this gets out, I'm finished," I laugh into Anston's ear, putting my arm around his neck. The world around me shines with colourful, flashing lights and spins like a carousel at night.

"I'll drive you back later, you'll climb over the fence, and no one will ever know you were gone."

Intoxicated, I have to giggle. "This is the last time you talk me into it."

"You don't regret it, do you?" Anston asks, stroking my back gently.

I shake my head, because ever since I've known Anston, he's the one I have the most fun with. He might have the craziest ideas, but he has become my best friend. We move in gentle circles around the edge of the dance floor as he strokes my hair, then gazes at my lips.

I don't like this. "Ans?" I ask, raising my eyebrows reproachfully. He swallows, his Adam's apple bobbing up and down, smiles awkwardly, and presses his lips together. "What, Nuri?"

"Why were you staring at my mouth?"

"You're imagining it." If there's one thing I really don't

want, it's for our friendship to break down because we've kissed or had sex. No, I'm not risking our friendship.

When I turn back to the dance floor, the two fit men I was dancing with earlier have gone.

"What time is it?" I ask. Anston lifts his wrist to look at his watch. "2:50am." I grab his hand to look at the watch face for myself.

So late? "Damn! We have to go back."

"Now? Already?"

We still have a half hour's drive. It'll be at least 3:30 a.m. before I get to bed. I might be able to have a quick lie down after I take the twins to preschool, but I'll be totally done in if I keep on partying now.

"Yes, now. I'll go to the toilet quickly, then let's drive back."

Unexpectedly, Anston buries his face in my neck. I feel his breath on my skin and then his arms holding me more tightly. "Just another half hour, okay?"

"No, Ans. I want to go back." I refuse to be persuaded and unwrap my arms from his shoulders. "I'm just going to the toilet, then I'll come and find you. You can decide what you want to do while I'm gone." After three drinks my bladder is about to explode.

I totter my way through the clubbers on the dance floor – it's absolutely packed. I can't stop grinning because right now, at this moment, my world feels so untroubled and carefree, as though there were no problems, no stalker, no nightmares, no worries or anxieties.

I sneak into the men's toilets rather than standing in the long queue for the ladies, then run back over to the bar at the other side of the club in my brightly-coloured crop top and short shorts. Anston has bought another two drinks and is sitting on a bar stool, waiting for me.

I roll my eyes when I see him, although I have to smile too. But my smile doesn't last long, because a hand encircles my waist from behind, pulling me back forcefully.

"What's all this, little flower?" I feel an icy shudder run

down my spine. “Are you trying to make me even more jealous than I am already?”

“How long have you been here?” I gasp.

“How long have you been so disobedient?”

“I can do what I want, okay?” Just as I turn towards him and attempt to free myself from his grasp, he lifts me up by the waist and tosses me over his shoulder. Damn, he’s strong.

“Hey, fuck! Put me down!”

“Out of the way, she’s drunk!” he calls over the dancers and the hammering bass, like a god in the underworld commanding his entourage. People actually do make way for him, as though there’s an emergency, and he strides towards the exit, carrying me.

“I am not.” Well, maybe a bit, but not so drunk that I need to be taken out of the club. “Demon!” I shout, flailing on his shoulder like a wild animal and clawing at his leather jacket with my nails. I’d rather break my nails than let them touch his body. I shove my hands under his jacket and scratch his back roughly. He flinches briefly, but doesn’t appear to consider putting me down.

He just laughs at my half-hearted resistance.

“I love your vicious streak.”

He only puts me down when the doorman opens a massive steel door into a dark, smoky alley, which I certainly didn’t come through when I entered the club earlier.

“Okay, you prick! You’re not pulling that stunt again,” I shout at him, as soon as my high heels reach the cracked asphalt. I shove him off me with all my might. Unusually, he is wearing a motorcycle helmet which hides his face.

My shove barely moves him a centimetre. He kind of lurks, tilting his head to one side, as I take another run-up and charge at him. Agile as a practised fighter, his hands deep in his jacket pockets, he turns aside, laughs under his helmet, and watches me as I stumble forwards, towards the brick wall. To avoid colliding with it – the wall would surely emerge as the victor – I push myself off it, grabbing a dustbin lid as I turn. Furious, I hurl the metal cover at him.

"Go away!"

"So much spirit, little flower. Did you grow thorns overnight?" he says, catching the lid with an outstretched arm and throwing it forcefully back in my direction. It misses me by a hair's breadth and crashes loudly into the wall behind me, making me jump and put my hands over my ears. "We'll have this kind of fun every day when we're living together."

"Living together?!" I snort, then stick my middle finger up at him. "Never in my life will I live with you, you devil!" He hasn't heard the final whistle.

Slightly dazed, I look around the narrow alleyway, where skips, rubbish bins and empty wooden pallets are stacked against the walls. Grey smoke is billowing from a manhole cover. To my left, probably more than twenty metres away, is the main road in front of the club. Cars are speeding past and people are walking by.

Demon takes two strides towards me, seizes my throat, and pushes me against the wall. "You still think I'm joking. But you will soon see I'm serious."

"You're messed up."

"No, just obsessed with you. Since the very first time I saw you," he corrects me, rubbing a gloved thumb over my chin.

"Same thing. I'm serious when I say your behaviour isn't normal."

"Normality is not something I have ever striven for, my little flower. Undo my belt."

"What?" He pushes his hips against me and I feel him bulging against my waist.

"Do I have to repeat myself!" I grab his arm and turn my face to the side in order to get away from him. He laughs again, rough and mysterious. Then he pushes the dark, mirrored visor of his helmet back, so I can see his eyes for the first time. I have to tilt my head back slightly to look at them properly as he towers over me by almost half a head. Although the alley is in semi-darkness, in the golden glow of the streetlights I can make out dark blue eyes and a few black strands of hair falling over his dark brows. What I do see of him draws me magically towards him. I've never met a man with such strikingly beautiful eyes before, eyes that cast such a spell on me.

"Now?" He interrupts my thoughts, lowering his face. "Last night I licked your pussy. It's only right that you reciprocate. Or don't you dare?"

I gasp, my lips parted, then step on his hard boot. "Here in this minging alley?"

"Right here, to teach you a lesson."

Teach me what? Before I grasp what he means, he detaches my fingers from his arm with his other hand and pushes me down in front of him. My bare knees scrape on the rough, damp tarmac. Fuck, he is rough.

"What are you waiting for? I know how often you have wished my penis was inside you. Undo my belt." He grips my chin again, forcing me to look up at him. "You need to learn that I get less kind and caring if you let yourself get felt up by strange men all over the place. If you can be that dirty all evening, then you can definitely be it with me. Because believe me, I'd have no problem leaving Anston or the two men from the club dead on your doorstep first thing tomorrow morning, to make you understand how serious I am about you."

"You wouldn't do that," I hiss.

He snorts. "Just you see." He strokes my chin with his thumb. "But you can also just make things right again. You know how. Show me you belong to me. Be a good girl and suck my cock."

He obviously wants to test me and is giving me a choice. A macabre choice.

If he thinks I'm going to back down just because I've scraped my knees on the pavement, or that he can intimidate me with empty threats, he's made a mistake.

"Okay, you think I don't dare? Forget it. I'll blow your cock in this manky alley. It's just about your level." Angrily, I undo his belt, unzip his black, slim-fitting trousers and pull them down. Holy shit! His cock is fucking big. Impressive.

"Princesses get fucked in bed. Women who try it on with other guys get fucked in a dirty alley." His amused undertone provokes me even more. "Now open your mouth and do your job, like a good girl."

"Bastard."

"Yes, but the only bastard you ever come with," he says, reminding me of last night. I glare at him angrily, because he's right. Then I grip his shaft, which I can't even fully close my fingers around. He puts his hands in my hair, and I submit willingly to his alluring domination and lick the smooth tip of his penis. He tastes different from what I expected, tart and pleasant. His taste instantly creates an insistent throbbing in my pelvis.

"Don't hold back. Open your mouth."

It's not that I don't want to, it's just that I don't want to give him a blow job now because he's been so rude to me. But yes, even if his sick brain is almost impossible to understand, I get that he's jealous. He just forgets that we're not actually together.

I moisten my lips, then take his hardness in my mouth. Centimetre by centimetre, his huge cock pushes between my lips. Although the men I've had sex with have never made me climax, that doesn't mean I don't know how to satisfy a guy.

He'll be amazed, and then I'll go. As I pull back and take his cock even more deeply and wetly into my mouth, I can hear him breathing under his helmet. His cock is now fully hard. Then I slow down and he buries his fingers deeper into my hair, directing me and showing me the pace he needs. His tart flavour isn't too overwhelming and it lingers on my tongue, awakening in me the sick fantasy of feeling him inside me, right here, amongst the rubbish bins and stacks of pallets. Instinctively, I squeeze my thighs together more tightly so as not to let on how much I want to feel his mouth between my legs again.

I hold his shaft and suck harder with my lips, increasing the speed.

"Fuck, I had no idea...," he gasps.

That I can do this? I look up at him with his big cock in my mouth, and our gazes meet. "... you were so... good..."

Believe me, you won't be getting another blow job from me. This is just payback for last night, so I don't feel in his debt. Is that really true, or am I deceiving myself?

For the first time, Demon falters briefly, takes a step back and leans his shoulder against the wall behind him, to steady himself. My knees slide painfully over the rough tarmac, then I add in my hand and carry on blowing him. Before long, he regains the upper hand, reaching into my cleavage and massaging my right breast, pulling it out and twirling my nipple.

"That's good, rose. Hell..." He groans deeply, and looks up at the night sky high up between the buildings, relishing my ministrations. Breathlessly, without taking a break, I continue the blow job, massaging his balls and creating a vacuum with my tongue and lips, exerting more pressure with the aim of driving him out of his mind.

He looks down at me, his eyes narrowed, then seizes control again because he is about to come and doesn't want me to stop too soon. Like he did a few nights ago. And I would fucking love to do that, just before his orgasm, just before he explodes with pleasure, stop the blow job and leave him standing there. But he continues to direct my head, thrusting deeper and faster into my throat as though he were in a state of intoxication, so that I gag for a moment.

"Now... damn... now..." Less than five seconds later, his cock pumps and his pelvis tenses. "Like that! Fuck, fuck, fuck. Swallow it all," he says in a rough, breathless voice from under his helmet, before he gives a deeper and more intense moan than I have ever heard from a man having sex before. It sounds strangely beautiful, as though the sounds were meant for me alone. As though I were the only person capable of eliciting these animalistic groans from him, as in the same moment his warm semen floods into my mouth. Some of his cum trickles down my throat, warm and mild. I would swallow it all, if he hadn't been such a cold-hearted bastard.

Breathing heavily, he releases his fingers from my hair and strokes my head, as I remove my lips from his cock, which really is the biggest and best-tasting one I have ever had in my mouth.

"Lick it clean," he orders. I glance up at him, then pull back. "Lick. It. Clean." I turn my face to the side and spit out some of his semen. "Lick it clean yourself."

Shakily, I go to pull myself up onto my bleeding, smarting knees, and then I feel hands under my arms.

"What's all this?" I turn and am surprised to see a man standing behind me. He has tattoos all the way up to his chin, he's wearing black clothes and he's looking at Demon. His stare is dark and penetrating. His black hair is combed back at an angle and is gleaming in the light of the street-lamp. It's cut shorter at the sides and has jagged lines shaved into it.

A bouncer, judging by his stance and dark clothes. "I've been molested and I want to go back into the club," I explain.

"I wasn't talking to you," the guy replies harshly. He's not even looking at me, he's staring at Demon, who is calmly zipping up his trousers.

"Why did you follow me?" My stomach ties itself in knots as, in my drunken state, I realise the man behind me is with Demon.

"That's not important. Who is she?" The man turns me roughly to face him. And fuck, he looks even more brutal and threatening than he did a few seconds ago. As he looks at me with dark, penetrating eyes that scour the depths of my soul, Demon pulls me towards him by the shoulder.

"Touch her once more without asking, Lexton, and I'll put a hole between your eyes!"

Lexton's eyes widen as he opens his striking, well-defined

lips and stares from Demon to me. "Fuck, so she's not just some throwaway chick you've grabbed for a blow job?"

Heedless of Demon's warning, Lexton grabs my chin, looks down at me, and scans my face. "This is the one you were stalking on Instagram earlier."

One lunatic is bad enough, but two will be the death of me. And a third, who suddenly appears at the end of the alley, will obliterate me. With Demon seemingly distracted, I seize the moment and rip myself free from his grip.

"This was nice, but I have to go," I hiss, then run back towards the side entrance of the club. I head up the steps that lead to the doorway, tear open the door and dart inside before one of the two devils can catch me. Looking back repeatedly, I bump into a doorman and run as though my life depends on it. After just a few metres, the floor is shaking beneath the soles of my feet and the bass is thrumming in my ears. One metre on, just before I reach the dancing, partying crowd, I slip in a puddle.

God! No! As I fall, I bang my shoulder hard against the wall, sending a painful jolt through my body that immobilises me for a moment. Before I can pick myself up again, heavy boots enter my field of vision. My stomach clenches as I look up at the black trousers.

"You should wear different shoes next time you run away from me, little flower. But I'm definitely not complaining." And then, without asking, he lifts me off the floor.

"Did you hurt yourself?" *Is he serious?*

"I'm fine, except for my sore knees. Put me down."

"I'll take you back. The chase is over." *Chase? Is everything just a cruel game for him?*

Two men are waiting at the exit to the club, the one with all the tattoos is calmly smoking a cigarette. The other looks at me questioningly. He has ash-blonde hair, and softer, less prominent and predatory facial features, but looks just as grim as his friend.

"Stop gawping and go back," Demon's voice thunders from under the helmet.

"Who is she?" Lexton asks instead. Without answering, Demon walks down the alley with me in his arms.

"Wylder. What is this shit? Where do you know her from?" The guy with the blonde hair catches up with us.

Wylder? Demon is called Wylder? What a strange name. I've often wondered what he might be called. I never thought of Wylder. Although it suits him. Wylder makes me think of being wild, unrestrained, obsessed. That describes his character very well. Wylder. I like his name. Very much.

Stubbornly, as though his associates, friends, doormats, or whatever they are to him weren't there, he carries me to his black motorbike, which is parked behind a skip at the end of the alley. He sets me down just before we reach it. It happens so quickly that I can't back away.

"Don't ask any questions, go back. That's an order." Interesting to know it isn't just me Demon talks to in this brusque, commanding tone.

Lexton sneers, gives me a condescending look, and snorts. "She's a one-hit wonder." Then he shoves his hands casually into the trouser pockets of his black suit, under which he is wearing a turtleneck sweater, and marches his tall, muscular frame around the corner of the alley.

The other man stands still for a moment, watching as his boss gets on the motorbike then pulls me to him by the waist. "Get on, Nuria."

"She doesn't look as though she wants to go with you."

Demon turns to him as he starts the engine. "She does. Her boyfriend has already left without her."

"How do you know that?" I interrupt their conversation, lift the visor and push his fingers off my waist. He revs the bike repeatedly.

"Look at your phone. He messaged you."

"I can't. I left my handbag in the cloakroom."

Unfazed, Demon hands me the small black bag with the silver chain, which has been hanging from his handlebars the whole time. How... How does he always do that? I get out my purse and phone. I read Anston's messages on the screen.

3:10: Where are you?

3:24: I can't find you. Tell me where you are?

3:37: Did you meet those two guys and leave the club?

3:43: Helloooo?

3:56: Nuri, don't be mad, but I'm leaving now. I'm sick of this shit.

That was quarter of an hour ago. *¡Carajo! Fuck!* Ans is always quick to get pissed off when things don't go his way.

So what now?

"I'll take a taxi."

"Without any cash?" Demon takes my bag and holds it out of my reach. Although he is wearing a helmet, I could swear there's a smug grin under there.

The blonde guy looks down, laughing, and scratches his temple. "I'll hitchhike then. No problem," I hiss, annoyed that he's stolen from me.

"Not an option."

"Because I might meet a monster who's even worse than you? It's not likely."

"You understand each other so well," observes the pretty boy.

"Just bloody get on, Nuria!" His barked command makes me flinch. "I'm going with you, whether you ride with me or get the bus. Take your pick."

He used to follow me home from all my night shifts. I'd love to annoy the hell out of him and take the bus, just to spite him. But I'd be making things worse for myself because I wouldn't get any sleep at all – the bus to the village takes over an hour. And then I'd still have to walk a mile, drunk, to get back to the estate.

I kick his boot angrily, then step onto the footrest, take hold of his shoulders and climb onto the back of the black Kawasaki, behind him.

"Good girl," he says, then takes a second helmet from the handlebars and puts it on my head without any warning. Great! My stalker is even caring. I dig my nails into the leather once again. Without success. "I'll see you later, Quest." He's already turning the bike. At the end of the alley he reaches back with one hand and pulls my bottom closer to him, then he accelerates and drives onto Brisbane's main street.

It feels bizarre being so close to him now, when I have otherwise just seen him through the window or at a distance, following me, and when he's revealed so little about himself. Sure, I gave him a blow job a few minutes ago, but this sort of intimate closeness feels strange. Lovely, but unsettling at the same time.

Since leaving the nightclub we've been tailed by a large, dark SUV, presumably containing his two friends. What does it all mean?

Has Demon followed me to Australia with these friends, or associates? Why? Why are there suddenly three men on my heels?

Although Lexton seemed more than surprised when he came across Demon and me in the alley. Lexton knew nothing about me, which means Demon hasn't said anything to him.

Once we've passed over a long bridge and left Brisbane behind us, the SUV catches up, flashes its lights, and briefly pulls alongside us. Demon and I simultaneously turn our heads towards the vulgar car, and Lexton now sticks his head out of the passenger window, pointing ahead with his index finger, and then to the left. Demon nods before accelerating onto the three-lane highway, making me cling even tighter to his jacket. My adrenaline skyrockets. The cool night wind bites into my bare arms and legs. I am clearly not wearing the right outfit for a motorbike trip, but Demon seems to be starting some kind of race, and accelerates even more. Is he crazy?

My heart beats wildly, as though I'm on dope. The combination of travelling at speed, the twinkling lights of the skyscrapers, and the roar of the bike creates a feeling of endless happiness, like a drug high.

If he makes one wrong move, we'll fall, and my bare arms and legs will be covered with grazes from top to bottom. So I have no choice but to rely blindly on Demon not to undertake any risky manoeuvres that could cost both of us our lives. The SUV catches up, then Demon leaves it far behind. His friends turn left, while Demon leaves the highway via the right-hand lane.

Some ten minutes later he is racing along the country road. Up ahead, the night sky is covered by a delicate purple veil of clouds. As the bike stops next to the wall out of range of the CCTV, the first rays of sunlight are creeping through the dense forest.

I lift the helmet off my head and get off the bike, my knees shaking.

As I walk past him, he grabs my elbow and spins me round to face him.

He straightens my top out over my breasts and holds my chin with his other hand. He strokes my lips with his thumb, as tenderly as if he were touching them with his mouth. He has never kissed me before. Not directly on the mouth.

Sitting on his dark Kawasaki, he pulls me closer to him and leans his head against my forehead, still wearing his helmet. "Don't pull any shit, or I'll have to punish you again, you understand?"

I smile. "What if I like your punishments?" *You didn't actually say that aloud, did you, Nuria?* Sometimes I should think before I speak.

"But you want to get rid of me, don't you?" says his deep voice from under the helmet. Now he grips my chin and tilts it upwards. I know he is searching my eyes from behind the visor, looking for the same obsession he has developed for me.

"Nothing has changed there."

"Liar," he drawls.

Fuck. He can see through me. But I mustn't let him know that.

I step back quickly before I can fall into his clutches again, grab the handle of my handbag, and run to the entrance gate. His bike roars behind me before turning onto the road and disappearing into the trees at the end of the driveway. I can hear the powerful engine for another minute as the bike speeds along the country road. Deep inside me I feel that this evening has changed something. I just don't know exactly what it is, and whether or not I like it.

I turn back to the gate, open my left hand and enter the code, whose numbers change weekly. I have noted it on my hand so I don't forget it. The gate hums and I enter the estate. It is 4:19 a.m. No one should see me at this hour. And if I hurry I might still get two or three hours' sleep before it's time to wake the twins and get them dressed for preschool.

I enter the house as quietly as possible, taking off my heels and climbing the stairs to the second floor.

Then, out of the corner of my left eye, I glimpse a shadow by the banisters on the floor above. Or did I just imagine it?

Demon can't have come back. I get a queasy feeling. I race over the soft carpet to my door, getting out my key as I go, and slip into my private rooms.

I hurriedly lock the door behind me, switch on the light, and scan the rooms. When I am sure I am alone, I go to the bathroom and look down at my grazed knees.

Princesses get fucked in bed. Women who try it on with other guys get fucked in a dirty alley. Demon's words run through my mind. Then I wash the last traces of him off my face, clean my teeth and slip into my pyjamas. Ten minutes later I'm in bed, asleep.

CHAPTER 13

Nuria

A token of love can be so great
until it breaks you.
Who will pick up the pieces at the end
when there are no more left?

3rd April

I love him in a way I've never loved a boy before. Like I've never looked at anyone before. My heart beats so loudly whenever he stands next to me to get his books out of his locker. I ought to know these kinds of boys are dangerous. I see how the guys on the football team show up with a different girl every month.

Jazeem is no different. He is popular, looks amazing, and has the body of an Adonis that makes all the girls swoon. I don't want to keep going on about it, that's not my style. But who else am I going to talk to about it?

My parents? Hardly, Monairs aren't allowed to get emotional. I don't have a friend I can tell. Jess and Lilly don't really count as friends, even if I do hang out with them every day in the canteen and on the steps after school. It's true that I'm one of the popular girls – no one mocks or bullies me. I'm very happy about that. But it wasn't easy getting in with them. And there's no way I'm going to tell them I have a thing for Jazeem. They'd make fun of me, and I don't want that. It's difficult to make your way up the ranks and become one of the in-crowd, but it's easy to get rejected and fall out of favour again.

I've often seen other girls getting bullied because of their looks. Seen them being put down just because they have glasses, or spots, or braces, or the wrong clothes, or the wrong figure. Properly put down. Teenagers can be cruel. If you're lying on the floor crying, they'll kick you even harder.

I know what I'm talking about. I went through it myself two years ago, at a different school. Since then I've had a pact with myself to stay in with the rich kids. The ones who are always perfectly styled and made-up for school. And what can I say, it has helped.

Although I'm a different person now, a different Ranja, school is so much less stressful. Of course, the tide can turn at any time, if people start whispering about you behind your back or you do something the other girls don't like. Like making fun of the wrong boy, or wearing the wrong colour nail varnish for the season. Fatal mistakes. Idiotic, but fatal.

That's why I can't talk to anyone about my feelings for Jazeem. My mother has no time, my brother is an arsehole, my friends are fake. That's why I'm starting this stupid diary. My therapist thinks it will help to write it all down, to work things through.

So here goes. Here I am – Ranja Monair.

This is my first entry, longer than I expected.

More tomorrow.

It's weird reading something so personal about someone you don't know. But I don't currently have any other way of finding out more about this strange story. I turn the page, curious to read the entry for 4th April, but Ranja's next entry isn't until 17th April, meaning she ditched her resolution after just one day. *That could be me.* I can't help but smile.

I reach into the bag of crisps next to me on the bedside table and as I shove two Cheetos in my mouth, my phone lights up. Chewing on the crisps, I grab my phone, unlock it and see a message from an unknown number. Demon.

Stop eating so much junk, *corazón mío!*

Irritated, I turn the screen off, before looking around the room. How does he know what I'm eating again? My eyes are glued to the drawn curtains. He can't see through the windows into my tiny ground-floor apartment any more. There must be hidden cameras. But where are they?

Provocatively I fish a whole handful of Cheetos out of the bag and stuff them into my mouth. He will see, and the knowledge that it will drive him mad not to have control over me puts me in an unashamedly good mood.

Just as I am about to put my phone down without answering his message and carry on reading Ranja's diary, a new message pops up.

Don't ignore me!

Oh yes I will! I love being in control – and he hates giving it up. I smile, then put the phone face down on the bedside table. I take another crisp out of the bag, push it between my lips and lick my fingertips pleasurably. The back of my neck tingles and my pulse quickens as I wait to see what happens next.

My phone vibrates. He's calling. But there's no way I'm answering. When the vibrating stops, I turn back to the diary to carry on reading.

But my phone vibrates again. Dammit! I reach for the phone, see the anonymous number, and reject it. As I go to put it down, he calls again. And I reject the call.

Stop it! Each time I reject his call, he immediately phones back. Until at some point I give in and answer.

"Don't you have any hobbies?"

"You are my hobby." I hear his deep voice and the sound of ocean waves in the background. It is just after midnight. Where is he right now? Why should I even care?

"If you cancel me again or hang up..."

"Then what? You'll come over and confiscate my crisps?"

I hang up, and can hardly suppress my laughter. In his mind he will surely spank me, make me suck his cock again, or worse. Although, to be honest, I find it more exciting than bad – which should give me pause for thought.

He is the devil and he is dragging me further into the abyss every day, corrupting me, luring me into his hell, where I will ultimately burn.

He calls again. "Did you forget something?" I ask.

"NURIA!" he growls into the phone.

"I can eat what I like."

"Of course, only you should look after yourself and your body."

How stupid. "I won't get fat, don't worry. And if I did, would that be a way of getting rid of you?" I speak my thoughts aloud.

He snorts dismissively. "That wouldn't happen in this lifetime. I'll always like your body."

"Because you've already seen all of me? Which is not true vice versa."

"Meaning?" he enquires. I hear a voice not far away from him. A male voice saying something in a hushed tone.

"So far, I haven't seen anything except your eyes and your cock. Kind of pervy. Do you have a fetish, or are you maybe disfigured and don't want to show yourself?"

A moment passes and he does not respond. "You will like what I have to offer. But you know that already. Soon, when we share a bed, you'll be able to explore every part of my body with your hands, your mouth and your tongue. And no, I don't have a fetish. Apart from you."

"Share a bed?" I can't help imagining him climbing into bed with me naked, taking hold of my chin like he did a few nights ago, and ordering me to explore every part of his body with my tongue. And yes, I imagine him to be muscular, strong, and sporty. Not brawny like a bouncer, but athletic. When my lips reach his fucking huge cock, he will take me by the hips, throw me down on my stomach onto the bed and push himself into me from behind.

Fuck... Don't think that. Stop! Why am I having these wild fantasies about him, when I've never had them about any other man before? It... it isn't healthy.

I narrow my eyes and press my thighs tightly together.

"I'm still planning how big our bed will be when we leave Australia." What? "What would you prefer? A box spring bed with a soft headboard, the right height for me to stand up and fuck you from behind? Or one with a metal frame that I can tie you to when I need to punish you? It's a difficult decision."

"I'd prefer a coffin that I can shut you in and nail shut."

"Sex in a coffin sounds like a fetish. I had no idea that you were into such morbid shit," he says, laughing enigmatically. "I now realise that I shouldn't leave these kinds of decisions to you."

"Because I don't need to make any. We're not sharing a bed! Ever!" Not even a coffin!

"But the idea of it turned you on. I know what you look like when you're excited." *Fuck! Which corner is he watching me from?*

"I'm angry, not excited, there's a difference."

"You're lying. Shall I calm you down? I already know how to do it. And how we can work off those crisps again." *We? He's such a dog.*

His dark laugh penetrates my heart. Since I can't win this battle of words, I end the call and put the phone back on the bedside table.

Although I expected him to, he doesn't call back. I catch myself repeatedly checking the screen, because somehow, as strange as it may sound, I hope he will.

I am crazy, gradually becoming as infected by this madness as he is – as if he has sown a malignant seed in my mind, which is now beginning to germinate.

I also have an idea about how to work off the Cheetos. One he won't like.

Demon wants to control me? I don't think he really knows who he's dealing with.

After eating some more crisps, I put Ranja's diary down and slide further down the bed.

With a smile on my lips, because I am absolutely certain he is still watching via a camera he has installed somewhere in the room, I slowly unbutton my pyjama top.

Out of the corner of my eye, I notice the screen on my phone light up, as expected. I have his full attention. Without reading the message, I smooth the fingers of my right hand over my stomach up to my breasts. As I do so, I move the pyjama top further apart to give him a good view of what he wants but can't have right now.

My lips slightly open, I massage my left breast, rubbing my thumb over my nipple to make it hard. The more I touch myself, the wetter I get. I twist my hard nipple, sigh and arch my back.

"God," I breathe and close my eyes. As I take my hand off my breast and run it down over my stomach to the waistband of my pyjama trousers, my phone rings.

But how...? I switched it to silent. It can only vibrate. Could Demon change the settings? That would mean he's controlling and monitoring my phone.

The phone doesn't stop ringing, so I pick it up and answer the call.

"It's not a good time right now," I explain in a tone that is both cheeky and aroused. I can hear his agitated breathing.

"Do you want to kill me? Stop it!"

"What?" I ask innocently, although I know exactly what he means. Keeping the phone to my ear, I lift my left hand to my mouth to lick my index and middle fingers before sucking both fingers noisily and wetting them.

"Stop touching yourself, I said. Your body belongs to me." The pure arousal is audible in his voice.

"Worried I can take care of myself better than you?" I taunt. He growls, then laughs darkly.

"No one can make you scream louder than I can. Not even you, because I know exactly what..."

As my wet fingers glide under the waistband of my

trousers, I spread my legs further apart and touch myself, letting out a breathless gasp.

"... what did you... say?" I breathe into the phone before slowly circling my clit with my fingers, applying a light pressure that makes me moan. "*Mierda...!*"

I turn my head to the side in pleasure. The phone slips out of my fingers and falls to the mattress, beside the pillow.

I use my free hand to firmly massage my left breast while pushing two fingers from my other hand inside myself.

"Fuck, I'm nearly there," I whimper, thinking of Demon the whole time. Thinking about him lying between my legs, licking me, pushing his fingers inside me and stretching me, getting me ready for his big cock.

I move my fingers rhythmically inside me, just like he would, then spread the wetness over my pearl and circle faster.

Completely immersed in the fantasy, I shut my eyes and bite my lower lip. "God, more, more..."

Just then my telephone rings again and tears me away from my appalling fantasies of Demon. I pick it up with my left hand, press the button on the side, and take the call.

"Did you... want to... say anything else?"

"Nuria!" he growls ominously. "Stop it! Immediately! I order you to stop touching yourself! Not when I can't be with you."

"Too late," I whimper, and put more pressure on my clit. "I... can't...," I let out a tortured groan, "... stop."

I hear him take a deep breath and curse, and I know without seeing him that he would like nothing more than to storm into my room.

I take my fingers out of my pyjama bottoms just before I climax, my legs shaking even more violently.

"Good, well done," I hear Demon say, who presumably thinks that I am going to obey his order. *How wrong he is.*

The next moment I push my feet out of my shorts and fling them out of bed with my right foot, then sit up on my knees, turn around, and place the phone on the edge of the headboard against the wall.

"What are you doing? I told you to stop."

"As if I'd listen to you," I retort with a smile. "See you later, Demon." I end the call again, which will definitely make him mad.

I would love to see his face, to know whether he's tearing at his hair, hitting a wall, or knocking over a chair, because all he can do is watch.

I steady myself against the headboard with my left hand before touching myself again with my right hand, kneeling up, and sliding my fingers between my thighs. My pussy is still wet, my clit is aroused, and my nipples are tingling with excitement. As I push my fingers inside myself again, the screen lights up in front of my hazy vision. A video call.

This could be entertaining. I want to see him, damn it. To look into his eyes when I come.

I take the video call and see before me, completely shrouded in darkness, the dimly illuminated outline of a face. When I blink, I see the lighter contours of a skull. He is wearing a cloth mask that reveals his eyes and covers the rest of his face in a lifelike skull.

"Do I need to come over and put you over my knee to make you stop?!"

"If you could do that, you would have...," I say breathlessly, moaning lustfully, "... been here... ages ago..." I pleasure myself more intensely, pushing my fingers deeper and faster into my wet pussy before lifting them to my mouth and licking them.

"You wish I was with you, my rose," he replies, and unfortunately he is right. Because yes, I really want to feel his hands on my breasts, my stomach, my bum, and his tongue on my clit.

Without answering I lift my hips up and down and move my pelvis in circles. I bite my lower lip, whimper, and feel the orgasm about to hit at any second. My pussy grips my fingers more tightly, my clit is swollen, and I feel like I am about to explode. I look down, screwing up my eyes, and imagine Demon lying between my knees, pushing my buttocks apart and pressing his face into my pussy as he licks me to climax. But what I want most of all is for him to grab me by the hair, push me forward, and then take me from behind, fucking me hard like an animal, taking everything from me.

"Look at me!"

"I… can't."

"Look!" And as I lift my eyes, his dark blue irises glint at me. So damn beautiful and evil at the same time. My body trembles, I groan louder and can't suppress my fantasy any longer.

"Fuck, Demon! Faster! Deeper!" I cry, before whimpering as I circle my pearl more firmly and am caught up in the orgasm. I am so hot and can't think clearly as I shout "More, more, more!" and bite down on the wood of the headboard. I circle my clit faster and faster, squirming and whimpering in a way I've never done before when doing it to myself. I hold my right breast, turn my nipple firmly and cry out again until I can't stop.

"Fuck, like that. Take me, fuck me, use me, Demon!"

I bend forward and let myself sink onto the mattress and finger myself harder until the first orgasm gives way to a second.

"Shit! Damn. If I was with you I'd get hold of your round arse and fuck you in every fucking hole, just like you're begging me to."

This thought takes hold of me. Utterly immersed in the game, I rub my bud harder to draw out the climax until I can't take it anymore. My pulse is racing, my arm is tense, my throat is hoarse from moaning and screaming. Sweating, my heart pounding, I collapse.

Breathing heavily between the pillows, I feel for my phone on the headboard.

"Seen enough?" I ask, my hair dishevelled. He narrows his eyes.

“Nowhere near enough. There will be consequences for this.”

“I can hardly wait,” I reply, as I end the call and the phone slides out of my fingers. The blood is still rushing in my ears as I feel the addictive thrill of the orgasm throughout my body. I feel intoxicated, liberated, and superior to him like I haven’t in a long time.

I roll slowly onto my back, lay my right hand on my naked breast and bend my legs. Is Demon already in a car, ready to carry out his punishment? Will he really spank me? Yes, fuck yes, that’s exactly what he’ll do. And why does this thought make my heart race even faster?

At least I was able to take control for the first time. Checkmate, Demon. You don’t win every game.

CHAPTER 14

Nuria

Dark secrets can
poison your soul.
They eat away at you from the inside
until only
despair remains.

I shut my eyes for a moment, breathe deeply, and pull the covers over my naked body. Then I try to shake off the thoughts of Demon and immerse myself again in Ranja's world.

17th April

Something terrible has happened.

I know I was going to carry on with this diary, but things have been going well recently. Or mostly well. There was nothing exciting to report, at least. But today everything has changed.

Jazeem is with Jess!!! At least that's what everyone was saying in school today, and it's been hard to miss. I saw them making out at Warren's house party. They went upstairs, and, to be honest, the idea of them fucking in a room somewhere on the first floor killed me. But that's how he is, I knew that. It wouldn't be so bad if he had just had a quickie with Jess. But why, WHY are they now together?

Does Jess know I like Jazeem? Is she into him too and just not telling the rest of us?

It broke my heart to see them standing by Jess's locker, their hands all over each other. Everyone, absolutely everyone, could see Jazeem pushing my friend against the locker and putting his hand up her skirt. It feels like a betrayal. Like a lie I've believed all these weeks! Why is he doing this to me?

I know a lot of this is just for show. I know who Jazeem really is. I know it, but having to watch while they tie their tongues in knots still kills me. I can't do it anymore.

I hardly said a word to Jess today, although she was constantly wanting my attention. I avoided her and kept coming up with excuses not to have to talk to her. I didn't even want to look her in the eyes.

Because deep down I know the game is rigged. I shouldn't be so naïve as to believe she doesn't know I'm in love with Jazeem. Friends know that kind of thing. And fake friends do too, because they want to know even more about you. So they can use that knowledge against you someday.

After class I walked by the sports field. There were a few girls sitting in the front rows, of course, cheering on their boys while they played. Jess was perched among them. The new queen of the football team. Shit! She was loving it. I felt like throwing up.

I waited behind the glass doors in the gym, near the changing rooms, prowling nervously up and down. My heart was pounding. No exam ever made me feel this worked-up and jittery. I felt like I was going to faint.

As the boys gradually began to arrive in the changing rooms, I plucked up my courage and waited for Jaz.

"Have you got a minute?" I asked him in a low whisper. Drenched in sweat, his helmet clenched under his arm, he ran his hand through his brown hair, exuding that seductive, manly scent of his that I love so much.

"Now?" he asked irritably, looking up and down the corridor. I nodded resolutely.

"Now."

"Okay then." He suddenly grabbed my hand and pulled me into a nearby room belonging to the cleaning staff. He didn't want to be seen with me, as usual. I hate that. He flipped the

light switch next to the door before I rushed inside, and followed me in. "What is it?"

"Can you tell me what this is all about?"

"What what is all about?" Annoyed, he turned from the door and faced me. I know how much he hates difficult conversations.

"You know what. We had an agreement, or doesn't that stand anymore? You can be seen in public with other girls, but there shouldn't be anything going on between you." His grass-green eyes sought mine, then he came up to me and held my face. His fingers smelt of chewing gum, salt, and earth.

"The boys are always saying stupid things about me never getting off with anyone."

"What?" Since when? "Why are you only telling me this now?"

"Because we're not together, Ran. Don't you get it? I don't have to tell you everything all the time. It's nothing to do with you where I am, what I do, who I meet."

Those were his exact words, and they cut my heart in pieces. I know how little I mean to him. That I am just disposable. Dammit, I can't help loving this boy everyone has warned me about. The son of the Vegas family. The family my father hates more than any other, because they are his competitors in the ore mining business. They run huge businesses that bring in millions and they don't give each other an inch. Dalcho *and* Xastra *aren't just family empires, they're massive corporations with a long history of fierce rivalry. If my father found out I was spending time with the Vegas family's son, he would cut me off. He complains about them every evening – really, every evening, without exception. I, on the other hand, don't care about the family business. Zain will step up at some point and take over from Father. I don't want anything to do with it. I want to travel the world, study marine biology and research whales in New Zealand. Status, money and fame don't interest me at all.*

"So doesn't the time we spend together mean anything to you?" I asked, my eyes full of stupid tears.

"You know what we have isn't a long-term thing, Ran. If it gets out that we're meeting up, I can guarantee my father will send me abroad to some shitty private school. I'm so close to getting into the Tigers. *The trainer is coming next week to watch us play and..."*

"I know," I interrupt, clinging to his sweaty top. "I know how important sport is to you. You can count on me, I'll always support you and I won't take any time away from that. But you have to understand, Jess has only made a move on you to show off. She doesn't love you. She's a fake, two-faced, superficial bitch..."

"I don't love her either. But she has connections to one of the Tigers *players, and..."*

In that moment I understood. He was shagging Jess and hanging out with her in public so he could use her contact.

I took my hands off him and stepped back. I've never been so lost for words. Of course everything revolves around his career, which I've never stood in the way of in the half year we've been secretly dating. I even agreed to the stupid deal that meant he could carry on amusing himself with girls at parties, while I had to stand by and watch. I went along with all that shit because he always said to me that at some point things would be different. When school was over, we could be together properly, move into an apartment together and have the relationship we wanted.

But now I understand what he's really like. Until today I thought there was a spiritual connection between us. Obviously I was wrong.

"Ranja, where are you going?"

"Sorry, I need some time." Upset, I left the stuffy broom cupboard. While Jaz was allowed to put himself about in public with my fake friend, Jess, our meetings always took place in storerooms, in the woods, on a beach miles away somewhere, or in the car, because we couldn't risk anyone seeing us together.

It was exciting for a while. Now it's horrible. There's nothing I want more than him. I want him so much. Just for me. Is that too much to ask?

I love him so much it hurts. It's destroying me. I don't know what else I can give him other than the promise that I will support his career, and that I won't undermine his fame or his talent. That I love him just the way he is.

The pressure I feel is unbearable. I can't talk to anyone about it. Anyone I tell could betray us. Only my therapist listens to me. And even he doesn't help. The need to let the pain out is growing stronger each day. It's so intense that what I really want to do is start cutting myself again.

With every line of this diary, the hole inside me grows bigger. I fight back the tears at Ranja's despairing words. The sentences contain so much pain, loneliness, and sadness. This entry was written six months ago. I leaf forward to see when she wrote her last entry. 6th June, just before the summer holidays.

At first I thought Ranja was just in love with Jazeem. I had no idea they were secretly a couple. That she was enduring so much for him, and for their love. Could Ranja's disappearance have something to do with her relationship with Jazeem? With her distress? Did she really go away? Did she quit school and pack her bags because she couldn't stand the pain and the secret meetings anymore? Or did she slip up – did someone find out about the relationship?

If anyone knows more about this, it has to be her unbearable brother, Zain – although the two of them apparently weren't close. And this diary. But I can't read any more this evening. It is already past 1 a.m. and I want to get some sleep and then go for an early run tomorrow morning.

I look at my phone one last time, but there's no message from Demon. I sigh in disappointment, and then shake my head. I shouldn't be disappointed; I wanted to make him explode, after all, I wanted to win. Demon is using silence to punish me for my disobedience and the fun I had earlier without him.

I hide the diary between the mattress and the headboard of the four-poster bed and then switch off the light. I lie there in the dark, thinking for a while. Of Jaz and Ranja. Of Demon and his messages.

Although I can't be certain, I think he will visit me tonight. And I can hardly wait.

CHAPTER 15

Demon

I crave her more and more each day,
the other half of my soul,
that once I didn't even know
existed in this world.

I watch her sleeping, from the armchair I have carried to her bedside. As I do every night. As I do every hour I spend in her presence. Something draws me to her, magically. Something I can't name. Something I can't fight. Something I don't want to fight. I have never felt anything like this. Since I saw her for the first time and fell hopelessly under her spell.

It was about six months ago, a damp, rainy evening, when I went into the *Luna Ilena.* An out-of-the-way but popular bar in Barcelona, mostly frequented by locals.

I sat back in an alcove where no one would notice me, in order to observe the woman on the list. I went through the photos on my phone repeatedly, checking Nuria Endrinal's dates and distinguishing features. And then suddenly there she was, standing right by my table.

"Are you in a gang, or a rapper, or a biker?" That was the sentence that awoke something in my soul. Not her looks, her expression, or her smile, but her voice. It might sound strange, but her voice was the first thing I fell in love with.

Did I ever think that something like that was possible?

No, dammit.

Was it possible?

Fuck, yes!

I finally put down my phone, where I had been studying pictures of her that had been taken secretly from a distance. Then I saw her. In real life.

"Do I look that bad, *corazón mío?*" I asked coolly, staring into her eyes down to the bottom of her wounded soul.

"Bad? No, just..." She licked her velvety lips as she sought the right words, unable to take her eyes off me. "I'm sorry. I didn't mean it," she muttered, the last words to herself. "What can I get you?"

I gave her a piercing stare. I'm not interested in what the people my clients approach me about look like, but her charisma blew me away. Nuria was wearing her reddish-brown hair tied up in a ponytail, making her seem both cheeky and innocent.

Two loose strands, braided into little plaits, framed her expressive, arched brows, and her large, intense eyes.

In that moment I wanted to twirl the strands around my fingers and smooth them back from her face, so I could see the green of her eyes more clearly.

My flower is not classically beautiful, like the women you see on billboards, social media, or porn sites.

No, she is perfectly imperfect. Perfect with her light freckles, the little dimple on her right cheek when she smiles, and the prominent scar under her jaw.

She is marked by life, like I am. After her voice, her pretty face wasn't the only thing I fell in love with, there was also the pale scar on her slim neck that carried on down to her lower jaw. I was impressed she didn't try to cover it with a scarf or a polo neck, or conceal it under her hair.

I hadn't known about the scar. Yet it was the one thing that piqued my curiosity and whose story I wanted to know.

"I'll have a Guinness," I replied in a low voice, before turning back to my phone. She nodded, and looked at me for a second longer than necessary. Feeling her gaze on me, I raised my head.

"Is something the matter?"

I already knew she was studying me for signs that I belonged to a criminal gang. She could look for a long time and still not find out who I was.

"No, nothing. I'll bring your Guinness over now."

A shrill whistle sounded over the clamour of voices and music in the bar, and was followed by a shout.

"Hey, bunny! Come over to our table. I have a raging thirst!" The idiot three tables away shouted to Nuria, and she turned towards him.

I watched as she briefly pursed her lips. She hated being called that. But not as much as I hated how the guy was talking to her.

As Nuria went over to the macho, tattooed skinhead in her black mini-skirt, white, short-sleeved blouse, apron, and seriously hot heels, I looked more closely at the hollering idiot. He slapped Nuria on the arse without warning.

Motherfucker!

If there was one thing I despised more than people who begged for mercy, it was toads like this, who groped women who didn't belong to them without asking permission. And unfortunately, I wasn't the sort of man who just stood by and watched. Nuria belonged to me now. And not just because I was meant to be tailing her.

Every night I kill this guy in my dreams. Every night I relish his cries of pain. Every night I look forward to being able to kill him all over again the following night. Nuria will never have noticed, but that after that encounter with her, the pushy guy never came into the *Luna Ilena* again, because his remains were already being devoured by worms.

From the moment I offed the guy that night, and maybe before then, I knew I wanted to see Nuria again – every day. It was a new feeling for me. As if there were an invisible cord that made it impossible for me to stay away from her.

The more I resisted, the tighter the cord became. Until I accepted the leash around my heart. I gave in to my insatiable desire for her and, from then on, I wanted to see her every day.

The memory of this first meeting makes it even sweeter to

watch my rose sleep. It gives me a thrill every time to think she could wake up and find me in the room. Every time I imagine getting into bed with her and taking what – after our earlier encounter – it's obvious she wants. What I want. Her. Her body. Her lips. Her pussy. Her soul. All mine.

I twist the stem of the white rose in my fingers, and with each whimpering noise she makes I tear out the petals. It causes me pain to watch her toss around restlessly every night, whimpering quietly. She suffers. In her dreams, she suffers. And I don't know why.

I don't understand her. I can glean next to nothing about Nuria's dark past, no matter how much I dig.

I know where she was born: Madrid. I know that she is twenty-two years old. I know her hobbies: running, partying, and reading. I know she doesn't have many friends, that she works hard to support herself, and that she hasn't any professional training.

Having completed her schooling with fairly average grades, she moved out of her family home. She has two siblings – brothers – and no other relatives. She left Madrid at eighteen; I've no idea why as the chats and messages I've found don't even indicate whether she was living with a boyfriend or a friend. She only has one remaining grandparent – a grandmother, who lives somewhere in the wilderness of northern Spain.

I've found nothing at all on her between the ages of seventeen and twenty. Not even an ATM withdrawal, a money transfer, a passport check, or a mobile phone connection. It's as if, from 31 October three years ago, she ceased to exist. She only resurfaces on 4 August, about eighteen months ago, at which point I can link her with a newly registered bank card, passport, and mobile number.

What did you do in those three years, little rose? Where were you? Are you a criminal who went underground with false papers? Did you leave everything, absolutely everything behind, and somehow manage to stay under the radar of all surveillance systems? Were you on the streets?

Life on the streets is hard, violent, and merciless. It would explain her nightmares.

It's just before 3 a.m. when things get worse. What is making her so afraid? I could wake her up, console her, lie down with her, but I want to know more about her nightmares. To know who or what she runs away from at night. A name will come out at some point. It can't be me. As much as I like to torment, punish, and even torture her a little, I would never go as far as whatever it is she fears in her dreams. And besides, I know she has been suffering at night for longer than she has known about me.

I am standing over her in bed, watching her shake her head and struggle for breath, when I hear footsteps in the hallway. The next moment I hear the door handle move.

Fuck! I didn't lock the door, because I didn't come in through the door. I immediately drop to the floor like I'm in the army and slide noiselessly under the bed.

How humiliating. The footsteps get closer and they definitely aren't one of the children she looks after. They are heavier, louder. Lying on my stomach, I turn my head to the side and see black trainers with white laces standing next to Nuria's bed.

What's going on?

The person doesn't make a sound. What if they attack Nuria? Just as I decide to crawl out from under the bed and pull my knife out of my boot, I hear the footsteps receding, followed by the soft creaking of the door and the click as it is pulled shut. I immediately slide out from under the bed and straighten up. I want to know who – apart from me – has gained access to her room without being asked, what they wanted, and where they are going.

I walk quietly past the dressing room and am about to go round the corner to the door when I hear a whispered "Demon" behind me. I freeze briefly.

"Wait...," Nuria calls, her voice breaking.

"I have to go." It kills me to have to deny her when she is finally asking for me.

I take a fleeting look over my shoulder and see Nuria reaching for the switch on her bedside lamp. I pull the hood over my hair to avoid being seen by her.

"How long have you been here?" The light flicks on and, snarling quietly, I clench my fists in the front pocket of my hoodie and lower my face.

"A while."

"Like every night?"

"Always, my flower." Then I continue my pursuit, pulling my mask over my face, and tearing open the door. The hallway beyond is pitch black. I listen into the darkness and hear footsteps not far away. Lexton and Quest are waiting at the gate. They know about the strange goings-on in this house, like the attack on Anston. I bet it was Anston or Zain in her room. But why? Why would someone sneak into a sleeping woman's bedroom, like I do, only to disappear again after a few seconds? Perhaps because they are obsessed with her, too? The footsteps go upstairs.

I reach the end of the hallway and, hiding round the corner, look up the staircase. I see a shadow. In the same moment, someone grabs the back of my jacket. My reflexes kick in and I spin around and seize their neck, mechanically pushing them against the wall.

Nuria stares at me in the pale moonlight, wide-eyed and panting.

"Shit, you're scaring me," she gasps.

"Don't sneak up on me!" I growl in annoyance. At the same time, I breathe in her flowery scent and feel the warmth of her body, which excites me instantly. Fuck!

My eyes flicker briefly to her cleavage.

"I've repeatedly said the same to you, and nothing has changed."

I smirk under the mask, then lean in close to her face. "Someone was in your room."

"Yes, you."

I roll my eyes impatiently. "A stranger."

"You're a stranger to me."

"Dammit, Nuria," I hiss, and carry on listening for telltale sounds nearby. Suddenly the wall lamps on the floor above come on.

"Hello?" calls a deep male voice.

"Mr Monair," Nuria whispers.

"Hello? Is there someone down there?" *Fuck.* He must have heard us. There's no way he can have seen us over the cameras because they're all turned off. Or maybe the fact that they are turned off has put him on the alert.

I immediately place my hand over Nuria's mouth, then push her back to her room. She stares up at me, wide-eyed, and stumbles, because she can't keep up with me while walking backwards. I quickly lift her, carry her into the room, and close the door quietly behind us. She reaches past me to turn the key. "Go," she whispers.

"Uh-huh, and how?" I'm damned if I'm going to show her my secret way of accessing her rooms.

"However you normally get into my room."

"I don't have wings, in case you haven't noticed. We're on the second floor."

"Then you'll have to jump," she teases. The next moment, there's a knocking at the door. Still in my arms, my flower jumps.

"Nuria. Are you awake?" Mr Monair calls from behind the door.

I don't really care if I'm found with Nuria, or if she gets thrown out for bringing strange men back to the house – then she'll have to come to me more quickly. But Mr Monair looked armed to me, and I have no desire to have a bullet pulled from my ass by Lexton.

"Open the door," I whisper, setting her down carefully and brushing my hand over her tousled hair.

"But..."

"Go and open it!"

She does as I say, turning to the door, and I seize the opportunity to creep over to the sofas, take a book from the shelf and activate the mechanism in the shelf without Nuria noticing. Then I slip through the gap in the wall panelling between the fireplace and the shelf.

"Mr Monair," she greets her host father.

"I heard something in the house. The cameras aren't working. Did you notice anything unusual?"

I watch through a gap in the shelves as Mr Monair comes into Nuria's room and looks around everywhere. Nuria, in her dark purple pyjamas, scans the rooms and shakes her head.

"No, no, I haven't." The raised colour in her cheeks and the slight tremble in her voice give her away. Give her away to me, though apparently not to Mr Monair. *You need to work on your lying, little rose.*

Holding a shotgun, he checks that no one is hiding anywhere in Nuria's room. He looks behind the long, heavy curtains and under the bed, and goes into the bathroom. He checks the wardrobes, apologising for the intrusion. Then suddenly that wanker Zain appears behind him in the hallway.

"Has something happened?" he asks. All he's wearing is a pair of black shorts.

"I heard a noise and came to investigate. The cameras are turned off. Did you see anything?" Mr Monair asks.

Zain gives Nuria a threatening look, which I don't like, but then shakes his head. "I haven't seen anything suspicious."

He and Nuria exchange a glance that makes me intensely jealous. He knows Nuria is hiding something, I can sense it.

"Where's Henry?" Nuria asks, walking to the door and rubbing her bare upper arms.

"Good question." Mr Monair, clad in dark blue pyjamas, raises his fingers to his mouth and whistles. "Henry. Here!" When nothing happens, he looks worried. "He always comes. Something's wrong. I'll look downstairs. Wait here. This isn't our first break-in. If the Vegases and their bastard company are behind this, I swear I'll shoot first and ask questions afterwards!" With this threat, Mr Monair leaves the room. Zain shuts the door behind him, which drives me into a rage. What is the guy planning?

"You should take care your nocturnal visitor doesn't get shot."

I ball the fingers of my right hand into a fist and my knuckles crack.

"Don't be ridiculous. There is no nocturnal visitor. Or have you found some evidence to support your claim?" Nuria asks.

Zain looks around her rooms, his raven-black eyes alighting on the discarded white rose by the armchair.

"What's all this again?" Zain strides over to the rose, picks it up and holds it in front of Nuria.

"A rose. So?" She shrugs her shoulders in a bored manner and folds her arms over her chest, accentuating the contours of her breasts. I'm not the only one who notices. Zain's eyes range over her breasts, then over Nuria's perfect, bare legs, which belong to me. They will be wrapped around my body, when I take her. The grazes on her knees are partly healed. And those don't escape Zain's notice, either.

"Something's not right here, and I'm going to find out what it is." Until now the two of them have been standing facing me, but when Zain presses the rose roughly into Nuria's hand, he turns his back to me and... I gasp at the sight. Long, deep welts are scarred across his back. *What in God's name...?*

He pushes Nuria roughly ahead of him so she can't see how damaged he is. Although I certainly can. But how could he know I am in one of the estate's secret passages? He probably doesn't even know about them.

"Good luck, you bastard," she calls, without looking up. "You won't find anything because there is no secret visitor. I bought the rose myself because... because I love white roses." A pleasant shudder goes through me. She loves my roses. I knew it.

"If you believe that...," he sniffs, "Why white roses, of all things?"

"Because..." Nuria licks her lips. Think of something clever.

"Because I bought it for Ranja." The eldest daughter, perhaps, who moved out months ago?

Zain narrows his eyes dangerously. "How..."

"How do I know you have a sister that no one here talks about?" Nuria retorts, tilting her chin to look up at him and steadfastly meeting his gaze. How I admire her courage. "Because Hailey and Maily talked about her. They both miss her."

"Don't say her name again, okay, slut?" I am so close to jumping out from behind the shelf and breaking his neck.

"What did you call me, you miserable motherfucker?!" she replies confidently.

The jealousy I feel towards this bastard seems to be unfounded. I should still teach him a lesson, though.

"Slut! Even if I don't have any proof you're smuggling someone in at night yet, I'll find some. Then you'll be for it, and hopefully you won't go weak at the knees when I claim my dues and you honour our bet!"

My stomach churns as he takes hold of her hips and pushes her further towards the closed door. What is that bastard planning to do with her? In that moment I decide to make a move. *No one touches her!*

"I won't lose the bet. Let me go!"

He traps my flower between his body and the door. I open the shelf to break his neck after all. Right now. If I don't do it he'll hurt her or harass her. And I won't allow that.

I locate the light switch next to the bookshelf and press it. The main light goes out immediately, before Nuria or Zain notice me. I pull myself out of the gap between the wall and the shelf, reach for the knife in the side of my boot and release the blade. *Goodbye, you annoying bastard!*

"Why did the light go out?" Zain asks.

"Don't do it!" I hear Nuria's voice – and know straightaway that she is talking to me.

"Do what?" Zain wants to know.

Cut his throat! I've had enough of his irritating presence, his insinuations that he could get her to sleep with him!

"Is there someone here?" he asks.

"Fuck, yes, and he'll kill you unless you get out right now," Nuria warns him. "Just go!"

And before I can get to the son of a bitch, the door opens and Nuria pushes Zain forcefully out into the half-lit hallway. Zain turns around, his face distorted, and stares at me as if he's seen a ghost. The game is up anyway, and I couldn't care less if he runs to his father now and tells on us. He's just a joker I'm going to get rid of because he's in my way.

I hurl the knife towards him, simultaneously grabbing Nuria and kicking the door shut with my foot. It falls into the lock with a loud crash, making the floor shake.

"Are you mad?" my rose shouts.

"Lock the door."

"He'll tell everyone. Fuck! What are you doing?!"

"If you'd let me finish what I was doing, he wouldn't have been able to tell anyone anything," I reply, letting her go. "Lock it."

"You're completely mental!"

"Too right!"

Once she has finally turned the blasted key, I grab her, push her against the door, and hit it hard with the flat of my hand, next to her head. "I'll kill that wanker for touching you."

"You won't!" she counters. "He is the son of the family I'm staying with."

"Why should I care?" I laugh joylessly, before her little fists rain down on my chest. How ridiculous.

"You won't kill him."

"He can hear you," I tell her. What are the odds his ear is pressed to the door and he is waiting to beat me up or shoot me as soon as I step out of the room? *Such a predictable fool!*

"Damn," she curses. "Damn, you ruin everything."

"I ruin everything?" I repeat grimly. "He's the fucker who called you a slut and touched you without asking! Do you really think I'm just going to stand by and watch? Do you think I'll let this happen to you, or to me? Let a complete weirdo take the thing I want away from me? Do you think I'm not going to castrate this bastard and then slit his throat? You're wrong!"

She doesn't say anything. Not a damn word. I'd like to punish her right here, right now, throw her down on the bed and let her make amends for this mess!

"What's going on in there?" I hear Mr Monair's voice and raise my head. Nuria takes shaky, frightened breaths. *Fuck! Time to go.*

I let go of Nuria with a jerk, and turn away from her with a threatening murmur, looking for the secret passageway.

"Where are you going now?" she hisses quietly.

"Sort your own shit out, if you don't want me to."

"Hey, that's not fair. What am I supposed to tell them?" *As if I care!*

I reach the bookshelf, and turn around. "I've half a mind to kill you, now you've protected that bastard. I don't give a shit what you tell them. How about the truth?" Snorting derisively, I climb into the darkness, close the shelf, and head into the secret passage from where I can still hear the hammering on Nuria's door.

I need to try other ways of bringing her to me in Boston, protecting her, keeping her with me so that no bastard can have her for himself, touch her, harass her, insult her. Why doesn't she see that she'd be so much better off by my side?

And why don't I see that I shouldn't give a shit about what she wants!

Every decision she makes is more reckless than the last. And with each day that passes, I start to suspect there is something bad going on in this place. Someone taking the pathetic Anston out of action. Someone sneaking into Nuria's room at night. There's something nasty going on here. What if it could even cost Nuria her life? I don't know what it is yet, but I'll find out!

CHAPTER 16

Demon

Anger and rage are the
weapons I have forged.
If anyone gets between my queen
and me, they'll face a torturous death,
one that will last forever.

"The cops are at the Monairs' place," Lex informs me, chewing gum, as I head to the bar in the mansion questioning my entire existence. "Man, there's some serious shit going down. What happened?"

I take a glass roughly off the shelf and pour myself a large slug of Macallan, trying to ignore all the chatter from Lexton, Quest and Cameron.

"Wylder. What the hell happened in there?" Cameron asks again. I snort, then down the drink. The whisky burns as it travels down my throat. It doesn't completely wash away the frustration and anger, although it briefly calms my thoughts about Nuria.

"Explain!"

"What do you want to hear?" I say, turning to face them. "That the family's son saw me before I could kill him? That they suspect there's been a break-in?"

Lexton, in his black roll-neck jumper and suit trousers, gets up from the Chesterfield sofa next to the crackling fireplace. "I've no idea what's got into you lately, Wylder, but talk to us. Who is this woman? How long have you known her? Why are you running around after her? We know she's from Spain, because that's where your last investigation was. So what the hell is this?" Lexton turns to the boys. "We have a right to know what's going down here. Not to put any pressure on you, we just want to stop you making any stupid mistakes. Otherwise we'll fly back to Boston, like you should be doing, instead of getting mixed up with the disappearance of these girls..."

"Shut your mouth! Keep out of this! It's not for you to ask questions. You..." My dark gaze scans the faces of these men, whom I trust completely. Who are at the highest levels of leadership in my organisation, whom I trust with my life. "You follow my orders and there's no need for you to know anything else unless I choose to inform you about it. Is that clear? If you're not happy here and want to go back to snowy Boston, I won't stop you. Take a flight home!"

Cameron, who travelled here a week ago, twists the signet ring on his middle finger thoughtfully and raises his eyebrows. Dressed in a loose, muscle-fit T-shirt and grey jeans, he flops back onto the couch and runs his fingers through his thick, copper-coloured hair. "I'm not questioning anything, I'm staying. If you've fallen for the woman, then that's your business. Don't get involved, Lex."

"Are you really in love with her? That Nuria, who gave you a blow job in the alley last week?" Lexton asks instead, making a face that suggests I'm mentally ill.

I look up at the ceiling in irritation. "And she did something tonight that really pissed you off," Quest speculates. "What? Does she even know who you are?"

These endless, irritating questions "She'll find out."

Quest's eyes widen as he gets up from the armchair beside Cameron. Cameron, however, laughs mischievously. "That's sick. She really has no idea who's visiting her at night?" He leans back on his elbows, looks at me and grins in amusement. "Why don't I come up with shit like this?"

"We're not here because of the missing person cases at all, are we?" Quest asks. "Did you actually leave Boston to continue the hunt for your sisters' kidnappers? Here? In fucking Australia? Why would they be here?" *Why not?*

I have reached a point where I probably have to tell them some of the truth. "You're right. I'd have expected no less of you. I suspect they're staying here and taking on more contracts from the Zetos." I feel, deep inside, that some members of the criminal organisation known as the Zetos are here – kidnapping, selling, and possibly murdering women. Their network extends all over the world.

"Do you think that's likely?" Lexton asks. "Why? Wouldn't they be better off fulfilling the contracts in South America? Smuggling goods into North America would be much easier. Or are you really only here to see Nuria, because she's working as a sweet little au pair?" Sweet. He has absolutely no idea. She's not a sweet au pair, she's a queen.

"I came to Australia for both reasons. To investigate the cases and to keep an eye on Nuria. Is that a problem for you?" I take a step towards him, causing Lexton's jaw to tense up.

"No, why would it be? It's only a problem if you're not thinking straight and you start making mistakes. I'm sure I speak for the others, too: I'm not going to spring you from an Australian prison because you've broken into the house of a filthy rich family so you can fuck your girlfriend."

"That's below the belt, even for you," Cameron remarks. "When did Wylder ever show an interest in a woman other than to drag her into his bed and fuck her? Let him have his fun."

"Do you love her?" Lexton asks. "Tell me. I want to know whether I'll have to stick my neck out for her when she becomes your partner."

"What if I do? Would you die for her, Lexton? Like you'd die for me?" I ask, looking down and observing every emotion that passes over his face. He opens his mouth, inhales, and then his brows twitch.

"Fuck, you're actually serious for once?"

"Deadly serious," I assure him.

Cameron whistles the wedding march. "Damn, I'm looking forward to going back to Boston and you making an official announcement to the organisation. The women will cry their eyes out."

I go over to him. "It won't come to that. None of you talk about it. If I find out anyone has been passing on information..."

"You'll get angry and throw us out?" Quest finishes my sentence, placing his hand theatrically on his bare chest – he's just wearing jogging bottoms. "Of course. You have my word. I won't say anything to anyone. If she's so important to you, then she's important to me too." Quest nudges Lexton, who's next to him. "What d'you say, Lex?"

Lexton groans, looking at me as if he'd expected me to give a different answer. "If it's really serious between you and the girl, what else can I say. Yes, damn it. I'm in, I'll stay in bloody Australia, sweating like a wolf."

"You could just take your stinking jumper off and put a T-shirt on," Cameron observes, laughing.

"No one asked you." Lexton never takes off his roll-neck jumper; it's become his trademark and, more importantly, it hides his scars.

"And you, Cam?" I ask. Cam jumps nimbly off the sofa.

"You can always count on me. No matter how many women you want, I'll protect every one of them." He's such a nutcase.

"Good. We've cleared that up then," I say.

"And what just happened? Why are you so worked up, and angry with your princess? What has she done?" Quest asks.

I turn back to the bar irritably.

"He's gone quiet again," Lexton remarks, like he's my therapist. "Let's ask him later. We don't want to overwhelm him." *Wanker.* Couldn't he just keep his mouth shut for once when he notices that I'm angry? No, he has to push the knife even deeper into the wound and turn the blade.

"I want to meet her," says Cam unexpectedly. "Why not introduce us?"

“Perhaps I will,” I reply, turning to them with another drink in my hand and surveying their questioning faces.

“What do you mean?”

“Just what I said.” They’re going to meet my rose.

CHAPTER 17

Nuria

How can you miss something
you have never had?
And long for someone
who is leading you step by step into darkness?

"You still have a fever." My hand is on Maily's forehead. She's been in bed with a cold since yesterday, with a temperature, a cough, and a runny nose.

Jacky has gone on a spa break to Melbourne with her friends for a few days. Although she said she'd cancel the trip and stay at home with the children, I knew what she wanted to hear: "You go, Jacky, I'll look after the girls."

She left this morning with two little Louis Vuitton suitcases, smiling happily and impeccably dressed in a cream Chanel suit, matching Prada shoes and a broad-brimmed sunhat.

I don't really know what to think of this woman. She's friendly enough towards me, but she's also very superficial. Less so in relation to her children, though she's very focused on the family's image.

Mr Monair, who has told me to call him Richard, is at work and won't be back until 10 p.m. Zain is at home, either hanging around on the upper floor or working out in the gym. The guy is a complete puzzle to me. After the incident a week ago he didn't rat me out to his parents or the police.

There's something strange going on. And I don't like it. Why wouldn't he tell the police that I obviously knew the man who hurled a knife at him? It doesn't make any sense. I guess I don't know him very well. After all, even I don't really know who Demon is. What he looks like, what he does for a living, where he comes from.

He is not a Spaniard – I've often clocked his American accent. But he speaks my mother tongue fluently, as though he has lived in South America or Spain for a long time.

So what should I have told the police when they asked about him?

Yes, I know the intruder. He has been stalking me for a number of months, he followed me to Australia and he sneaks into the house every night. Oh and I once gave him a blow job. Is that important?

Is that what I should have said to the four officers Mr Monair called that night? No, probably not. The police in Spain weren't able to help when I repeatedly reported the stalking. Why should the Australian authorities be any better equipped to deal with it? I don't have any more useful information to offer about Demon than Zain does. The most I can say is that he has piercing blue eyes and an impressive cock.

Damn! Why am I thinking about that right now?

Perhaps because I haven't had a single glimpse of Demon since Mr Monair busted us? Because he hasn't sent me a single message? Because he seems to have stopped stalking me? Because I miss him?

I've been tearing my hair out about why he hasn't been in touch. At first I thought he was pissed off with me. Demon is bloody proud. If someone bruises his ego he retaliates by punishing the person or pushing them away. At least that's how he's always been with me. But then it occurred to me that he might not be able to get in touch. Perhaps he's gone back home, wherever it is this devil lives. And then I've been having these crazy thoughts that something might have happened to him.

Because regardless of how often I pick up my phone and open our chat, there's never a message from him. Even when

I've tried to provoke him. He's not been online. It's as though the ground has swallowed him up.

My fingers have itched to message him on more than one occasion. But I couldn't bring myself to do it. On the one hand, I want nothing more than to get him out of my life. On the other hand, I kind of miss him. I think so often of his deep, sonorous voice and his piercing eyes under the motorcycle helmet. See his tall, imposing figure in front of me and long for his masculine aroma, mixed with that smoky, woody scent. Imagine his hands around my waist, and his tongue that has made me moan. I can't get him out of my head.

The police will carry on looking for the intruder, but they won't track Demon down unless he wants to be tracked down. He's obviously a phantom and is very well acquainted with the layout of the property and its secret passages.

The day after his last visit, I searched the whole bookshelf in vain for levers or buttons that would make it move aside the way it had done for him, without success. Every evening I stand in front of the shelves, cursing, and feel all along them. Nothing happens. I can't find the secret passage through which Demon has obviously been entering the property unnoticed whenever he wants to.

In spite of the radio silence, I am convinced he's still watching me. I feel it. And sometimes I think I see him standing behind a tree in the garden at night. Now and then, if I look down from my second-floor window in the middle of the night, I catch the red glow of a cigarette. But I'm still not entirely sure it's actually him. The last time I think I might have seen him was four nights ago. Since then, things have been unusually quiet as far as Demon is concerned.

What if the police have caught him after all? No. No, they can't have. What if his obsession with me is over? And if so, why aren't I glad? Isn't that exactly what I wanted? Why don't I feel relieved?

"I'm going to die, I'm sure I am." Maily's quiet murmur drags me from my thoughts, and I place a cool cloth on her forehead.

"You'll feel better very soon," I comfort her. "Hailey, please get changed."

Hailey is watching her evening TV programme and calls to me from the sofa in the playroom. "I don't want to yet."

"It's time for bed." It's after 8 p.m. already.

"No!"

I'm not giving in. Otherwise they'll just push the boundaries even further. "Get changed, okay? I'm going to come to the bathroom and we'll clean your teeth."

"Then will you read Ranja's fairytales to us?" Maily asks, her voice groggy. I turn back to her and tuck a strand of dark blonde hair behind her right ear.

"Oh yes. We have to find out whether Ranja has found the mermaids' cave."

"She has. I know she has," Hailey says, focused on getting changed and getting into bed now after all, so she won't miss the story. "I'm hurrying."

I pick up Ranja's diary, which I read aloud to the girls every night. Obviously not the diary entries about her and Jazeem, but a made-up fairytale about mermaids, lazy princes, talking birds, and magic dwarves. I have written an extra-long, made-up story and I put it inside the book every evening, so the twins think I'm reading from Ranja's diary.

After Hailey has got into her nightdress, cleaned her teeth, and combed her hair, she runs quickly out of the en suite bathroom and slips under the covers with her sister.

They haven't asked about their mother once this evening, which makes me kind of sad. Do they even realise Jacky isn't here? They definitely know about her trip, but as a child I always asked when my mother was coming back if she'd gone away. I could hardly manage a day without her.

"You can start now. Read, Nuria!" Hailey looks at me with large, expectant eyes, while Maily lowers her feverish gaze and puts her head on the pillow.

I pull the covers up over them both and open Ranja's book. "Where were we?" I flip through the book to my story, which is written on an A5-sized piece of paper, and start reading.

Hailey's little hand seeks out mine. It's hard to believe how much the two girls seem to like me now, despite our rocky start. I've become very fond of them, too.

I take Hailey's fingers in my hand, then carry on reading. After one page, Maily is already asleep, while Hailey hangs on my every word, spellbound. My stomach turns when I think of their big sister Ranja's real story, which I continue reading every night before I go to sleep.

At 8:40 p.m., I stop reading. Hailey is yawning, although she's begging to know what happens next. "Tomorrow, little moth. Then I'll read more. It's time to go to sleep now."

"Will you carry me to bed?" she asks.

I put the books down, then lift Hailey carefully out of her sister's bed and carry her to her own. She watches as I adjust her covers. "What are we doing tomorrow?" she asks sleepily.

"What would you like to do, Hailey? Shall we ask one of your friends over to play, if Maily still needs to rest?"

Hailey shakes her head. "No, we're not allowed to bring friends home. Papa doesn't like it." *How strange. Why would he want to deny his children like that?*

I hand her a plush hippo to distract her.

"Okay, sleep well, little moth." I kiss her on the forehead, then take Ranja's diary, switch on the nightlight by the door, and turn off the main light.

I shut the door quietly behind me, and find Zain waiting for me. He's leaning against the wall in the hallway and eyes me up and down, like a foreign object that has no place in this well-to-do family.

When will he stop being so hostile towards me? He doesn't have to like me, but he could at least leave me alone. Zain, who is wearing a grey Ralph Lauren polo shirt, sand-coloured khaki trousers, and Jordans, slowly pushes himself off the panelled wall.

"What is it?" I ask.

"Do you have a moment?"

"For you? No," I retort, earning a cool grin that quickly

fades again. I hurry past him to the door of my room. Just as I put my hand on the door handle, his hand appears in my field of vision and holds the door shut.

"I want to talk to you."

"But I don't want to talk to you." Though I do turn around to face him. His green eyes travel across my face, study my eyes, glide over my nose to my lips.

"Where did you get that book from?" He suddenly reaches for the diary with his free hand, trying to tear it out of my fingers.

"That has nothing to do with you!" I try to loosen his grip. He won't let go.

"It very much does have to do with me. It's my sister's diary."

"It can't be that important to you. No one in the house talks about her except for the twins," I reply.

"For good reason. Give it here!"

This lousy sod is really getting on my nerves. "What kind of reason can there possibly be for getting rid of all traces of a member of the family?" Because isn't that what he's planning to do with this book, too: take it off me and hide it, or destroy it. I won't let that happen. Although I didn't know Ranja, her story is important to me; someone has to remember her. And the twins might want to know more about her one day.

"You ask too many questions, Nuria. This isn't something you should be sticking your nose into."

Is he threatening me? "Too late. I'm not giving you the book." I carry on wrangling with him as though we were on a football pitch.

"Do I have to get violent?" he asks.

"Just you try!"

I jab my knee upwards, but he moves out of the way before it can make contact with his crown jewels. *Shit, he's quick.*

"Nice try." Now that he's standing half a metre away and has let go of the book, I quickly reach behind me for the door handle. He comes at me again and I hit him over the head with the diary. He stares at me, confused by what I have just done. I seize my opportunity and slip through the door, hastily pulling it shut.

"Give it to me!" he yells through the closed door.

"No!" I answer defiantly. "I'm going to finish reading it."

"But I want to read it too." *What?* I turn to the door in surprise. "But surely you know what happened to your sister. Why do you want to read it?" I'd assumed the Monairs hadn't told the two girls anything about their sister's disappearance because they were too young.

"Use your brain. Because I don't know what happened," he says agitatedly. "Give me the diary, Nuria. I'm Ranja's brother. I know my parents don't talk about her because something happened that made her disappear – from one day to the next. All the answers could be in that book. If my parents get hold of it, I'll never find out what's in there," he continues. I don't know what to think. Because his mood is switching, from his customary anger to despair. It could be a cheap trick to make me open the door. But what he is saying might also be true. This is his sister we're talking about, after all.

"What did your parents tell you had happened to Ranja?"

For a moment he's quiet, very quiet. "They said Ranja had been admitted to a clinic, because..." He sighs, and his voice grows quiet, more brittle. "Because she was self-harming again. They had diagnosed her with borderline personality disorder, and in-patient therapy was supposed to help get it under control. But, dammit...!"

"But dammit, what?" I ask.

"I've been to all the local psychiatric clinics, phoned around, spoken to people, and my sister hasn't been admitted to any of them."

"Perhaps she's there under a different name." I know how highly the family values their reputation.

"I've been to every single place within a hundred-mile radius, Nuria, I'm telling you. I showed them all a photo of Ranja. I'm her relative, the clinics have to give me information. None of them recognised her. She wasn't there. She's been missing almost six months now, she hasn't been in touch, or left me a message. She wouldn't do that, do you get it? At first I believed the shit my father told me, but now… Please, Nuria, give me the damn book. I've been looking for it for weeks. I've no idea where you found it, but give it to me."

My breathing shallow, I listen to his every word and debate what to do. If he's lying, he's being very convincing about it. I chew nervously on my left thumbnail, looking at the notebook in my right hand and agonising about what action to take. "I haven't finished reading it. I'll give it to you when I'm done. You have my word." First I have to know the truth, in case Zain is lying after all and intends to destroy the book.

A sigh of disappointment and frustration comes from behind the door. "Can I trust you?"

"And can I trust you?" I ask.

"I didn't blow the whistle on your criminal boyfriend, the one who almost killed me. So yes, I would say you can trust me."

Now I turn the key, open the door, and stare at Zain, who actually looks dishevelled. I have never seen his black pretty-boy hair so tousled. His dark eyes move instinctively to the book in my hand, which I put behind my back. "I'll take a leap of faith. We'll make a copy. I'm keeping the original."

He raises his eyebrows. "It sounds as though there's a 'but' coming."

"But…," I begin. "I want to know why you didn't give the game away about me and my night-time visitor. Tell me." Demon almost did him in, after all.

"You want a reason?" He takes a step towards me so that there's only thirty centimetres between us. Every one of my muscles is tensed to breaking point, ready to dodge an attack if he tries to take the book again. "Yes."

He looks slowly down at me, deep into my eyes. For so long that it's difficult to hold his gaze.

"Because I want to know how he can walk around the house without being caught on camera."

"I don't know that either."

"You know. You must do. Is there a loophole in the alarm system?"

"Why are you so keen to know?"

He narrows his eyes, with their unashamedly long lashes. "Because I'm sure my sister knew about it, too, and left the house without being seen."

Is he telling the truth? Or does he just want the information so he can use it against me?

"Why do you think that?" I enquire.

"You don't trust me."

"Not one bit," I say, because he can be an arse, like so many rich, spoiled brats – in spite of the other side of himself he has just shown me.

"I know Ranja must have left the house somehow, because she was in a secret relationship with a boy from her school. Jazeem." *He knows about that?* "Perhaps you've already seen the guy's name in her diary. He won't come clean, no matter how many times I ask him. And believe me, I've tried everything to get him to talk."

"How do you know about their relationship if you haven't read the diary?" After all, Ranja and Jazeem were intent on keeping it a secret.

"Because I went into her room one night and found her crying in bed, with a bottle of vodka. That's when she told me about him." I examine Zain thoughtfully as he continues. "She never told me how she managed to sneak out of the house at night without being seen though. But now she's gone, that's exactly what I want to know."

He moves away from me and seems to be waiting for my reply.

Although I'm really worried I'll regret it, I look determinedly at him. "Okay. I'll give you a copy of the diary. For real."

Zain is visibly relieved, and inhales deeply.

"Thank you." *Thank you?* Of all the answers I would have expected from him, thank you wasn't one of them. It seems

I've made the right call. He would never behave so uncharacteristically if he wasn't genuinely worried about his sister.

Hopefully.

Hopefully he's not lying to me.

CHAPTER 18

Nuria

Whenever the back of my neck tingles
I know you are with me.
In me, in my thoughts,
my heart, my soul.
What if you aren't there anymore?

Zain's dad's study is an elegantly furnished office with tall shelves for files and books standing behind a huge, solid-wood desk.

The photocopier light traverses Zain's face as we make the copies together. He checks his watch nervously at frequent intervals. "Dad'll be back in a few minutes."

"Let's copy the rest tomorrow then."

"No. I want to read it tonight."

"It's over a hundred handwritten pages."

He looks at me like I'm a puppy that has fallen into a pond. "I'm a quick reader."

Of course he is. I roll my eyes in feigned annoyance.

As Zain turns over the next page, I glance behind the curtains into the garden. Mr Monair's – no Richard's – office is on the first floor. I have a good view of the metal gate and the drive behind it. If I see headlights on the road I'll quickly switch the office light off so that no one can see us. The slender sickle moon is fighting its way through the tattered clouds.

It looks beautiful, and at the same time my neck tingles, in the way it only does in the presence of a certain person.

When I tear my gaze away from the driveway, suddenly, out of nowhere, a dark figure with a hood and mask is standing by the window. Startled, I stumble back.

"Demon." Is he back? After the initial shock, relief floods my chest. So he hasn't left or given up on me? For some reason I am happy to see him, and a smile steals across my face.

"What is it?" Zain asks. He must have heard my gasp. The curtain closes again but Zain goes over and opens it. "Is my-Dadback?"

This time there is no silhouette of a man standing there. He's gone, but my heart's still racing like I'm sprinting. "No."

"What gave you such a shock then?" he asks, turning round from the window to face me, not knowing Demon is there again, standing behind him. I can't breathe. *Don't do it!,* I think. *Don't pull any shit, Demon.*

Goosepimples spread across my body as I grab Zain by the arm and pull him away from the window. "He's here."

I hurriedly close the curtains. However much a sick, reckless part of me, buried somewhere deep inside, might have longed for Demon, reason triumphs in the end. Demon is capable of anything if I give him a reason to be jealous. I'm currently in a room on my own with Zain, the guy he threw a knife at without so much as a second thought only a few days ago.

"Who?" Zain tries to grab hold of me. "Your boyfriend?"

Boyfriend? Hardly. "Yes," I lie. "He was standing by the window."

Zain's eyes widen, then he turns around, opening the curtains with a jerk. "Are you mad?" I say. "Do you want to die?"

By now I am fairly certain Demon won't kill me. Although he wouldn't hesitate to kill anyone who got between us. There's no one at the window now, and I shut the curtains again in panic. The thought that one shot would be enough to make Zain sink to the floor beside me with a hole in his head makes my heart feel like it's about to burst out of my chest.

"Would he really kill me?" he asks. "Is your boyfriend a murderer?" Coming from his mouth this sounds so... so... so utterly horrifying and wrong. But he is right.

"Put it this way, he hasn't done anything in my presence so far. But yes, he is capable of it."

"Who in the hell are you with? Is he blackmailing you? Are you really together?" This is starting to get complicated now. What should I tell him? No, we are not together. He is stalking me, and I get weak in the most stupid moments, even though I bite him and kick him, and ought to report him to the police? Because that's exactly how it is. No one will be able to understand why I fall for my shadow more and more with each passing day. That I'm addicted to the thrill, that the idea someone out there is protecting me is somehow calming. He might be extremely possessive but there's a considerate side to him somewhere. I don't even understand it myself.

"It's complicated," I say evasively. Just then I hear a loud bang on the windowpane. Horrified, I turn around.

"Duck!" I warn Zain. I pull back the curtains and see distant headlights approaching the house from the long driveway.

Kneeling by the window, directly in front of the photocopier, Zain looks at me.

"Your father's coming."

"We're not finished yet."

"We'll copy the rest tomorrow. Come on, let's pack up."

I've no idea how I ended up working with a guy I hated with a passion just two hours ago, instead of handing him over to Demon. This doesn't mean I now trust Zain blindly – not in a million years. He could still betray me. But as long as I keep hold of Ranja's diary and Zain only has the copies, I hold all the cards.

I quickly grab the book from the photocopier, while Zain switches off the light. Then we leave his father's office together, and he locks the door. Arriving at the staircase, we hurry up the stairs. We part ways, me turning off on the second floor, while he heads up to the next floor with his rolled stack of papers.

"Your boyfriend must like me after all, if he warned us like that," he calls with a grin.

I doubt it. Before I can reply, the front door opens and I slink into my room like a weasel.

I look up at the ceiling, my breathing coming in gasps. That was close. I need a few minutes to settle my adrenaline levels and I decide to have a shower and then read some more of Ranja's diary in bed. Presumably that's what Zain's planning to do tonight as well.

My eyes blink open in the middle of the night. I heard a crash. *The book...* I fell asleep while I was reading, but why is the light not on?

Suddenly I find myself staring at four dark figures wearing bright neon masks with x-shaped eyes and broad grins.

"Pay-back time!" I hear Demon's muffled voice behind the red neon mask. Then a cloth is tied over my mouth.

"What?" I splutter through the gag, panicking, as in the same moment the blanket is torn from my body and the masked men lift me out of bed. Two hold my arms, two my legs. Before I can grasp what is happening I am lifted out of bed and find myself standing shakily between the four men.

"Demon, what's going on?"

Behind me, someone seizes my chin with a gloved hand and lifts it to his chest. "We're getting to know each other. Enjoy it, little rose." It's Demon. His fingers stroke voluptuously down my throat to my collarbone and my breasts. His hand glides under my pyjama top and cups my right breast.

"Do you trust me?" he asks. Although I shouldn't, because I don't even know whose face is really behind the mask, I stare at the other three masked individuals who are standing in front of me, and hesitate for a few seconds.

My common sense is screaming *no*, as my heart races in

my chest. But my curiosity has been awakened. It's possible that now, for the first time, I might actually find something out about Demon.

"Just say the word, and you'll be back in your bedroom faster than you can blink."

"What do you mean?" I mumble, turning my head towards the glowing red neon mask.

"We're taking a trip."

"Where to?" I ask.

"It's a surprise. So, yes or no?" He pushes me to make a decision. In principle, he could take whatever he wanted without my consent.

"I bet she won't go," I hear the guy in front of me say. He's wearing a black hoodie like the others, and a neon yellow mask.

He shouldn't be so sure.

"Give her time," Demon insists, in a lightly threatening undertone. The man with the glowing green mask flops nonchalantly onto my bed.

"If she's staying, I am too. This bed is damn comfy." I haven't heard that voice before. I'm pretty sure I recognise the voice of the one with the yellow mask, though. That guy in the alley behind the club. Lexton.

I breathe in as deeply as possible through the gag. "God, I'm going to regret this. So bloody much," I murmur, tilting my head back to look at Demon. He continues to massage my breast playfully, his thumb circling my nipple.

He inclines his head. "And?"

"Yes."

"Yes what?" the guy with the blue smiley face asks me, as Demon unties the gag from my mouth.

I gasp for breath. "Yes, I'm up for your trip."

"I never expected otherwise," Demon replies, lowering his face to mine and placing both his hands on my cheeks. If he weren't masked, it would look like he wanted to kiss me.

The guy in my bed suddenly sits up.

"Then we should get a move on." Demon is already putting

a blindfold over my eyes. Another of his friends handcuffs my hands in front of my body.

"What are you doing?"

"So worried, all of a sudden?" Demon laughs smugly with a husky undertone. "You trust me, don't you? I'll bring you back safe and sound. You have my word."

"No, no, I'm not worried," I counter, before a jolt passes through my body and I am lifted up in the air. "I just don't want to hurt myself while I can't see."

His men laugh.

"Most people would have wet themselves in fear in her shoes, and she's thinking about bruises." The voice belongs to Quest, whom I saw days ago in the alley and who is now wearing a blue neon mask.

"No worries, little rose. I'll look after you. Let's go, boys."

How long were they standing around my bed? I don't even want to imagine how this trip will end and what Demon has dreamed up. But excitement is fizzing in my stomach like an adrenaline rush. He is back. Finally.

CHAPTER 19

Nuria

I am addicted to the rush
he gives me, although I know very well
that a demon will inevitably lead me
to ruin.

Minutes after Demon has carried me through what I assume is a stuffy secret passageway on the Monair property, I feel fresh air on my face. We are out in the open. A heavy metal door slams shut and I hear the clatter of keys and the sound of a grille being closed.

"Where are you taking me?"

"Somewhere you'll like," Demon assures me.

"To a cellar?"

"Much better than that." Instead of coming over as threatening or frightening, Demon is in a strangely cheerful mood. I have often experienced him as rough, harsh, almost annoyed, or even agitated, but rarely amused.

Shit, what have I let myself in for? The question circles around my head. The next moment I am set down, and then shoved blindly into what feels like a car. Hands grab me by my waist and under my arms, manoeuvring me into the back seat. Immediately afterwards I find myself wedged between two guys. I know they're sitting next to me because I can hear them breathing as they put on their seatbelts.

Someone fastens mine, and multiple car doors slam shut. The engine starts and the car reverses. I fiddle nervously with the fingers of my bound hands.

"Could you at least give me a clue about where we're going?"

Someone takes hold of my chin, not roughly, but almost carefully, as though I were fragile. "To school," replies a rough, deep voice that must belong to Lexton, the grim-looking, tattoo-covered giant.

"School?" I repeat, confused. "What school?"

"So many questions," remarks an unknown voice. "Here. Take my hoodie. So you don't catch cold."

It isn't especially cold, but I'm only wearing short pyjamas. Unknown hands place a jumper around me. It smells of a sensuous men's fragrance. *Amber & Vetiver.*

Okay. Okay, what kind of kidnapper gives their victim a jumper so they won't freeze? Of course I want to trust Demon, but I'd be lying if I said my trust was unconditional. The jumper warms me, smells good, and makes me feel like I'm not sitting half-naked between these guys in dark clothing, who might otherwise have got ideas.

I am on the brink of feeling sure Demon's not going to kill me. At least I hope not. But I do know he's prepared to do a lot of other evil things. Things that could permanently damage me, break me, hurt me.

My pulse races as I listen intently for every sound. Music is turned on, a window is wound down, and then my nose detects cigarette smoke.

"Give me a drag," I say to Lexton, who's on my left. A hand grabs my neck. "I don't think Wylder wants you to smoke."

"She can if she wants," I hear from the front. Now I know Demon – or rather, Wylder – is driving.

"All right. Be a good girl and open your mouth then."

I snarl, then open my mouth, and Lexton places the cigarette filter between my lips. I inhale, knowing all eyes will be on me.

I blow the smoke at Lexton provocatively, grin, and move forwards to ease his hold on my neck.

"This is some cheeky girl you've got yourself here, Boss."

Boss. Why do they all call Demon Boss?

"I love her temperament. 'Don't intimidate her too much. I want to see her fire later."

Fire? What fire? Then I get it: we are on the way to an orgy. My heart stands still.

He wouldn't do that to me, would he?

"Okay, stop, stop the car," I shout immediately. The car does an emergency stop, hurling me forward into the seatbelt.

"What is it?" Demon and the strange men whose faces I have seen as little as Wylder's chorus. "Do you feel sick?"

"Sick? No, I've changed my mind. I'm sure you're all nice boys." I babble stupidly as I try to extricate myself from the situation, and earn a sneering laugh.

"Nice boys," Lexton growls in my ear. "I haven't been called that by a woman since I was sixteen."

"She's wimping out," observes Quest.

"Do you want to go back?" Demon asks me. "Why?"

"Why? I thought it was us going on a trip. The two of us, not all five. I know how this is going to end, and no..."

All of a sudden it's damn quiet in the car, and someone takes hold of my cheek. "Yes, it will end with *that.* I'm not going to lie to you, little rose." So Demon knows what I mean. I'm not mistaken. "But you're going to like what's in store for you." His thumb strokes my lower lip. "You can say no at any time, or be taken home. But tonight is the night I take what belongs to me. And that's you."

I can't breathe for a moment, as he voices his intentions aloud so openly. "So? Should my men get out or be there when I take you? You choose. Because me not fucking you is not an option."

I slap his hand away quickly. "No, that is an option. I'm not going to be fucked by a sick, faceless stranger," I reply confidently, although his words make me melt inside.

"I'm still a stranger to you?" he snorts arrogantly. "Dammit, rose, you can't stop thinking about how it'll feel to have my cock inside you."

I swallow instinctively and press my knees together more tightly.

"I don't think this is meant for our ears," Quest observes. "I'm getting some fresh air." And, as though acting on an invisible command, Demon's men suddenly all get out.

"I'm getting out too," I decide, feeling for the buckle between the seats with my bound hands.

"Funny, Nuria. You're not getting out." I hear the clicking sound of the car doors being locked.

"I am getting out, Demon."

"Don't you trust me anymore?" he asks, undoing his seatbelt. Suddenly, he climbs into the back seat, sits down next to me, and unbuckles my seatbelt. Only to lift me onto his lap a moment later.

"How can I trust you if I don't know who you are? Or whether you're going to kill me?"

"Haven't I proved to you multiple times," he says, straightening the jumper I'm wearing and adjusting the hood, "that I don't want to mistreat you, or hurt you, or kill you?"

He pushes a strand of hair behind my ear almost tenderly, then takes hold of my backside and pushes his hard-on between my thighs. "I just want you to be mine. I want this moment to be something special. My boys need to know how bloody important you are to me, and that you are the woman I have chosen to spend the rest of my life with."

His words sound so meaningful, so final, so decided, as though no counterargument could possibly change his mind. And the more he proves to me, tells me, how important I am to him, the more I fall for him. Because I want someone powerful by my side, someone to protect me, be there for me, love me unconditionally. Looks don't matter to me. But I still want to know who he is.

"And you won't give me the option of deciding for myself whether I want to spend the rest of my life with you?" I ask him.

He gives a sonorous murmur behind his mask. "You already know you want to. Your body knows it." His hand moves from my right buttock, pushing between my legs. I gasp in excitement. "Your thoughts, which I have been occupying for weeks, know it. Your soul, which has longed for me all the nights you have stood at the window looking for me in the garden and every time you checked your phone for messages, knows it. You want it. Deep in your heart. You want me. Only your morals stand in your way."

I absorb and internalise every word he speaks. Each one makes my heart sing. I swallow hard, lick my lips, and can't deny I have missed him.

"Tell me I'm wrong, and I will let you go forever."

Astonished, I raise my eyebrows. He is risking everything with this question and would be willing to give me up if I lie to him. Because yes, it would be a lie to say that I am not attracted to him.

So I turn my face to the side without answering and close my eyes behind the blindfold. Suddenly I feel his warm lips on my neck, his tongue on my lower jaw, then, as I turn my face to him, his mouth on mine. Our first kiss. And it pulls me completely into the canyon of darkness and sin.

My pelvis begins to throb as goosebumps spread over my body under the thick hoodie, and I slide closer to him as his tongue devours me. I return the kiss, and an inner whirlwind rages inside me, one that can only be calmed by responding to him even more intensely.

My lips rub moistly over his as he takes my lower lip between his teeth, bites into it and then kisses me hungrily again. Meanwhile, I move discreetly against his hard-on, which is pressing more firmly between my legs. I hear his aroused groan, which I have thought of so often before falling asleep at night.

"Fuck, I really want to fuck you here, but I want this moment to be something special."

"Same here," I reply, whereupon he bites into my chin.

"Shit, you are perfect."

His hands push their way under my hoodie, as my bound hands also wander, sliding under his hooded sweatshirt. He wasn't lying. I feel his smooth skin and the firm, defined chest muscles underneath. My hands travel upwards until they touch his face. Then he moans into my mouth as I make out something uneven.

I pull my fingers back like I'm acting on a warning signal, as if I'd burned myself. "Touch me wherever you want, whenever you want, however you want." His fingers encircle my wrist and push me down onto his hips. "That's what I'm going to do when I fuck you in every position you can imagine."

I have to smile, then I push the mask off his face, feel for his neck under the hood and blindly seek out his lips. My fingers move through thick, silky strands of hair, a few centimetres long. This time I kiss him passionately and greedily, letting him feel my nails under his hoodie, losing myself in his intoxicating scent of cedarwood and lemon.

In this moment he lets me take control as our tongues encircle each other. He holds my left buttock firmly, rhythmically pushing my hips back and forth, igniting an insatiable desire in me, like nothing I have felt with any man before. He is perfect. Perfect for me, with all the dark facets of his character.

I've no idea if I am sick or possessed or simply in love, but I push myself up higher onto my knees so I can pull down my pyjama bottoms.

Hands stop me. "So insatiable, little rose? Not here. I told you."

Gasping, I lower my pelvis again, as he strokes my bare thigh with his fingers. "First you turn me on, then..." An index finger is placed on my lips.

"Be patient. You'll soon know why."

Suddenly there's a knocking on the window to my left.

"Should we run back, or stop a car and nick it so you can fuck in peace?" asks the guy I don't know. Demon groans irritably. "Cameron," he mutters, letting go of me and then removing my hands from his body. But not before he's kissed the knuckles of my right hand and let me feel his teeth.

"The windows are already steamed up," I hear Quest say.

"But the Escalade isn't rocking. They're not shagging yet," Lexton chips in. "So, are we carrying on, or – FUCK!"

The screech of tyres from a fast-approaching car shocks me out of my altered state. But the sound is quickly replaced by the roar of an engine.

"Shit! Fuck! Out of the car!" Lexton yells.

Before I realise what's happening, something hits the car Demon and I are in at full speed. My back is rammed back hard into the passenger seat and I gasp in pain.

"Wylder!" someone calls, as I cling on tight to Demon and hastily push the blindfold away from my eyes. The Escalade is shunted across the road. Then I hear shots. I tear my eyes open in panic, and stare at Demon's mask as he opens the door. "We have to get out. Go."

As I look over my shoulder I see that the heavy SUV we are in is being pushed, metre by metre, towards the guardrail on the clifftop.

More shots ring out and I feel like I'm in a film. *This... this can't be happening!* At the same time the shots make me want to scream. They awaken something in my memory, bringing something long-forgotten to the surface.

Demon lifts me easily onto the back seat next to him, before leaning forward to the driver's seat to release the central locking mechanism. "Get out, take cover behind the car. Cameron!" he shouts.

"What's happening?" I ask, as I watch him draw a weapon from the waistband of his trousers and get out.

"No questions. Get out, go!" My stomach ties itself in knots.

He reaches quickly past me to the door handle and pushes the door open. Hands seize me under the arms and I slide along the backseat of the Escalade.

"Got you, little fox." I am confronted by a masked man with red, glowing X-shaped eyes, a smiling mouth and naked upper body. Cameron.

"Duck!"

Bullets hit the SUV again, windows shatter, the engine of the other car roars. Crouching, I peer round the bonnet, though Cameron, who has also drawn his weapon, tries to stop me, wrapping an arm around my upper body. My gaze travels to the black pistol. The name is on the tip of my tongue. Why... Why can't I remember? It begins with a "G".

G... G... G...

I wrinkle my forehead, racking my brains and lost in thought. Though it's not remotely the moment for that.

More shots ring out, ripping me from my reverie. The white Jeep that rammed the Escalade reverses suddenly, only to race past Demon and his men, wheels spinning, as they continue shooting at it, before jumping out of its way.

The blood rushes in my ears and I sink to the tarmac by the back wheel, breathing shallowly.

Breathe. Breathe. Breathe.

Every breath is pure agony, as though I've forgotten how, and the attack has paralysed my body.

"How is she?" Demon enters the corner of my field of vision and drops to one knee in front of me.

"Good, she's good," Cameron reassures him. "What the hell was that?"

"The Zetos," Lexton says. "You were right, Wylder. The motherfuckers are in Australia too. Who would have thought it. This is going to be fun."

Fun? This is Lexton's idea of fun?

Demon cups my face, then checks me over thoroughly for injuries and scratches.

"Zetos?" I gasp. "What are the Zetos?"

Quest comes over to us too, one hand lodged casually in his trouser pocket and the other holding a pistol, which he sticks in the waistband of his ripped black jeans.

"You don't want to know, beautiful."

CHAPTER 20

Nuria

What if the real danger is not
the enemy who loves you?
But your friend, who hates you?

I can still feel the residual fear from the attack in the back of my neck. Nobody has explained who these Zetos are or why they attacked us. Everyone just carries on as though nothing happened. How often must they have experienced this sort of thing, to be able to brush it off so easily?

We continue our journey in the battered Escalade, arriving at a mansion that resembles an old English manor house, right on the edge of a steep cliff.

If I'm being honest, at first sight it's even less inviting than the Monairs' house was on my first day. Large sections of the bay windows and stone facade are covered with vines. The driveway is surrounded by a poorly maintained garden with withered grass, crumbling stone walls, and two empty fountains that have seen better days. I notice that cameras have been installed on the empty gateposts at the driveway entrance.

The dark stone building looms up at us out of the darkness like a creepy haunted house.

Lexton leans forward unexpectedly, then turns his masked face towards me.

"Did any of you idiots notice that she isn't wearing her blindfold now, and she can see where she's being taken?"

I grin triumphantly at him. "You can take your mask off too, Lexton, I already know what you look like."

"How?" Cameron asks, turning round from the passenger seat.

"Because he surprised her and Wylder in an alley when he thought –" on my right, Quest smirks and reaches behind me to shove Lexton's shoulder – "that the Boss needed help." His smirk turns into an amused laugh that even makes me giggle.

"Doing what?" Cameron asks curiously, scratching his bare, muscular chest, where I now admire elaborate Māori tattoos over his pecs and left arm.

Next to me, Lexton and Quest start laughing like teenagers. I smile to myself.

"Doing what?" Cameron repeats, as Demon parks the flashy SUV in front of the stone steps and the towering, moss-covered porch.

"Welcome to Hell's temporary home," Demon says ominously, turning to me. "Put on the blindfold."

I sigh. "Really?"

"Really. You're not here for fun, you're here to make amends."

"Oh fuck, if this ends like it did in the alley then...," I say, before Lexton blindfolds me with the black cloth. My wrists are still in the handcuffs.

"What happened in this alley?" Cameron probes. "Why does everyone except me know what happened? Tell me."

"Yeah, if you'd gotten your ass in the aeroplane a day earlier you'd know what we're talking about, Cam," Lexton explains in the overbearing tone that makes me shudder every time I hear it.

The doors are already being opened. I am lifted out of the car and then carried to the house. Although I can't see anything, I know we're heading towards the entrance. Gravel crunches under the soles of Lexton's shoes – he's carrying me in a very uncomfortable position.

The door opens with a creaking moan and I am greeted by the scent of furniture polish, leather, and wood.

"I can walk," I say, trying to persuade Lexton to put me down.

"I'm not convinced. We saw you kissing the wall, and then the floor, in the club."

I hear Demon and Quest laugh nearby. "I won't forget that sight in a hurry." Yeah, you enjoy making fun of the fact that I slipped over in a fucking puddle. Anyone would fall over running away from devils like you.

"I was drunk and wasn't in control," I counter, holding on more tightly to Lexton's hoodie and snorting in annoyance.

"Not when you blew Demon's cock, either?" Lexton asks. "You seemed pretty cheery to me at the time."

"What?" Cameron blurts behind us. "That's how you got to know her?"

"I wouldn't say they got to know me," I hiss in his direction, although I can't really make anything out. Right now I'm wondering why I'm here, why I'm being carried like a rag doll into a building where the boys could do anything to me. But somehow they don't seem all that ruthless. Okay, they're carrying weapons, they're violent, and definitely aren't shy or nerdy, but with every minute I spend in their presence I feel more comfortable, almost safe.

"She thought I was a doorman and was going to rush to her aid." *Go on, laugh at me, you heartless, tattooed blockhead.*

Multiple footsteps echo around what is clearly a very large room. The footsteps are not muffled by carpets, so the floor must be covered with stone slabs, concrete, or tiles. I hear the click of a lock, followed by the creak of a door hinge.

The room has a warm, flowery scent. A scent I wouldn't have expected in an old house like this with these thugs.

"Put her down, Lex," Demon orders in his usual authoritative tone, the one that creates that tingling sensation under my ribs.

My heart starts to beat faster again, because I know what's coming next. Demon has already told me, and so, because I know what his version of payback is going to look like, I go down on my knees in front of him.

"Oh yeah, what's this?" Quest asks, and hands seize my shoulders. I immediately start to blush. *Mierda! No!* Have I knelt down in front of Quest?

"We're still learning," Demon says to me in a strangely amused tone. "You're kneeling in front of the wrong person, my rose." Then I am helped up, the blindfold is taken off my face and the handcuffs are removed from my wrists.

And what I see between the two masked men takes my breath away. A sea of white roses covering the floor of a huge hall, with floor-to-ceiling windows on my right and a mirrored wall to my left. The fresco on the ceiling above us is lit by flickering candles, which have been arranged in the corners of the room like a church. I go over to Demon, but I can't tell which one he is. The faces of the four men are now covered in identical masks and they are all wearing black hoodies. Including Cameron.

"What sort of game is this?" Then suddenly, as though it has been prearranged, I am spun around by several hands, fingers stroke my face, my legs, my buttocks, take off my jumper, undo my ponytail, and caress my bare arms. My breathing becomes shallower as I desperately try to find out which of the men is Demon.

No one speaks. Only when somebody stops me moving and grabs me around the middle, their face lowered, do I suspect that it is Demon.

"In front of the others?" I ask uncertainly. He tilts his head then suddenly tears my pyjama top open, scattering buttons onto the parquet floor.

He drives me backwards into the sea of flowers, while someone behind me intercepts my stumbling steps and pulls down my pyjama shorts. They land around my ankles and I am driven further back, leaving the shorts behind. Goosebumps spread across my body before the man before me raises two fingers and motions towards me. In the next moment my field of vision darkens again. I am turned around, and completely undressed.

"Everything okay? Or should I be worried you're about to faint?"

"I'm okay," I answer. Demon is standing in front of me, talking to me again, so I am able to recognise him.

Hands hold my breasts, massage them, tweak my nipples, while my own hands are pulled in front of me. Are those Lexton's hands on my breasts?

"Undress me," Demon orders, and I blindly feel over his hoodie. I hold the seam of his jumper with my fingertips and then pull it over his head, until he helps me and the jumper is torn out of my hands.

I feel his fingers gliding over my spine. Someone touches my hair, more hands disappear between my thighs. "How does it feel?" Demon wants to know.

Strangely, it feels bloody good. Unfamiliar, but not intrusive. I reach for his mask and take it off, then possessively run my fingers through his thick hair and tilt my face. Before my lips can seek his, his mouth meets mine. God! The kiss that follows momentarily takes away all my fears. Our tongues circle one another hungrily and ever more greedily. Fingers part my wet labia, gliding back and forth until my pelvis is filled with an irrepressible desire.

"Fuck, she gets wet quickly," I hear Lexton say. If it's his fingers between my labia, he's moving damn slowly.

"I know. Her body responds to me instantly," Demon groans, biting my lower lip tenderly and leading my hands to his belt. I open the buckle, sink ever deeper into the kiss and the feeling of nightmare and pure desire. Never before have I been so obsessed with being fucked, with feeling a man deep inside me.

After I have pulled down his trousers he lets himself sink backwards and pulls me on top of him. Like in the car before, I feel his hard, defined stomach and chest muscles, then his fucking big, heavy cock. As I bend forwards to kiss him, taste him and explore every centimetre of his body with my lips, fingers push inside me from behind. I inhale sharply, a hand already holding my hair.

"Don't get distracted. Suck it. Cameron wants to see how good you are," Demon orders.

I hear a snort to my right. "She could also demonstrate by sucking *my* cock." Demon's growl vibrates in my body.

I smile, then wet Demon's glans with my tongue and move my pelvis rhythmically in time with my fingers.

Then I take his hard-on into my mouth, going deeper each time I go down. His pelvis tenses, his mild, smoky taste settles on my tongue. I listen to his rough moans.

"Damn, she's taking him deep," observes Cameron, who has evidently been involved in these kinds of dark orgies before. At the same time, my clit is circled wetly, while two fingers thrust inside me and take my lust to new heights.

As I continue to suck Demon's cock, increasing the pressure, my buttocks are pushed apart and something drips between them. As I continue, panting and shaking, a thumb is unexpectedly inserted into my anus. I whimper. Hands continue to massage my breasts, more firmly, possessively.

Meanwhile, Demon moves my head in the rhythm he needs. "Like that, little rose. Very obedient. Take it even deeper."

I carry on with my efforts until he takes control and fucks my mouth. I completely block out everything around me. My knees tremble violently on the rose petals before the hand disappears from my hair and takes hold of my hips. In the same moment, the blindfold is removed from my eyes and I come face-to-face with a huge snake, its mouth open wide, tattooed on a bare, well-defined torso. The light bathes Demon's muscular chest and upper arms in a golden glow, and I notice two cuts on his arms.

I groan in disappointment to see he is still wearing a mask.

"Get on me," he commands, raising his right hand imperiously. I place my hand in his and his slender fingers intertwine with mine. Several black rings are tattooed around his wrist, and I am briefly fascinated by them before I look down at his masked face and slide onto his hip.

He holds my hand like that of a queen who is about to settle on him. I briefly bite my lower lip.

"Ride me now, before I can't take any more and I fuck you like you've wanted me to this whole time."

Smiling, I bend towards him, hold his shoulders, and lower my hips.

Centimetre by centimetre, his massive cock enters my pussy. Gasping, I close my eyes, because the feeling of being filled to bursting by him is so overwhelming.

"More, or am I too big for you?" he teases. Although it's true. He is infernally big.

I shake my head, because I hear Lexton snort, then lift my pelvis and lower it again, taking him inside me with a whimper.

"Shit," I whisper.

"Fuck yes, shit," I hear Demon groan under the mask, as a shiver runs down my spine. Our eyes meet for a second, until I move and start to ride him. Faster and more intensely until, on the fourth thrust, he is completely inside me, and I know immediately that I am addicted to the feeling of having him so deep inside me.

His friends are gathered around us, watching us and enjoying the show as I ride their leader. "She's got some fucking good moves," Quest remarks. "I wouldn't mind swapping."

"Ride him faster," Lexton commands, coming closer, and I obey. I increase the speed, focusing on Demon's mask. What does he look like under there? Are his lips open? Well-groomed, dark stubble is visible around the edge of the mask and I can see a prominent Adam's apple. There is a certain charm to riding a complete stranger, someone so mysterious. I would never have expected it to be such an unbelievable turn-on.

He runs his hands over my body as though I were his most costly possession, holds my breasts, strokes my stomach. But although I can't look into his eyes, I know that any moment now all his composure will be gone.

Suddenly, when I am feeling like I could move on top of

him forever, he takes hold of my throat and spins me over. The next moment, I find myself back on all fours as he holds me by the hips, pulls me towards him and pushes his cock inside me. I cry out in shock. He takes me from behind relentlessly, hard and uninhibited, as though otherwise I might run away from him and go over to his friends. Skin meets skin as my nails claw the rose petals. "Perfectly prepared, Lex. You should thank him, little rose."

"Thank him?" I gasp shakily.

"Do you want to overwhelm her so soon?" Lexton asks in surprise. *What does he mean by that?*

"You're refusing?" Demon asks, breathing hard behind me. "What about you, Cameron? Do you still want to find out how she gives head?"

"Hey, no way," Lexton interrupts, before Cameron can walk over to me. What kind of godless idea does Demon actually have in mind?

In the blink of an eye, Lexton kneels down in front of me, takes off his jumper and opens his trousers.

"Will you permit me?" He massages his hard-on, which is tattooed along half its length, in his hand. I turn my face to Demon, who is still fully inside me. I frown, panting heavily.

"Are you serious?" I ask. Demon lowers his face to mine, grabs my buttocks, and pushes them apart.

"Of course I'm fucking serious. They're like brothers to me."

Sweating slightly, I turn to Lexton. "Open your mouth, baby, or Demon won't fuck you anymore."

This sentence earns Lexton a dark look from me. "Oh yeah, that look is killing me. You can happily do your job looking like that."

I bare my teeth at him, and he rubs the tip of his penis along my lips. Then I open my mouth with a groan as Demon starts circling my clit.

"You belong to me, never forget that. I just hire you out for services. Services you'll enjoy." He is so utterly depraved – I can't begin to imagine how he got this way. Yet this game is more than exciting. I open my lips and take Lexton's cock in my mouth. He strokes my head. "Nice and wet and deep, can you get it in?"

Better than you can imagine. I have a lot of respect for Lexton. I don't want to turn him against me, because he is absolutely capable of killing five men at once. I respond to his movements, taking his considerably more bitter-tasting cock deeper, sucking it and moaning as Demon finally starts fucking me again.

After just a few minutes, I succumb to them both completely. Lexton moans deeply, looking up at the ceiling: "You weren't exaggerating. She gives fucking great head," as I increase the pace and apply more pressure with my lips, blowing him deeper and feeling how, after a few minutes, he is no longer in control and I'm taking over.

He pushes into my throat, he can't get enough, and my fingernails claw at his thighs. Quest and Cameron look on in silence as I am used by two men at the same time. And hell, Demon has incredible stamina, taking me more and more savagely and so deeply that he touches a point inside me where it makes me feel like the ground is about to give way. But I want to make Lexton climax before I come. I can't reach orgasm too soon, I want to have time to enjoy it.

And then, just when I feel I could explode at any moment, Lexton's cock pulses and he thrusts deep inside my mouth several times and curses crudely.

"Fucking hell, she's better than any prostitute!" Then his cock pumps and I taste his cum on my tongue. It runs down my throat, mild and warm. "Fucking awesome." He looks down at me, his upper body tense, ruffles my hair and squints at me, his lips open.

I swallow his sperm to allow myself to breathe more easily. He thrusts into me once more, before I can't take any more, groan loudly and let go of his cock.

"Now, come for me!" Demon orders, unleashing all his strength and taking me so hard that I'm going to be bruised all over. Whimpering, I lower my upper body and surrender myself completely to him, writhing in front of him and screaming his name, "God, Demon!" as the first wave of the orgasm crashes through my body. It feels like I've been electrified. My skin tingles all over, my legs won't stop shaking, I'm breathless, and my pussy contracts tightly. I can hear him cursing and moaning too.

"God! So tight!" He inhales sharply, moaning and thrusting deep into me three times before coming inside me. The sounds he makes are the only thing I've been able to think about over the last few days, whenever I've closed my eyes in a quiet moment. They are meant just for me. Mine. Just like this man belongs to me. And fuck, the thought that this strong, muscular, mysterious man is mine makes my heart beat like crazy.

CHAPTER 21

Demon

She is the drug I lust after.
My queen, whom I honour.
My downfall, standing inexorably before me.
But I don't want to let her go.

"Why in front of the others?" she asks, as she lies across me, naked and warm, my fingers circling over her back. I have never felt her so close to me, as though we were one. Merged into one soul. The boys left a few minutes ago.

"To show them you mean everything to me. That you belong to me. I have never been so sure about wanting a woman by my side as I was about you a few minutes ago."

"What a twisted way of thinking," she observes with a giggle, as my fingers comb through her long, dark brown hair. Her silky tresses flow through my fingers. They feel so soft I want to bury my face in them.

"You enjoyed it. Or am I wrong?"

There is a moment of calm silence. Whenever she doesn't contradict me, I know she agrees with me. Deep in her heart, she longs for more. I have led her down a sinful path and she doesn't want to turn back. That gives me a sense of satisfaction. It proves to me how similar we are. "What time is it?" she asks suddenly, sitting up and casually grabbing my left hand to read my watch.

"04:24. Holy shit! I have to get back."

"You're staying."

As she attempts to climb off me, I hold her waist and press

her to me. "You're staying," I repeat. "Or do I have to tie you down?"

"I have to get back to the Monairs'."

"It's Sunday. You have a free day and you're going to spend it with me."

"Maily's ill. I'm not free today."

She lifts her picture-perfect face, frowning. I can't suppress a grin behind my mask. She is so unutterably beautiful. The candlelight accentuates her large eyes, her naturally full lips, and her slightly prominent cheekbones. Her hair, wonderfully tangled from the wild sex, falls over her shoulders and her perfect, round breasts.

"So you don't know everything," she says.

I lift my face slowly, until my mask touches the tip of her little nose. "I know almost everything," I growl menacingly.

"And I know nothing about you." She narrows her eyes distrustfully. "I don't know your name, or what your face looks like."

"But you've seen other parts of me that most people don't get to," I joke and enjoy the sigh she gives at the allusion to my cock.

"Who are you really, Demon?" she asks, holding my face. I am terrified she is going to tear off my mask. But I don't stop her, because I know she knows this will all come to an end if she finds out who I am.

"Someone who is absolutely crazy about you, little rose." I toy sensuously with a strand of her hair, gliding the tip of it over her face like a paintbrush. "Someone who wants to protect you, to possess you at any cost, and is your future husband."

She raises her right eyebrow as she moves her thumb over the plastic neon mask. "How could I love a man who lives behind a mask?" Good question.

"The time will come when you can take my mask off. Until then," I drop her hair, slide my finger around her neck and lift her chin with my thumb, "you'll love what I give you."

Will she really love me at some point? Experience the

same intense, pure obsession and devotion as I have for her? But why did she choose the words *How could I love a man*, when she could just as easily have said *How could I be with a man?*

Does she have feelings for me? Is she already in love?

"And what if that's not enough for me?" she whispers, as I am on the brink of tearing the mask from my face myself, so she can see me. So she can see the face she will wake up next to every morning, after I've fucked her to exhaustion in my bed in Boston.

"You'll have to practise patience, little rose. There are reasons I can't show myself to you. Anyway..." Her eyes downcast, she seems to be weighing up whether she can be patient or if she will move on. "... you have already seen me without a mask."

She looks up straightaway, and there is a sparkle in her clear green eyes that doesn't come from the candlelight.

"When? Where?" she asks excitedly.

I suppress a smile again, without answering.

"You're lying to me." She sighs disappointedly.

"I have never done that and I never will." I can see her racking her brain, sorting through all her memories in search of my face.

"You'll know eventually," I assure her. "For the time being, I exist for you behind this mask."

Something like sadness flickers in her beautiful eyes. Mixed with a hint of disappointment, as she parts her lips and looks to the side, where the mirrored wall displays our naked bodies on the sea of rose petals.

"Are you part of a criminal organisation, on the FBI's most wanted list, and that's why you can't show yourself?" she probes further, with no idea how right her assumption is.

"How do you mean?"

"Those Zetos. They attacked you and your friends. That wasn't just an argument between guys who hate one another. That was... There were shots, they wanted to kill you. It was an attempted fucking murder in the middle of a country road. What do they want from you?"

Now she's started to ask the right questions. "They want me to die, and they want to kill my future bride too," I tell her, as she sits casually on top of me and lets both hands wander over my chest. She feels it. The need to touch me all over, the irresistible bond between us. She can't get enough of me, even now, when I have just been inside her and touched her everywhere.

"Future bride?" She rolls her eyes and snorts in amusement, as though it were a laughable idea, then looks away and, when I don't say anything, back at me again. "You're actually serious?"

I quickly grasp her throat. "Deadly serious. You still don't get it, do you, little rose?" Even my men have understood that this thing between me and Nuria is more than just a passing fad, not just a quick flirtation or fuck.

Gasping, she licks her lips. "You're always changing the subject." She holds my forearm, trying to pull my hand from her neck, but I don't let her. "The Zetos. Why do they want you dead? Where are they from? How do they know who you are? Where you are?"

"So many questions..." Sighing, I let go, but not before I have run my forefinger along the scar under her lower jaw. "Your assumption is not wrong. But I have no fucking idea how the Zetos could have followed us. They normally operate underground in the USA. They're based in Newport. They deal in weapons, drugs, exotic animals, and people. You can't begin to imagine the terrible things these people are capable of. You could never conceive of such cruelty and inhumanity, not in your wildest dreams."

Her slim body stiffens against me, even her nipples grow more erect, tempting me to push up the mask so I can take them between my teeth.

"What have you done to make them want to kill you?"

"So much, and yet not enough."

"Hey," she protests, hitting my chest with her little fist, so that I flinch in mock pain. "Stop speaking in riddles. You're like an oracle."

"So cruel," I tease, happy that the mask hides how much I'm enjoying myself.

"Sorry, I didn't mean to hurt you." Sweet how she immediately regrets her action. "Why are they after you?"

"Because my people and I have repeatedly got in their way. I will not let my business be ruined by these filthy scum, who flog cheap goods and auction off and enslave people."

She scrutinises me, her lips parted. "Business? What do you sell?"

I lower my face. "This and that." I hoist her up.

"Drugs and weapons too, right?"

I bite my lower lip and then stroke her cheek. "Clever girl. Why are you asking questions when you already know the answers?"

She looks genuinely upset at my words and goes to move away from me.

"I don't want to be involved with any of that, Demon."

I take hold of her waist just in time. "You are already involved. In contrast to the Zetos, my organisation doesn't trade in people and children."

"But the rest is bad enough."

"The Zetos aren't just my competitors, they murdered my family. That's why I'm out for revenge and I'm going to track down and kill every last one of those bastards, wherever they might be in the world." Pure fear flickers in her eyes. She writhes in my grasp until I let her go and she jumps frantically onto the flower petals.

"You're a murderer!" I prop myself on my right forearm and watch as she gathers her pyjama bottoms, her half-ripped top, and Cam's hoodie from the parquet floor.

"Are you surprised? You've known for a long time..."

"No!" she yells over me. "I didn't know. Not really. Definitely not that you're the head of a murderous organisation dealing in weapons and drugs."

"Coming from your mouth that does sound fucking terrible," I say calmly, amused by her stubbornness. She sticks her middle finger up at me.

Fuck! I love her temperament. Things will never be boring with her.

"If I could, I would smash another dustbin lid over your head to move your brain to the right place." She quickly slips on the hoodie, which reveals half of her round buttocks and long legs. From my perspective, an exquisite sight.

I murmur provocatively, "After that pathetic attempt you'd be lying under me screaming out your fifth orgasm quicker than you could say knife."

"Don't make fun of me!" she says, then turns on her bare feet and marches the three metres to the tall wooden door as proudly as a queen. As she pushes the handle I get up at a leisurely pace and put on my trousers.

She pushes the handle repeatedly before realising the door is locked. "Open the door, you fuckers!"

Laughing smugly, I smooth my hair and ignore her angry outburst. "Demon! Open the door!"

"Only if you get down on your knees and beg," I tease.

She hammers on the door with her fists. "Hey, Cameron, Lexton, Quest!" she cries. "Open the door."

"They won't listen to you. I give the orders, little rose, remember?"

She turns to me angrily, her fists clenched. What's the betting some object is about to fly in my direction?

God, I'm looking forward to taming her again. To grabbing her and fucking her until her fire fizzles out.

She picks up a jumper one of the boys has thrown on the floor, then runs towards me, brandishing it at me like a whip. *Cute.*

I grab the garment and pull Nuria towards me, making her spin around, so that in under two seconds she is standing with her back to me and the sleeve of the jumper around her neck. "Calm down. Or do I need to get angry?"

"Stop provoking me, you prick," she sniffs, her arms shaking as she reaches for the sleeve. She tries to free herself with all her might. I pull the noose tighter.

"I really don't like doing this, Nuria. But you need to watch your tone when you're speaking to me, and show me more respect."

I hook one leg around her right calf so that she loses her balance and drops to her knees. I loosen the sleeve around her neck so she doesn't fall over, replacing it with my lower arm and holding her hair.

"I don't respect monsters."

"But you don't mind being fucked by one?"

"I didn't know what you are."

"You still don't know, because you're jumping to conclusions."

She cries out in anger, until I let go of her tousled, chestnut-brown hair and place my hand between her thighs, touching her pussy, parting her labia. She gasps.

"You'd give yourself to me even now, wouldn't you? Even now that you know more about me."

My fingers glide eagerly through her increasingly wet pussy, reach her most sensitive spot, and massage her clit.

"That's not fair," she whispers, and the corner of my mouth twitches under the mask.

"Life isn't fair. I'm not giving you a choice. Give yourself to me now." I push her forward with my upper body, but not without first crossing her wrists behind her back. Consumed by lust, I undo my trousers and free my hard, heavy cock. And she follows my order, writhing in my grip, but opening herself to me.

"Demon," she snarls. "That is... This conversation isn't... OVER!" she groans loudly, as I take hold of my cock and push inside her. I'm halfway in at the first thrust. Panting, I look up at the angels painted on the ceiling, who are watching our rough sex.

I pull back out of her wet pussy, and then push back inside her even more deeply. The overpowering feeling of being completely at one with her is like a drug. She belongs to me, no matter how offensive, depraved, or criminal she finds me.

While she grew up in a modest, poor, well-protected world, the realm where I was created was harsh, cruel, and dark. She will eventually come to love the darkness, just as I have learned to.

I fuck her more and more quickly, observing how her anger dissipates and she gives herself to me more deeply and willingly. Breathing heavily, I rub her right buttock, push the jumper up around her shoulders and take what I have wanted this whole time. And the sight in the mirror in front of me gives me the rest. She stares back at me, blinking and moaning, like captured prey.

I circle her clit, twisting it so hard that she screams and begins to shake beneath me. My moment. I release her wrists and take a single-edged blade from my boot. Making sure she can't move away, I push the back of the knife between her teeth.

"Hold it. If you drop it, I'll mark you." I can see her alarm in the mirror. Nevertheless, she bites down on the blade with her teeth. "Very good, my rose." Then I pull out of her, making her sigh and utter a sound of displeasure.

I get up, walk around her, and take off the annoying hoodie, then lift her up and carry her over to the window. I can't resist her with the knife between her pretty lips. She turns her head over her shoulder and looks out of the window, where it is getting light. I hold her little arse tightly before I get to the window with her and push the whole of myself deep inside her.

She must have seen Lexton outside smoking, and now watching us. Watching me fuck my rose unrestrainedly at the window. Her face flushed, she narrows her eyes and groans even louder. She's so turned on that her pussy drips as it squeezes tight and warm around my cock.

"If you drop that knife, you'll be punished!" I threaten. She shakes her head, holds on tightly to my shoulders, and lets me lift her up and down on my cock again and again. I've never felt her so intensely and deeply before. It is the purest sin. I gasp under the mask as her body shakes, her pussy tightening so hard around my cock that I think she's going to crush me. I thrust into her faster and more greedily until she puts her head back and screams. The knife falls right in between us, landing with the blade to my stomach.

Lexton takes a deep drag of his fag and steps closer to the window, grinning broadly.

"Fuck," I curse, while Nuria lets go completely and groans, whimpers, and screams, completely intoxicated. Making my woman climax like this, seeing her like this, makes me endlessly horny, and after several hard thrusts I can't contain my insatiable lust any longer and I gush inside her. Growling, I sink deep into her one last time, before lowering my face, exhausted, and looking between us.

"Take the knife," I say breathlessly.

"What?" she asks in surprise, before licking her lips.

"Take it."

"Why?"

"To mark you."

CHAPTER 22

Lexton

Loyalty shouldn't be confused
with friendship.
Loyalty extends beyond death
when friendships have long broken.

What the hell has got into Wylder? I've never seen him like this before. He's completely obsessed with this woman. The Spanish girl is super-cute, of course, she gives pretty good head and she's definitely a great fuck, but what is it about her that's got him so hooked? Setting up the mirror room like this for her? Visiting her for hours at night?

And we all know where he's hanging out when he's not in the house. He's definitely not looking for the missing girl, who's the real reason we're here.

Wylder seems to have it really bad. Terminal.

While I'm looking at the battered Escalade outside, which is riddled with bullet holes, they are having sex again, while he carves the sign of the Dykats between her breasts, no less. Bro, he really wants to make her his queen. What if this country girl doesn't like Boston? What if she's wrong for him and he's just into her body, but she's actually just a cheap bitch like so many women, just after power and money?

Although... it's not as if I couldn't just off Nuria if she has bad intentions, or cheats on Wylder, or takes advantage of him, or gives away any information. Let him have his fun. If I find out she's harming him, I'll end her.

A fatal accident can be so quick and unexpected – I really shouldn't worry about it. She's screaming underneath him again as he kneels between her legs and takes her.

I'm smoking more post-coital cigarettes than Wylder because I'm continually hard. What I really ought to be thinking about is how the Zetos were able to intercept us last night. Those motherfuckers are becoming a problem. They know where we're staying, and that we're hot on their heels. It's time for me to check out their club, even if the Boss is against it.

"Please! Please! Demon!" Nuria cries huskily. "God! I can't take any more."

Wylder now takes his wife from behind against the mirrored wall, until they both fall to their knees against it. Breathing deeply, I roll my eyes, straighten my hard cock, and then step to one of the windows. When I knock on it, Wylder immediately looks over his shoulder.

"Shall I call an ambulance, or relieve you?" I offer. The two of them can't take another step, and Wylder's cock must be glowing.

Wylder lifts his middle finger slowly in my direction, and I know he'll be grinning broadly at me under his mask.

"Take care of the car," he calls through the glass. I act as though I don't understand, narrowing my eyes and cupping my hands behind my ears.

"What?"

He eventually releases his queen, lifts her up, and carries her over to the window. He opens it and sits Nuria on the window sill.

"Hey," she complains, covering her bottom, as though I didn't see it naked just a few hours before.

"Switch the car, Lex. The boot is fucked."

"Oh really," I reply and grab Nuria's neck. She stiffens and turns to face me. "Do you want the same model?" I ask ambiguously.

Wylder lowers his head, then seizes my wrist and removes

my hand from his property. "Yes, the same model. Take Cameron with you. Stay together and stick to the brief."

"Cam's asleep," I reply.

"You're not going alone. Not if the Zetos are in the area." What a big heart my old friend has.

"I'll give him a kick up the arse. That should wake him up."

Wylder laughs. "Keep me posted."

I salute irritably. I sometimes feel like I'm a little kid and he's my guardian. I do understand his concern for his people, though – we've been attacked more than once in the last year, and eleven of our best men have been shot.

He lifts Nuria off the windowsill. She cuddles up to him surprisingly quickly, given that she barely even trusted us just a few hours ago, and he shuts the window. I groan in frustration. *Shame I can't look after his little rose while he relaxes. I would have had a whole lot of fun with her.*

"Do you think we're going to hang around Australia much longer?" Cameron asks, biting into his chicken baguette with much too much mayonnaise.

"Are you homesick?"

"No," he replies. "But I like Boston better."

"The polluted city air, the noise, the crowds, the traffic, the litter, the cold rain... Sure, I get where you're coming from, buddy," I joke.

Cam gives me a murderous glance as I take a drag on my cigarette and blow the smoke out the open window. "Did you get out the wrong side of bed? You had some fun last night, unlike me."

I flip the indicator on the new car and turn into a pretty shady part of Brisbane with bars, late-night shops, and seedy businesses. *Knife West* is somewhere around here.

"Was she really that good? Or did you just not want to let on to the Boss that she gives shit head?"

"She was good," I assure him. "The best," I correct myself,

while Cameron almost chokes, his eyes wide. Then he scratches his head and looks around at the street.

"Hey, tell me... Where the hell are we?"

"In the roughest area of Brisbane." I park the new Escalade in a side street next to a rubbish bin and look out of the windscreen at the rough, faded facades of the houses in the alley. Most of the window shutters are closed, the fire escapes below them rusted.

"The Boss told you not to do any solo runs."

"I know that, genius. But the Boss is otherwise occupied right now, and I want to find the rats who tried to bump us off on the open road yesterday!" I snap back.

Cameron finally puts his baguette away, brushes the crumbs off his trousers and turns to me. "I'm not getting into any trouble if this goes to shit."

"I know that, you little wimp. That's why you're staying in the car," I reply with a quick grin, opening the car door and getting out of the SUV.

"Lex!"

Before Cam can object, I bend over to the side mirror, straighten up my roll-neck and smooth down my hair. *Everything looks perfect.*

Cameron jumps out of the car. "I'm calling Wylder!"

What a coward! "Say hello from me."

"Are you insane? He'll kill you. If the Zetos don't!" Cameron comes round the front of the Escalade and stands in my path.

"You think I'm a rookie? I taught you four years ago, showed you how to hold a pistol properly. So get your ass back in the car, give me fifteen minutes and I'll be back."

He looks worried, as though he thinks today's my funeral. "Chill out and guard the car." I put my hand on his shoulder, then head along the alley to the main street.

Knife West is round the corner, a bar with piles of cigarette butts in ashtrays outside and a *Closed* sign hanging behind the door. My invitation to enter. I can't see anyone inside. They'll definitely still be asleep. It's 5:15 a.m. I take my phone from the inside pocket of my jacket and call the number for the police.

A cop comes on the line straightaway.

"Queensland Police Service. How can I help you?"

"I'm standing outside the bar, *Knife West*. There's been a shooting." I tap on the glass door repeatedly to mimic the sound of shots. "There are two people lying injured on the ground. Please come quickly."

If my calculation is correct, they'll be here in five to seven minutes.

"What's your name?" the voice asks, before I hang up, draw my pistol, pull my roll-neck up over the lower half of my face and use the butt of the pistol to break the glass in the door. As I expected, the key is in the lock, so I am able to open the door and go inside the seedy joint. *What idiots.*

I stand in the doorway and look around the bar, whose floor plan I have previously studied in detail. There are tables to my left and right, ahead of me is the bar, made of polished wood with red upholstered stools, and further back a cigarette machine and a fruit machine. The stench of weed and cigarettes enters my nose.

"Hello bitches, Daddy's home!" I yell, before walking over the glass, the splinters crunching under my feet. Before long, a guy comes storming towards me, his skinny little arms poking out of a baggy vest, loaded with jewellery like Grandma's Christmas tree. He stares at me, then rushes back.

"Attack!" he yells. *What a bonehead.* A few seconds later, two bulkier guys push through the door, and I take them out with shots to the head before they can draw their guns.

"Was that it? Where's my welcome party?" *Fuck, I'm in a good mood today. I've just had the best blow job I've had in a long time.*

As the cowards barricade themselves in the back room, I shoot at the lock from a safe distance, kick in the door, and step over the dead guys in front of it.

"Sorry boys, I hope I'm not interrupting," I murmur, finding at least three guys in a red-lit room, surrounded by two half-naked women. Two women whose beaten faces immediately catch my attention. *Holy shit!*

Screaming and begging for their lives, the women crawl behind the sofa as a guy with stringy black hair and a goatee climbs over the coffee table – which is strewn with bags of coke and grass – towards me. I pull out my second gun, surprising them, then shoot the two guys, who flee instead of fighting me off. They slump against the walls like limp sacks before I point the barrels of both guns at the guy with the goatee. He puts his hands in the air.

"Dykats! How did you find us? Are you alone?"

"There's an army waiting outside," I lie.

"Liar," he retorts, training his gun on me. If he's faster to the trigger, I'm finished. I need an element of surprise.

"I hope the fuck was worth it," I say to the guy and nod at the terrified, cowering woman. His eyes stray to the half-naked woman for a fraction of a millisecond. *My moment.* I shoot him in the balls. "Because it's the last one of your miserable life." Before he can pull the trigger, he falls forward, yelling in pain, and lands on his face right by my feet, crying like a baby. I put my right foot between his shoulder blades, bend down, and grab his shaggy hair.

"Go to hell, number thirty-three!" Then I shoot the whimpering toad in the head. The thirty-third person I have killed – a number that is rising faster than I expected. The women, who don't interest me in the slightest, flinch in fright at the shot.

"Ladies, you'll soon be picked up. And hopefully we'll never see each other again." With these words, I open the door to my left, which leads to the private area and the back exit of the club, and push the corpse in front of it aside.

"Queensland Police!" I hear the police shout, then I hurry along the corridor and climb the stairs. There's a window ahead of me, which I quickly unlock and push up. Cameron is standing by the car directly beneath, looking everywhere, but not up. I throw an empty can that's lying on the fire escape at his head, and he finally tilts his head back. *Where the hell are his eyes?*

I throw the guns down to him so that I won't be carrying any weapons if the police stop and search me.

"Hide them." After I've thrown the second gun down, Cameron shouts, "Behind you!"

But it's too late, someone grabs my neck and slams my face so hard against the iron railing that I hear the angels sing.

"Lousy maggot. Think you can walk into my bar and bump off my people, and then just piss off, hey?!"

Before my skull slams into the railing a second time, I grab the handrail with both hands to slow the momentum, and stare at Cameron who is on his way up the fire escape to me. *Fuck! Stay down there.*

"Tell me, who are you?" the guy behind me asks, pushing me further forwards. I bend my arms and jerk free of his grip, hitting him in the face with my fist. My skull hurts like hell. The Zetos guy has his hair tied back and is wearing a muscle shirt; he narrows his eyes as he looks at me.

"Dykats!"

"You've got a brain after all!" I say, panting, pulling my knife out of my boot and hurling it at him. He swerves to avoid it and it misses his neck by a hair's breadth. I'm seeing double and my vision is blurring at increasingly short intervals.

The next second he storms towards me, puts his hands around my neck, barely seeming to notice my punch between his ribs. A fraction of a second later I am bent perilously over the railings. It's a fucking four-metre drop if things go wrong.

As I try to push him off me, the damn railing gives way slightly, and I feel a blade in his waistband. Cameron leaps up the last few steps, his gun trained on the Zeto guy. *Shoot already!*

But before he can pull the trigger, the railing rips from its fitting, and I plummet downward, with the bastard on top of me.

As we fall I quickly pull the knife from his waistband and ram it into the side of his neck, before I crash hard into the tarmac. A violent jolt blocks my lungs, my skull seems to have burst into a hundred pieces. Everything goes black. My body is overtaken by a wave of pain. But pain is a sign that I'm still alive, even if I must have broken several bones.

The ballast is rolled off my body. "Lex! Lex! Are you still alive?"

I snort painfully. It's difficult to breathe, even though he's rolled the guy off of me. "Lex!"

"Please... talk quieter. My skull's... buzzing like hell."

The next moment we hear footsteps. "Queensland Police, hands in the air."

A groan escapes my lips. "I want to see your hands," barks an aggressive cop, as I open my eyes a fraction. Cameron is kneeling beside me, his hands smeared with blood, staring aggressively at the cop as he reaches for his weapon. "Do as he says," I growl effortfully. Now's not the time for him to play the hero and end up getting shot. "Cam!"

Cameron shoots me a look. "Shit. This is..."

But he obeys the command and stands up, putting his hands in the air.

"And you on the ground."

"You want me to raise my broken hands?" I ask the two cops as they approach, not even managing to grin any more.

CHAPTER 23

Nuria

Should you let a demon into your heart,
just because he once
gave you an innocent smile
instead of a terrifying look.

"Where did you learn to cook?" I ask him, pulling my right foot up onto the seat of the chair and studying Demon's naked, athletic torso. He's standing at the hob in the dark country kitchen, his back to me, frying eggs, French toast, and potato wedges.

"From my sisters."

He has sisters? His arm and back muscles ripple with every movement. All he's wearing are a pair of black, low-slung joggers that reveal two dimples on his back, just above his hips. He keeps looking at his phone and watch.

"What are your sisters called?"

"They're called... Eden and Summer and... they're missing."

Missing? I fiddle nervously with the serviette, unsure what to do with this information.

"What do you mean, missing?"

"They were kidnapped five years ago during a break-in at our house."

"I... I'm sorry."

"Don't be. You couldn't have known." He turns to face me, holding a pan. A masked stranger, topless, preparing breakfast at just short of six in the morning, after I have hardly slept a wink.

"I learned to look after myself after I moved out. I didn't want to keep eating that fast food shite, so I cooked the things my sisters used to make and then tried other things too."

He slides French toast onto my plate with the spatula, along with two fried eggs and some potato wedges, then puts sour cream and berry compote in the middle of the table.

"You're fattening me up here, but I'm not allowed to eat crisps in bed?" I try to change the subject. He dips his head. I love this gesture because I can imagine him narrowing his eyes and question marks forming in those beautiful dark blue irises.

"Eat as many crisps as you like, as long as you listen to me the rest of the time," he replies sarcastically, putting the pan on the stove without taking anything for himself, and grabbing his phone. He unlocks the screen again.

"Don't you want to eat anything?" I ask as he sits down next to me, although I know the answer already.

"I'll eat later. Enjoy."

How does he know the crazy combination of things I like to eat in the morning?

Why am I even asking myself this question? He knows everything about me.

He picks up a piece of potato, dips it in the sour cream, and holds it to my mouth, which I open willingly. When has a man ever cooked for me? Never. Truly, never.

I sigh softly as I chew.

He looks at his phone again as a message appears.

"Has something happened?" I ask. I immediately think of the twins. But they are in the care of Mrs Warner. It's the weekend, when the housekeeper looks after the girls.

"Good morning, people." Quest comes into the kitchen, a hand towel slung around his hips. "Holy shit, she's still here," he exclaims, staring at me as though I've landed in the kitchen like a comet.

"Shit!" Demon snarls, at the same time. "That bastard!"

"What is it?" Quest and I ask in unison, watching as Demon jumps off his chair.

"Quest, stay with Nuria. Take her back when she's eaten." But... The words land heavily in my stomach, like a stone. Just when I thought I might have a chance to get to know Demon better, he wants to send me back again.

"Will do. Where are Lex and Cam?"

"Don't ask," Demon says aggressively before turning to me and caressing the back of my head with his hand and lowering his masked face to me. "I'll be in touch later, my rose."

He storms out of the door just two seconds later, while Quest inspects the stove.

"He obviously didn't cook anything for me. Lousy rat," he grumbles.

"You can have some of mine." I point my fork at the stack of French toast I'll never be able to finish.

Quest turns his athletic body towards me, smiles broadly, and sits down on the chair Demon has just vacated.

"Nice of you. But my boss will kill me if I take food from you."

"But if you don't accept my offer, I'll tell Demon you didn't respect my wishes, Quest. What do you think your boss will have to say about that?"

He shakes his head. "Fuck, you're just like him. How can I refuse if it's life or death?"

"Quite right." If I can't sound out Demon, it'll have to be Quest. He's come across as pretty trustworthy from the beginning – compared to the other boys he almost seemed gentle and considerate when he was tucking his jumper around me. I load up his empty plate with two pieces of French toast and some wedges, and he dives into the food. I hear the roar of a motorbike engine outside. I turn quickly to the kitchen window on my left, and see Demon get on to his bike, dressed in black, and then race off. What could have happened?

"Are those Zetos causing more trouble?" I ask Quest.

"I hope not. Maybe Wylder's got a new lead on the missing women."

"Missing women?" I ask, biting into a potato wedge.

"Yes." Quest cuts a large piece of golden-brown fried toast and dips it into the berry compote, then shoves it sideways into his mouth. Strands of damp, dark blonde hair fall over his eyebrows as he chews, looking at me with dark, honest eyes.

"Young women have been going missing for some weeks now. That's why we're here, because the trail led to Australia. Well," he corrects himself and grins broadly. "We're definitely also here because you're here and Wylder's totally lost his head over you."

His words are lost on me because I am thinking about these strange cases. Ranja is missing too, after all.

"How old are the missing women?"

Quest curls his lip, then thoughtfully scratches the three-day stubble on his chin with the knuckle of his index finger.

"They were in their final year at school. I think sixteen or seventeen years old. The two missing girls are called Vendra and Layla. They went to Wellington High School."

My stomach lurches abruptly when I hear him say the name of the school. I inhale deeply and choke on my food. So much so that Quest jumps up, pulls back my chair, and slaps me on the back. "Fuck, don't die, Wylder will skin me alive if you turn blue and start choking."

I wave my right hand frantically, reach for the orange juice on the table, and take two mouthfuls. My face must be bright red and there are tears in my eyes. Once I've recovered and can breathe freely again, Quest sits back down, looking concerned.

How embarrassing.

"Wellington High School," I say hoarsely, trying to move on from the incident. "Are you also looking for a Ranja Monair?"

Quest shakes his head. "No, no, her name isn't on the list.

Monair? Isn't that the family where you're working as an au pair?"

I nod, take another mouthful of juice, and frown. "Shame," I murmur.

"Is this Ranja missing?" Quest asks.

"Yes, since June."

"I can find out more about her, if you want?" he offers, getting up and leaving the kitchen. He returns a few minutes later with a laptop, which he sets on the kitchen table. He starts a programme, then points to a black screen, where in green glowing numbers and letters, all the key information about Ranja Monair is listed. From her phone number to her bank account details. Holy shit. He is… I look over the edge of the PC.

"You're a hacker."

"A fucking good one," he assures me proudly. "Is that the information you need?"

I shake my head, not seeing anything that might indicate whether she's been admitted to a hospital.

"Can you find out when her mobile was last used? Or if she's in a clinic?"

"Yep," he answers, as though it were the most natural thing in the world to find out private information about other people. I just hope I'm getting closer to some answers. Although I haven't finished Ranja's diary yet, I know from Zain that she disappeared very suddenly.

"The last call was on 5 June. It lasted 7 minutes and 41 seconds. Afterwards…" He types something on his keyboard and wrinkles his forehead. "There are no more calls, messages, or phone usage. The same for her online banking and debit card. The most recent activities were on 3 June and, wow…"

"What?" I ask curiously, standing up and positioning myself behind his chair.

"She withdrew 22,780 Australian dollars. That's the last activity on her account. Looks like she emptied her account and vanished."

So, did she move out voluntarily? "Can you find any admittance or insurance data about whether she was admitted to a clinic?"

Quest turns to me. "You've got a lot of questions. Give me two minutes." He opens a new window. His fingers fly so confidently over the keyboard that I feel dizzy. Now I know how Demon managed to track me everywhere. With Quest's help. The ease with which Quest can access information about people means it would have been child's play for Demon to get hold of my latest phone number, address, chat history, and online purchases. He definitely would have known I was booking flights to Australia before I clicked the *Book* button on the airline's website.

Fuck! There was no way I was ever going to escape him.

"Nope. No entries. After 6 June there's no sign of any private health insurance card being used, or any files being created in a clinic, no flights in or outside the country, and no passport use." My eyes widen as the programme writes line after line in response to Quest's enquiries. "Nothing. This Ranja really has disappeared. Or..." He inclines his head and looks at me with those warm, open eyes. "She's gone underground like a pro, which I can't really imagine a schoolgirl could do. Or..."

"Or?" I push.

"Or she's dead," he says, voicing the thought that has often crossed my mind. I remember Maily's words. "Dead. She's dead."

Gasping, I take my eyes off Quest and look back to the screen. Dead. Why? Did she take her own life, or was she murdered?

How did she die? Why do Richard and Jacky think their daughter is dead, while Zain hopes his sister has been cast out by his parents and sent to another school, or to a clinic?

And if Maily is right after all, why aren't Jacky and Richard making it known that their daughter isn't alive anymore?

What the hell really happened to Ranja?

CHAPTER 24

Nuria

The depths of the human soul
are deep.
Sometimes deeper than the devil's
darkest intentions.

28 April

I still don't know how to process this. How it could happen. What I should do now? Shit! Shit! My life is shit!

I cried for two hours in the bathroom when I saw the result of the pregnancy test. I even did a second test, just to make sure. Both results were the same.

I AM PREGNANT!

Shit! Shit! Shit! Shit! Shit! Shit! Shit!

What do I do now?!

The stupid test says I am at least three weeks pregnant. There are only two people it could be. And I don't want to have a child with either of them. They'd both want me to get an abortion immediately. I can't tell either of them about it. No, no way.

I have to find a way to deal with this myself. Somehow. But how? I can't talk to my friends about it. They'd laugh and call me stupid for not using proper protection – but they don't have any idea. They'd drop me, tell everyone, shame me.

I wish so, so much that there was someone in my life I could tell. Just one person. I can't tell Mum. She'd freak out. The family's reputation is everything to her. If it came out that her underage daughter was pregnant, she'd throw me out. I can't say anything. She'd tellDadimmediately, and that... that can't happen.

I have to come up with something else.

Breathing heavily, I put the diary down and sink back in the chair beside Maily's bed. My eyes dart over to Maily who is holding an iPad, having been allowed to watch a film for half an hour. Her cough has got worse, although her fever came down this afternoon. Mrs Warner has taken care of the children for the last few hours and spent the night in the girls' room after Maily was in tears outside my locked door, calling for me.

I feel awful that I wasn't there, that I spent the night with Demon even though Maily needed me. She wasn't on her own, of course – her father, Zain, and Mrs Warner were all here, but I still feel as if it was my responsibility.

Hailey is at a children's birthday party today. I dropped her off with the O'Brians an hour ago in the car the family let me use. So apparently she can meet up with friends, just not at the Monairs' house.

I spend the afternoon with Maily to make up for my absence, making her favourite food – little skewers with sausages, cheese, tomatoes, and cucumber – and reading more of Ranja's diary.

"You read very quickly," Maily observes, looking at me listlessly. The sound of shrill cartoon voices is coming from the iPad speaker.

"Yes. The story is very exciting."

"Has Ranja already written about why the princess in the fairytale can't come back to the castle?" she wants to know. I stroke her forehead gently as she looks at me expectantly through sad eyes.

"No, I'm not up to that part yet." I regard Maily thoughtfully and wonder to what extent she sees through my made-up story about Princess Ranja. "Are you really sure your big sister won't come back home?"

She nods, sticking out her lower lip. "Yes. She would have been back. Or do you think she's coming back?"

The feeling in my stomach betrays me: No. No, she's not coming back. If her siblings had meant so much to her, she'd have found a way to see them, visited them in preschool, or rung them. But she hasn't.

"I don't know, little moth," I reply, just as sadly. She sobs, and I put the diary on the bedside table and take her in my arms. "I'll find out why Ranja went away. She definitely won't have wanted to leave you, but she must have had to. She loves you more than anything, she's written that so often."

And that's no lie. In the entries where Ranja writes about her less eventful days, she's always writing about how grateful she is to have her little sisters. That they meant everything to her, and she wanted to spare them all the pain she had to go through.

After I have comforted Maily, there is a knock on the door. I'm hurriedly closing the book and pushing it under Maily's pillow when I hear Zain say, "Here you are."

Maily looks at me in alarm, warning me not to tell him about Ranja's diary.

"Maily, how are you doing?"

"Good," she answers briefly.

"Good, really?" Zain sits down on his little sister's bed to my right, in dark-blue Bermuda shorts and a white polo shirt, and tickles her tummy.

"You've got hot chocolate here, a little snack bar, and you're watching a film in bed. You should be doing amazingly, princess."

Maily giggles, pushes him away with her hands, and wriggles under the covers. "Stop, stop tickling me," she says, laughing and breathing heavily. Her face beaming, she bats his hands away to provoke him. Zain climbs onto her bed and tickles her again, and she tries to tickle him back.

I smile as I watch them both, then Zain gets up, inhaling

deeply, and straightens his sister's bedcovers. "I have to speak to Nutella quickly. Can you wait here?"

Nutella is about to stick it to him, I think, lowering my gaze and giving him a look of mock hostility.

"She's called NU-RI-A!" Maily tells him, like a teacher. "Nuria. Not Nutella."

"Nuria then. Will you come outside for a minute, Nuria?" he asks me, with an insistent look that lets me know he has something urgent to tell me.

"For a minute, sure."

Standing in the hallway, he checks repeatedly that there is no one around, then grabs my left hand and pulls me into a nearby guest room.

I look around in amazement.

"Where were you last night?" he asks suddenly.

I frown. He noticed my absence? "Out with a friend."

"Your nocturnal boyfriend?"

I look down at the carpet quickly before telling a half-truth. "No. With another friend. I was in Brisbane. Why are you asking?" I can't change the subject quickly enough.

"Because I want to know how far you've got," he replies, after he's closed the door and locked it.

"With Ranja's diary?"

He nods.

"The part where Ranja writes that she's pregnant," I tell him. "Did you know about that?" He looks more angry than surprised.

"No! No, I didn't know until last night. The bastard! I'll kill him."

"Jazeem?" I enquire as, without asking, he takes hold of my waist and pushes me further into the room. Only now do I notice that we're not in a regular guest room. To my right is a four-poster bed with mint-coloured bedclothes and a light-coloured rug covering the parquet floor, and to my left is a white dressing table with a large vanity mirror. All the pieces of furniture in the room look as though they have been emptied out. The room itself has light, feminine décor. There are three polaroid photos on the mirror. One shows three girls, all in school uniform and sticking their tongues out. Another shows Zain with a gorgeous young brunette girl. On the third, the brunette girl with a fringe is standing alone under a tree. This is Ranja's room. These are the first photos of her I have seen in any part of the house.

"No, not that son of a bitch. Jazeem didn't get her pregnant. She wrote that they were always careful."

How far has he read? I don't know anything about that yet. "Who did then?"

"You should read it yourself. I'll kill him!" Zain's fingers dig deep into my stomach but then he lets me go and paces back and forth by the bed with the wide, velvet-covered bench, beside himself with anger.

"Tell me."

"No." Agitated, he runs his fingers through his hair, closes his eyes, and sucks in air through his clenched teeth.

"Zain. How much have you read?"

"Everything, everything we were able to copy last night. Up until 22nd May. I'm just missing two or three entries before Ranja disappeared or..." He turns to me, his face so full of horror, anger, and pain. "Was set aside."

"What? Why?"

I walk slowly towards him. "Because she was pregnant by him and wouldn't get rid of the child."

"But she was only in the third week. I googled it. In Australia it's allowed until the twenty-fourth week..."

"She was in the twenty-sixth week."

"Without knowing?"

"Clearly," he says, staring at me. "And then she asked him for help."

"Who?"

He lowers his face, breathing deeply.

"Who, Zain? Tell me."

"My dad."

I briefly feel as though I can't get any air, as though the

ground has been torn away from under my feet, as though I have heard wrong.

"What? Please, what?" I repeat haltingly. "It can't be. That's..."

"Unimaginable?" he finishes, taking three steps towards me, and holding my shoulders. "Nothing is unimaginable in this place. D'you get that, Nuria?"

I lean back so I can look him in the eye. I haven't noticed anything suspicious here before now, besides Demon's nocturnal visits. The attack on Anston in his car goes through my mind, and the girl I saw in the garden on my first day. Sure, I sometimes had a bad feeling, but there was nothing tangible.

"I don't believe it."

"You don't believe it? Or you don't want to believe it?" he asks. "I've read it and I'm not lying. You'll read it too and, shit... I always thought that at least our wanker of a father wouldn't do anything to Ranja. I... I... I just didn't notice anything. But I should have noticed, shouldn't I?" he asks, completely beside himself, his face despairing. "As a brother I should have seen that my own father was abusing my sister, right? Why didn't she say anything? Why... Why didn't I realise? Was I so blind? I could have helped her, somehow, and..."

Utterly broken and trapped in guilt, his eyes well with tears. He keeps shaking his head, as though he himself can scarcely believe he's saying it out loud. As though he can't comprehend what his father is capable of. I see horror, disgust, and endless hate in those dark eyes that are so like his father's.

Before he goes any further, hates himself even more for not noticing, I throw my arms around him. "It's not your fault, Zain. You can't do anything about what happened."

"But I could have prevented it, I could... could... could have killed him."

"No," I gasp. "No, then you would have turned yourself into a murderer."

"Just like him, presumably?" Although my arms are around him, he stands there stiffly, not returning the embrace, every fibre of his body tensed, as if the hug is unbearable to him. "I don't care! I would have killed the monster before he hurt anyone else and made my sister disappear."

I let go of him slowly, realising that the embrace isn't consoling him, it's just making him more upset. Why? Why is a simple hug unbearable for him?

"Zain?" I interrupt his continuous stream of death threats and curses. "What did you mean when you said, 'Nothing is unimaginable in this place', and, 'I always thought that at least our wanker of a father wouldn't do anything to Ranja'?" I ask, holding his face and willing him to look me in the eyes. "Did he do something to you too?"

He looks at me for a while as though he's been struck by lightning, and I read the answer in his eyes. "So yes. What?" I ask.

He furrows his brow, pulls away from me as though I'm hurting him, and runs his hand over his face.

"Zain," I say his name calmly, but he blanks me, moves towards the door and turns the key.

"Keep reading, if you can bear it. Keep reading, Nuria."

He leaves me alone in Ranja's room, feeling queasy and unsettled, with a faint scent of lilac still lingering in the air.

11 May

I can't take it anymore.

It is 2:35 a.m. and he's just left. Like always, I feel bad, used, disgusting. If it wasn't for the quiet place inside my head that I crawl into each time I would definitely have gone completely insane. He switched the light on after he was finished this time, and he saw the cuts on my forearms. Then he switched suddenly, as usual, from being the monster in the dark who forces his way into my room at night because I'm not allowed to lock it, to being my father. When the light was on and he'd sat down on my bed, he took my arm and furrowed his brow in concern.

Concern?! As though what had just happened a minute ago wasn't a cause for concern.

"You need to stop this, Ranja," he told me. "If your mother sees she'll send you back to the clinic, do you want that?"

I choked back my tears, pulled my arm away from him and pressed it to my body. He stroked my back, which only made me feel sick. "If there's something on your mind, talk to me. You know that you can tell me anything, my child."

I just nodded, to avoid any discussion with him, like I've been doing for months.

"I'll figure it out," I assured him. "The exams at school are really getting to me right now."

"Of course you'll get a handle on it," he replied, putting his hand on the back of my head and kissing me on the forehead. Bile rose in my oesophagus. "You are a diligent and very obedient girl. I'm proud of you."

With these words he stood up and fastened his belt. He was wearing his white shirt and black suit trousers.

I sat on my mattress as though I'd been turned to stone, the place where I can barely sleep at night, disgusted with myself, and looked down. As I heard him turn the door handle, I murmured the words I felt were unspeakable.

"I'm pregnant." Part of me wanted to take the sentence back immediately, as soon as I had said it aloud, another part of me was relieved that now somebody else knew. Somebody. Hopefully my father. Not the monster that had been raping me for years.

The click of the door rang in my ears as his footsteps approached. "You're pregnant?" he repeated. I looked at him through my tears. Although I didn't want to cry, I couldn't help it. My lower lip was shaking uncontrollably. I hate it when I cry and can't stop.

"How far along are you?" he asked, as I hurriedly wiped away my tears, although new ones kept on coming.

"Twenty-five weeks. I was... at the doctor's... the day before yesterday."

There was an all-too-familiar silence. The same silence as when he comes into my room in the dark and I know what's about to happen. The silence that makes me scream, beg, and wail on the inside. He was responding, but as the monster, not as my father.

Over a minute passed before I dared to look at him.

There was pure madness in his eyes as he looked at me. Looked at me like something that could ruin his life. Like his enemy. Strangely, his expression then changed immediately, as though everything wasn't so bad, after all. He licked his lips, came over to me and stood by me. When he took my hand, I thought for a tiny moment that he would take me in his arms and comfort me. But he didn't. On the one hand I could have done with a hug from him, from theDadI used to idolise so much. On the other, it would have disgusted me, as his hands wouldn't have stayed on the parts of my body that were appropriate for a father and daughter.

His eyes examined the many cuts on my right forearm that I made with a razor blade only yesterday.

"Let me take care of it, Ranja. We'll find a way of making the problem go away."

I nodded. "You want to get rid of it?" I asked uncertainly, because I wasn't sure how he wanted to fix the problem.

"There's no other option. You can't keep it."

"But... but... I'm a week past the time... Where... where..."

"I'll take care of it. Now lie down and go to sleep. You've got to rest – you have school in a few hours."

Correct. Although I hardly ever get any sleep in the nights after he sneaks into my room.

He let go of my hand, sighed when he saw the cuts again – I quickly covered them with my hand – then went over to the door. "We should look for another therapist. Your current one doesn't seem to be helping you."

With these words, he left me to my own thoughts, feelings, and worries. And now I am sitting here. In an hour I'm taking my sisters, Maily and Hailey, to preschool, then going on to high school. I'm so tired. So endlessly tired and lost. Every day is a battle. Every day I have to face my father. Every day some-

one at school might notice my stomach getting bigger. Every day, the gossip and whispering could start. Every day I see Jazeem and Jess together. They've been a couple for almost a month now.

The boy I love, the only one who has given me any light in the darkness, has left me. Now there's just this hopelessness, this meaninglessness, this doubt.

I feel unwell, and my thoughts are racing.

In some places, the writing is smudged and the paper is slightly warped. How bitterly did Ranja cry as she wrote these lines? It pains my soul to think what she had to go through on her own. Her own father, who raped her night after night without her being able to defend herself. He's her father, for fuck's sake! A father should protect his daughter, help her, care for her.

Zain is right! I could kill him too for what he's done to Ranja! How can I ever look this monster in the eyes again without clawing his face to bits? How long did the abuse go on? For years, Ranja writes.

Straightaway, I think of Maily and Hailey. What if Richard preys on them too? I get goosebumps all over my body. No, no, please, no.

I close the book and push it under my pillow as my phone vibrates. It is almost 11 p.m. Both girls are in their beds, but the door isn't locked.

It vibrates again and I look at the screen, which shows an anonymous number. Demon?

Completely distracted and agitated, I grab my phone and answer the call.

"Demon, finally, what's happened? Are you coming over?"

"Demon?" Anston asks on the other end. "Did you actually just mean your stalker?" *Holy shit!*

I freeze. "Erm, I meant a friend who... I met here... at the estate. A member of staff. I'm supposed to call him Demon because he looks like a demon."

What kind of rubbish am I making up here? I silently pull a face and hit myself on the forehead.

"Aha, okay. And you want this employee to come over tonight? It's after 11. Is something going on there?"

How do I explain the whole thing to him now, so that it makes sense?

"That's right, yes. He needs to come over right now, we agreed that, because I think there's something... not right with the overflow in the wash basin. It smells foul. I can't sleep with it. He's got other jobs to do during the day."

"Sure. So he's coming over at night to clean your pipes." *Shit, that really does sound ridiculous when he puts it like that.* But I'm too messed up to think of anything better.

"Don't talk such rubbish! Nothing's going on, okay? He works as a handyman on the estate," I say.

"Of course," he murmurs, clearing his throat and then inhaling deeply.

"Why are you calling?"

"Why indeed? Perhaps because I'm flying back the day after tomorrow? Did you forget?" *Shit!*

"Yes, sure. I hadn't forgotten." *Which is a lie.*

"Of course you forgot. Just like you forgot to reply to my messages or to call me back. What's up with you lately? Don't you care about me now? You're always cancelling our meetings, you only answer my calls when they're anonymous, like your shitty psycho-stalker!" I immediately feel a surge of anger, because he shouldn't be calling Demon a shitty psycho-stalker.

"And now you've forgotten when I'm going back? Such a great friend. We all need someone like you." What an idiot.

"I've been busy and I've had a lot going on. One of the children is sick and..."

"You're having fun with the caretaker, sure. Who are you kidding? Demon is your stalker. Rhea told me you sometimes call him Demon. Is he here?"

"No," I lie, feeling really terrible. Like a traitor going against her principles. Which is exactly what I'm doing. Only weeks ago, I would have fiercely ruled out getting involved with Demon. I even left the country to get away from him, and now... Now the only thing I can think about when I'm not thinking about Ranja is him and last night.

Instinctively, I pull my top down a bit between my breasts, where Demon's mark is. Now and then it tingles and itches. It's a back-to-front D, with a Y above it, the vertical line merging into the D. Demon marked me, like he said he would. Sometimes I wonder whether I'm completely crazy for having agreed to it in the heat of the moment, or if I am flattered to bear this mark, whose meaning I do not yet fully understand. It's a mixture of both.

"Something's not right, Nuri. The other night at the club you just disappeared, leaving me sitting at the bar like a fool. If I don't matter to you, then say so. I can handle it. But don't lie to me."

Awful feelings of guilt awaken in me because I have to agree with him. I am a terrible friend.

"I'm really sorry, Ans. I didn't mean to leave you sitting in the club."

"Oh come on, save your excuses. If I really mean something to you, you'll be at the airport the day after tomorrow to say goodbye. Unlike the way you feel about me, you're important to me, Nuri. I wouldn't have come to Australia if I'd known we weren't going to spend even one nice evening together, and that you'd keep cancelling on me."

I look down sadly, breathe in, and nod, even though he can't see me. "I'll be at the airport the day after tomorrow. I promise."

"I don't believe your promises anymore. You've made so many promises lately then left me hanging. Come or don't come. Then I'll know whether or not you give a shit about me."

He hangs up before I can reply.

CHAPTER 25

Demon

I see you.
I feel you.
I am part of your soul.
Wherever you are, my rose.
I am the first to know.

"Count yourself lucky you're not a suspect!" I whisper angrily to Lexton, who has woken up in hospital after his surgery.

Lying in the hospital bed with a bandage around his head, his forearm in plaster, a black eye, a broken nose, broken ribs, and a neck brace, he has the cheek to roll his eyes irritably.

"But those swine won't be bugging us anymore, I took them all," he replies with a triumphant grin that makes me even angrier.

"So now you're proud of what you did?" I continue, grabbing the bed frame and leaning over him threateningly. "Because if you are, I'd be very happy to throw you out of the organisation."

"Just be cool," he counters, his voice hoarse. "Why so tense, Wylder? It's not like you're in need of a good fuck."

Behind me, Quest clears his throat. "Lex, don't provoke him. That stunt could have finished you, and you're making jokes. It really wasn't funny, what you did." I look over my shoulder at Quest and an incredibly subdued Cameron, who won't meet my eye.

"But the plan couldn't have gone any better, if only I hadn't missed that last fucker."

"But you did miss him," I reply, although I know that whatever I say, I'll be wasting my time. "As soon as you're halfway back on your feet again, you're flying back to Boston." I look at him unwaveringly. Lex has known me long enough to be aware that we've gone beyond the point where I'm willing to enter into discussion.

"Are you serious? You're punishing me for saving your ass and your little squeeze's ass too? Because I'm telling you...," he says more loudly, but then his face crumples in pain.

"Don't work yourself up," Cameron interrupts.

"No, I will work myself up. I did this solo mission to save yours and the others' asses." Lex looks at me grimly.

Oh, that's how he sees it? "That doesn't change the fact that you ignored my orders. Again."

He is my main man, no question. He always was and he always will be. Ever since I saved his ass from the cops in America ten years ago, when he got caught at a bank robbery that went wrong, he's been totally steadfast. My most loyal man, even. Because he owes his freedom – and the fact that he wasn't deported to Romania – to me.

If he hadn't been standing there in the street outside the bank back then, surrounded by armed police, with his hands behind his head, yelling about how he needed the money for his family and wasn't just some mangy criminal, I'd probably have ridden past on my motorbike without paying him any attention.

But his words struck a chord with me. So much so that I paid his bail, set him up with false papers and gave him a role in my organisation.

Lexton will always be my right-hand man, my shield, the man who would walk through fire for me. But his solo missions present more of a risk than I'm comfortable with. "What if some of the dead guys in the Zetos' district knew where the missing girls are being held?"

"You think the girls are still alive?" Quest chips in.

Of course I do. If the Zetos are involved in this thing they will have sold the girls. But not being able to question any of the Zetos makes the search significantly more difficult.

"They could also have been kidnapped or even murdered by other people," Lex says tersely.

"Possible, but unlikely," I reply, irritated, straightening up and glancing at my black smartwatch. It's just after 10 p.m. I've been at the hospital over six hours, waiting for the doctors to finish the operation and praying Lex would survive. Before that I had to pick Cameron up from the Queensland Police Service after he was questioned, and call Quest to the hospital after he'd dropped Nuria off at the Monairs' property.

To be honest, this isn't how I'd imagined today would go.

"You're not going to take any further part in the investigations, Lex. Quest will spend the night here to make sure you don't get any stupid ideas about leaving the hospital," I go on. "And Cam..." I direct a murderous look at him, "... will stand guard at the Monairs' estate tonight as a punishment."

Cameron opens his mouth to groan in annoyance, but catches himself just in time. I give him a wry grin.

"Yes, you go and have fun, now you've given me the earful of the century," Lex complains. I turn back to him.

"I will. Although it's not really about fun now, there's something much bigger going on."

Quest has told me about the Monairs' missing daughter, the one Nuria was asking him about. Something's going on at that estate.

The adult son has deep welts on his back, the oldest daughter has been missing for over four months without the family initiating a public search. The whole thing stinks to high heaven. There's no way I'm leaving my rose unguarded in that place with all these strange goings-on that I haven't got to the bottom of yet.

"That's why you need me here, Wylder," says Lex, reaching for my forearm with his good hand. "I'm no use to you sitting in this crappy bed, but as soon as I'm out of here..."

"*Vreau să fii în siguranță.*" *I want you to be safe,* I say to him in Romanian, so that the others can't understand us.

"*Și vreau să nu fii nepăzit. Cine va fi acolo să te țină în siguranță dacă mă trimiți?*" *And I want to protect you and make sure you're safe too,* he replies, his expression serious. I know his highest priority is protecting me. That he would die for me and he doesn't want to leave me unprotected. But right now he needs to be thinking about his own recovery.

"I'll be all right," I reply. He doesn't look happy about the decision. "I'll check on you tomorrow, brother." He gives me a concerned look as I move away from the bed. "If you're right, the girls are in the Zetos' hands and they'll be in the next container to America. Once we find them, our assignment will be complete." But if he's wrong, the students have been kidnapped by a madman and may no longer be alive.

And I still have this uneasy feeling that Ranja's disappearance is connected with all this, and that the Zetos only followed us to Australia to lie in wait for me. Which in turn means that we have a mole, who has been informing the Zetos about my movements.

I trust Lex, Cameron, and Quest to the death. But not all employees of my organisation. What if this person deliberately set me on the trail of the girls in order to deliver me up to the Zetos like a lamb to the slaughter? We must have a traitor in our ranks. That's the only explanation. Because all of this is connected somehow. I just don't know how.

It is just after 1 a.m. when I climb over the wall of the estate and drop down easily onto the soil behind the hedge. Any minute now I'll be breathing in the scent of my flower, clasping her hair in my fingers while I'm inside her. Feeling her and drinking in every passionate sound she utters, like she's praying to me. Just thinking about it makes me hard.

In the protection of the hedge, where the cameras can't film me, I first observe the estate, then use my smartphone to switch off the surveillance system. I see a message from Nuria, actually saying she wants me to come over.

Suddenly the light goes on in the third floor of the building. I see two people in Zain's room, standing close to the window. I squint and lift my phone to my face, using the camera to zoom in. I usually bring binoculars to observe my rose, but I don't have any on me today.

As I focus on the people in the window, every muscle in my body tenses up. Nuria is standing with Zain in his crappy room, giving him a long, intimate hug.

What are you doing, my rose? Why are you hugging that bastard who only wants to fuck you? You're nothing more than a notch on his bedpost, he'd discard you the very next day.

Bare-chested, the guy puts his arms around my property. Around my wife! I instantly see red and grind my teeth.

I put my hood up, draw my knife from my biker boot and jog across the lawn to the back of the building, concealed by the night shadows.

Reaching the corner of the property, I kneel by the grid over one of the cellar windows and lift it up. The screws were loosened days ago, allowing me to remove the grating effortlessly.

I nudge the window with my right foot and it swings open. I also opened the window some days ago and just left it ajar. So far, no one has noticed that the handle has been moved. After I get into the cellar, I pull the grating back over the shaft and make my way through to the boiler room.

From here, a corridor leads to the wine cellar where, behind the many shelves, a secret passageway is located. The property is crisscrossed with secret passages, like a Swiss cheese. I use my smartphone to light my way up the incredibly narrow stairs leading to the second floor. There are rat droppings and cobwebs everywhere. Woodlice and spiders scurry into the corners as I climb the rough stone steps and come to a fork. The passage on the right leads to my rose. I already know this route off by heart. The one on the left goes further up, to the third floor, where more secret passages connect to almost every room. The property must have been built to hide someone, or spy on them, or store something secret. And the labyrinth of passageways is very convenient for me.

I have only half-explored the left-hand corridor, so I don't know where I will end up or what awaits me. And my crazy thoughts about Zain and my rose are buzzing around in my head. Him seducing her, lulling her into a sense of security, claiming her for himself. I'll kill him if he does anything she doesn't want! At the same time, I'm praying my flower won't allow herself to be fucked by this son of a bitch. That she won't want him.

If she does, it'll end in a blood bath!

I dip my head inside the narrow passage, which can't be more than 1.8m high. When you're 1.95m it's a tight squeeze in these corridors and my shoulders keep on brushing the walls. Once I have gone up another set of stairs to the third floor, the passages get wider. How strange.

I use my phone torch to illuminate the corridor, which is around three metres wide. I continue slowly until I turn a corner and start to think I've gone the wrong way. *Fuck! Where am I?* It feels as though the corridor is leading in the opposite direction. And the clock is ticking!

I should have scouted out all the passages over the last few days, not just some of them. Still, I have a map of the corridors on my phone.

I frown as I open the document, because the passage seems to be heading towards a much bigger room on the fourth floor.

Puzzled, I carry on until I come to a wooden door with iron hinges and handle. I try to open it, but it's locked. Shame, but not a problem. I take a small leather case from my jacket pocket, which, as well as cash and fake passports, contains lock picks.

I want to know what's behind the door so, without stopping to think, I position my phone in the corner next to the door to illuminate the lock, then get to work. I crack the modern lock in around two minutes. There's a soft click and the door springs open. Nicely done.

The first thing that hits me is the disgusting, sour smell of decay.

"What the hell...," I curse, narrowing my eyes and holding my right wrist over my nose and mouth.

Only then do I shine the torch inside the secret room, whose walls are made of stone. It is cool and stuffy in here. And the room is not empty. Two children are standing in the beam of my torch. Impossible!

The boy and girl recoil in fear, hiding behind a stone pillar that supports the vaulted ceiling.

I move the phone to right and left and discover two more children, wearing dirty trousers, T-shirts and jumpers. Their hair is tangled and their hands and faces are dirty. And then the light falls on a covered, hunched form in the far corner. She looks bigger, not a child at all.

Cowering in the corners, the children look at me, before I raise my hands.

"Don't worry, I'm not going to hurt you," I reassure them. "Why are you here?" I lower my hood to make myself seem less threatening to them, although the scars on my face will definitely make them even more afraid.

None of the children says a word. The figure in the corner doesn't react either. No one answers.

But I don't need them to answer. I know why they're here. What they're here for. It's not just the smell of faeces and decay that makes the bile rise in my throat, it's also revulsion and mounting anger. There can only be one reason for hiding these children in this place: they're being abused by sick paedophiles. I can see the fear in their faces. Their fear of me. How often have they heard the words, "Don't worry, I won't hurt you," before that is exactly what happens?

I walk slowly through the room to look at the figure in the far right-hand corner. She's lying curled up with her head on her knees, as though she's asleep. Dark hair falls over her face, concealing it. There's a blanket around her legs, and at first glance she seems to be alive. But the smell coming from her is the unmistakable stench of death.

I crouch down by her, then lift her head. Pure horror stares back at me, making me inhale sharply. I have seen a lot of corpses, but not this advanced.

My stomach turns again at the thought that the children have been in this place with a corpse for weeks. I shine a light on her neck and I can't find a tattoo like the ones my sisters have. I exhale in relief. The woman isn't Summer or Eden. But who is she?

I carefully release her head with the words "Rest in peace," then look back over my shoulder at the children, who are standing close together, watching me from a distance. The oldest child, a boy of perhaps ten, is standing protectively in front of the younger ones, staring at me with dark, anxious eyes.

What do I do with them now?

The oldest, dark-haired boy snaps me out of my thoughts. "Someone's coming."

I raise my eyebrows in alarm, but understand immediately. "Okay. I'll come back. You have my word."

I have to go to Nuria and get her off the estate as quickly as possible, and then help the children before the situation here escalates. I carefully take photographs of the room, the corpse, and the children before leaving the room and taking a deep breath.

The swine who are responsible for this are going to bleed for it!

Back in the passageway, I resume my search for my rose and then hear footsteps. The boy was right.

Fuck! The footsteps are coming from the passage to my right, so I quickly go around the corner and press myself against the wall. If the person turns towards me I'll be on them before they know it.

But the footsteps go quiet, as expected, in front of the massive wooden door that I came through just a few seconds earlier. As I sneak a look around the corner I have to stop myself from ramming a knife in the person's back.

Mrs Warner is searching for keys in her blazer pocket. There's a woman involved in this filthy business? How evil does a woman have to be to lock children in this dark, cold room with a corpse? She's carrying a cool box in her right hand which she briefly sets down to open the door.

"Dinner time, brats." The door closes behind her with a bang, and I'm tempted to lie in wait for her and slit her throat when she leaves.

Although I'm itching to, I decide against it and wait until she comes out. Then I'll know whether or not the children have said anything.

Suddenly my phone vibrates in my hand – I'd turned the torch off to avoid being discovered.

When I'm sure Mrs Warner is with the incarcerated children, I look at the screen and see a message from Nuria.

jsmeah zru g

What? I know, without having to think about it, that she's in danger. Cursing inaudibly, I push myself off the wall so I can enter the passage Mrs Warner came from as quietly as possible.

My phone vibrates. A call from my flower. I hurriedly take the call.

"Hey, what's up?" But instead of an answer, all I hear are rustling and banging sounds, and the noise of breaking glass.

"Give me the phone!" It is a man's voice that I can't identify. Then there's more rustling, and then the call ends.

Fuck!

CHAPTER 26

Nuria

A friend can give you the most beautiful smile
to disguise their dark intentions,
while the monster
doesn't need to smile to do that.

Having assured Anston multiple times that I'll be at the airport punctually the day after tomorrow, I check my messages. Nothing from Demon.

What's going on with him? Why hasn't he been in contact? Will he surprise me again tonight, seduce me, drive me wild, and finally give me the chance to get to know him properly? What happened to his sisters? And why is he looking for missing women here in Australia? Is he hoping to find his sisters here? So far from his home town of Boston?

I suddenly remember him telling me I'd already seen him without his mask. When? When the fuck could that have been?

As far as I know, I've never been to Boston. So it can only have been in Barcelona. Where was it? I didn't go to that many places. Just the university campus, the bar where I worked, and my apartment. He seems older than me, so it's possible he was on campus, perhaps looking for his missing sisters, although we're more likely to have met at the *Luna llena.* And that doesn't make it any easier to get an answer, because I've served countless customers in that bar. How did he come across me anyway? Was our meeting a coincidence?

How can I have become so fucking addicted to him? To his

voice, his muscular body, his smell? And what I really long for right now is for him to be here with me.

I shake my head. I'm not addicted, not like him. I just think about him a lot, that's all. Right now, I long for him to be here, for his strength, because he's currently the only person I could talk to about what I've read.

I put down my phone with a disappointed sigh – he still hasn't messaged me, even though I really need him today after the awful revelation – and carry on reading Ranja's diary.

I haven't got too many more pages to go before I'll know what happened to her in the final days before she disappeared. But it's painful to read.

The next entry is unusually short, not even half a page.

22 May

What's going on here? How can I keep what I've seen to myself? If they know I've witnessed their horrific activities, they'll kill me. I need to report them to the police!

First I need to make sure I haven't been caught on the cameras, and delete any videos. Otherwise, I'm done for. And then... then... I have to get out of here! This house of horrors is driving me crazy! The things going on here are terrifying, evil, cruel!

Confused by her words, I frown and read them again. What is Ranja talking about? What has she seen? What's so bad that she can't name it? There's no mention of her pregnancy or her father.

I carry on reading.

27 May

They caught me! They know what I've seen and they've locked me in my room for two days and taken away my phone. This is so much bigger and more dangerous than I thought. This house is harbouring true evil. It feels like I don't have much time left to write down what I've seen. They're deciding what to do with me. I'm no use to them pregnant.Dadcould send me away, but there'd be no guarantee I wouldn't talk. That's why I think I'm probably going to die here.

She knew she was going to die? I ask myself. What could be worse than being abused by her own father, what could she be killed for talking about? Did she witness a murder?

If my father doesn't manage to convince his associates I'll keep my mouth shut, he won't have a choice. Because I could reveal what I saw a week ago, in the green hall on the fourth floor... I was just going toDadin the middle of the night, to suggest I could keep the baby, carry it to term, and give it up for adoption, but his study was empty. And then, from behind a sliding door that wasn't completely closed, I heard voices and strange noises.

The horror and cruelty make my entire body feel as though it's been electrified. The shock of these unspeakable things, of what the diary might still contain, of what is being done to innocent children on this estate, of what Ranja had to experience and witness, makes my heart ache. Just when I think it can't get any worse, Ranja seems to have experienced another tragedy.

Just as I was about to leave the study, I heard footsteps in the adjoining room and the voice of somebody I would never have expected to be there. It was...

I am about to turn the page when there's a knock on my door and I get a terrible fright. Is it the twins? Could Hailey and Maily have also been their father's victims?

"Nuria, are you still awake?" It's Zain. I exhale in relief before putting the open diary on the bedside table and jumping off the bed.

I still feel sick about what I've just read. About what I've found out about Mr Monair. I can't spend a single night longer on this estate and I have to talk to someone about it.

About the flood of emotions that overwhelms me. The rage, the sadness, the sympathy. The disgust, the fear and the doubt.

"Yes, I'm awake."

I open the door to Zain, who's standing there in a half-undone dark shirt and low-slung suit trousers, emanating his expensive aftershave. He looks as though he has calmed down since reading the entries this afternoon.

"Have you been out? Why are you looking so..." I gesture up and down his body with my right hand. Even his dark hair has an elegant side-parting, giving him the look of a male model. "... suave," I continue, when I've found the right word.

"Yes. I went out for a bit to get some headspace."

"Understandable."

I look around the hallway behind him to check there's no one who could overhear us. "Why are you here?"

"Can I come in quickly?" he asks, giving me his beguiling smile.

"Of course. I was just about to read the last few pages of Ranja's diary."

"That's why I'm here," he explains, closing the door and coming further into the room, apparently looking for something. When he spots the open diary on the bedside table, he goes straight over to it.

"I don't have the final entries. I thought we could read them together, then..." He turns to me with a concerned expression. "I think what's in there is going to be difficult. Unless you want to finish reading it on your own?"

I fold my arms lightly over my nightshirt, since the new pyjamas that I bought especially for this trip were ripped off my body last night by my psycho-lover. In just my black panties and a T-shirt, I feel somewhat naked in front of him. His eyes are wandering – admittedly not obtrusively, but still unmistakeably – over my bare legs.

"We can read the end of the diary together. I'm already on

the final entry, and you won't believe what Ranja saw. It's at least as bad, if not worse, than what happened to her."

Zain casts a fleeting look at the diary as I pick it up from the table. "Worse than what my rapist of a father did to her?" he asks incredulously. "Hard to imagine."

"It's bad. Very bad." And I need to get out of this house as quickly as possible. I can't stay in this place now I know what's going on here. The best thing would be to message Demon to pick me up. First thing in the morning I'll report what's happening here to the police, and present the diary as evidence. Only now do I fully understand the significance of this book. Why Ranja's parents were so desperate to find it, why her room was cleared out, why she disappeared. She was going to reveal a terrible, unspeakable, awful secret.

"It's best if we read it in my room. No one ever comes in there and we won't be disturbed."

I nod, even though I still don't fully trust Zain. There's no way he could have simulated the anger and despair I witnessed this afternoon. He hates his father so deeply for what he did to his sister. And we're on the same side there. Because I do too. I hate Richard Monair.

As I get to Zain's room, I type a message to Demon, telling him I can't spend another night on the estate. I don't want to be alone, don't want to lie alone in bed after Zain and I have found out even more terrible details about Ranja's life.

"I hope you like salami and pepperoni pizza?" Zain asks, pointing to a box on the coffee table, as he moves to the corner of the dark sofa. But food is the last thing on my mind right now. Zain's still holding Ranja's diary as though he's never going to let it go, as though it were his most precious possession.

I shut the door behind me and look around the room. It is furnished in a similar style to mine. There's a fireplace and TV on the wall to the right, with a dark leather three-piece suite positioned around them. To my left is a huge box spring bed, with the blankets and pillows carelessly thrown back and two shirts lying on it.

Zain opens the lid of the still-steaming pizza box.
"Zain," I interrupt him.
"Yes?"
"Do you know what goes on in this house?"
"What do you mean?" he counters, frowning questioningly.
"Well, I mean, yourDadwas with your sister at night... You know. And I don't want to upset you or ask you directly, but did you go through the same thing as her?"
His reaction tells me my suspicions aren't wrong. His charismatic smile disappears temporarily, he lets go of the pizza box lid and straightens up. Suddenly, he puts the book down on the cushion of the three-seater sofa and takes off his shirt.
"What are you doing?" I ask, presumably wearing a perplexed expression.
By way of an answer, Zain throws his shirt over the back of the sofa and turns around so that his back is towards me. I am filled with horror at the sight of countless wide, scarred welts on his back. The bulging, partially healed scars denote immeasurable pain.
"Oh my God," I blurt out, going over to him and examining his skin more closely. I can't help stroking them, which makes his breath tremble, as though my touch could hurt him.
"Who did this to you?" I ask. Although I can already guess the answer.

CHAPTER 27

Nuria

Every woman needs a monster by her side,
to make her feel safe,
because there are a great many beasts
lurking in the streets.

Zain slowly turns around. “My Dad. Every scar represents disobedience, an infringement of his rules. It began when I was a child. I have never shown them to anybody before, only you.”

Breathing heavily, I raise my eyebrows, shake my head in disbelief, and can’t help giving him a hug. “I am so… so fucking sorry.”

He stands there stiffly, then he gives in and unexpectedly puts his arms around me.

“I thought he was only like that with me, I didn’t know he was hurting my sister too, and…,” his back muscles tense under my hands again, “… abusing her.”

“It’s very likely he wasn’t only doing it to the two of you,” I say.

“What do you mean?” he asks. I lift my face to look into his eyes and loosen my embrace.

“In Ranja’s last diary entry, she describes a scene she witnessed. She writes about children being abused by associates of your father in a room behind his study.”

I’ve hardly finished my sentence before he opens his shapely mouth and gives me a confused look.

“That can’t be true.”

"It is true. It has to be true. That's why your parents wanted the diary. I don't know whether your Mum's involved, but I know yourDadfound out your sister had seen them. That's probably why she disappeared. Not because she was pregnant by your Dad, but because she'd seen things she shouldn't have seen. Things that shouldn't have happened."

"Don't ever call himDadin front of me, Nuria. That monster isn't my Dad."

"I wanted..."

"It's okay. Don't worry. You can't understand how I feel inside right now. What I'm feeling right now. I hoped so much that he hadn't touched Ranja." Raw pain flickers across his face as he brushes a strand of my hair behind my ear. "I thought he wouldn't hurt her, not like he did me. I never saw scars on her back, so I assumed..."

The corners of his mouth twitch as he licks his lips, seemingly battling grief.

I touch his arm again, to comfort him. And this time he accepts the embrace straightaway and leans his face against my shoulder.

"It's not your fault."

"But... I should have spoken to her. I should have asked her if he was doing the same things to her as he was to me."

"It's difficult to talk about this kind of thing, Zain. It was hard for her to talk to you about it too." I stroke his back gently, feeling his inner turmoil and self-doubt. When he lifts his head and takes my face in both his hands, it's me that stiffens. I never thought he would do this, but he leans towards me and places his lips on mine.

In contrast to how it is with Demon, an unpleasant coldness surges through me. I feel nothing, neither the desire to return the kiss nor any feeling of connection. It feels completely alien and wrong.

After a couple of seconds, I abruptly pull away from him and lift the back of my left hand to my mouth. "This... isn't happening. It's wrong and..."

Zain covers the distance between us in a single step. "Why? Because your secret boyfriend will kill me?"

Why does it sound so ridiculous coming from him? "Yes, damn it. If he finds out, then..."

He holds my head and goes to kiss me again, more forcefully this time. "Stop it, Zain. I don't want this." I quickly turn my head aside. "I know you're going through a lot right now and you think this sort of closeness will help, but it won't. And anyway, I have someone..." I stumble over my words. *What do you want to say? Someone you love?*

"Someone I mean something to." How inane does that sound?

"You mean something to me too, Nuria. And anyway, he's not here, and you're clearly not with him properly. Or am I mistaken?"

I am much more than with Demon.

"That's nothing to do with you, Zain," I keep him at a distance. "I don't think it was a good idea to read the diary with you." As I free myself from his grip to pick the diary up off the sofa, his reflexes are triggered and he grabs my wrist.

"The book stays with me."

"No, I'm reading it to the end," I insist.

"So that you can run to the police with it?"

What did he say? I slowly turn towards him. The pain and suffering that were previously written across his face have been replaced by an evil glint in his eyes. I hardly recognise him. What's going on here?

"You're not getting the book back, Nuria. I'm lucky you haven't read on to the next page." As I watch, he turns the page and then reads out a sentence in a voice of feigned shock. "*Zain, my own brother, is part of this monstrous gathering.*"

I open my mouth in horror as painful cramps begin in my stomach. *Shit! Shit! How could I have been so stupid?*

He wanted to have the book the whole time in order to find out what his sister had written, to find out whether she mentioned him.

"It was all lies. You...," I whisper to myself. His mock anger at his father, his concern for his sister, his friendly side.

"Not all. I wanted to find out more about you, your boyfriend who found the secret passages, and that other friend of yours who kept waiting for you outside the house."

"Anston?"

"Yes, Anston. That guy was too pushy for me, so I had to send him for a little sleep. He had no business on our property! But your nocturnal visitor is worse than that Anston."

So it wasn't Demon, it was Zain who drugged Anston in his car, to prevent him from stumbling upon any of the Monairs' secrets.

"Why?" I ask.

"You might well ask." I strain against his grip. "To catch him and silence him. You know too much. But I don't know who your nocturnal visitor is, so I wanted to lure him in."

The scheming bastard!

"He'll be here any minute, won't he? You know I'm going to shoot him." He murmurs the last sentence so quietly into my ear that I see red.

"Dad!" he calls his father, before I strike out with my right elbow and jab him in the ribs.

"You miserable rat! You utter wanker!" I yell at him, turning away from the sofa and hurrying away. As I run I unlock my phone and hurriedly type a message to Demon. But before I can tear open the door and flee, I am thrown roughly to the floor. My chin cracks on the parquet floor and my teeth are painfully rammed together, making my eyes fill with tears. *God!*

I tap on the red phone icon with my outstretched hand. *Demon! I need you. Please, please, please answer!* Although I am terrified Zain and his father will attack him, I still believe he has the upper hand. I hear a dial tone as I struggle under Zain.

"Get off me!"

"Give me the phone!" Zain growls, reaching for my hand as the telephone is taken from me by another hand. I look up in horror and see Richard Monair in front of me. *"Mierda!"* I curse.

"That's right, *Mierda.*" He puts my mobile in his back pocket, then grabs his son by the hair. "Can't you even handle a woman?" He pulls Zain up, and I free myself from under him and crawl forward on my forearms. Once Zain's weight is off me I go to stand up and run away. But my plan is thwarted when a hand grabs the back of my T-shirt and pulls me backwards with a powerful jolt.

"Get in here! Come on!" Mr Monair snaps at me, and apparently at his son, too. I stumble to a halt in Zain's room. Before I can come up with another way of escaping, Mr Monair shuts the door behind himself and puts the key in his trouser pocket. *Fuck! What now?*

I spin around on my bare feet, rush to the coffee table and grab the three-pronged candleholder.

"Stay away from me!" I threaten, my voice shaking but determined. I know what will happen if I end up on the floor again. They will silence me, kill me, and possibly torture me first. Just like the endless spiritual and physical pain they caused Ranja. This family is sick, rotten to the core!

Mr Monair laughs at my improvised weapon, adjusts his shirt sleeves, and takes two steps towards me.

"I never thought you'd be so bold and feisty, Nuria. I thought you were one of those girls that would burst into tears straightaway and beg for their life."

I return Mr Monair's cynical grin with a poisonous look. I'll fight to the end.

But suddenly there is a chasm behind me. This abyss. I can smell the salty sea, hear the roar of the waves. What's going on?

"You won't shoot me." Surprised, I hear the same words coming from Mr Monair's mouth as the ones that plague me in my nightmares. His lips are moving, but the wrong words are coming out. Petrified, I examine his tall figure, which is unexpectedly being wreathed in dark clouds before my very eyes.

"I will!" I reply, with less determination than a few minutes before. But I'm clutching a candlestick in my hands rather than a pistol.

Suddenly a man steps out of the darkness and it's not Mr Monair's bronzed, angular face, but a dark blond man with eyes as black as the darkest night. He's wearing a black shirt with an upturned collar and a white jacket. Before I understand that I am caught in my own nightmare – a daydream, a flashback – someone takes hold of my throat and I am catapulted back to the here and now. I am pushed hard against the wall between the windows.

"Take the candlestick off her and gag her," Mr Monair orders. My only weapon is ripped away from me and I lift my hands up to the fingers that are boring brutally and painfully into my neck. Panicking, I struggle for air, writhe in his grasp, and try to kick him. With every second that passes my tear-filled vision turns blacker at the edges. *No! No! I have to do something!*

As Zain returns with a silk scarf and tries to put it between my teeth, everything suddenly goes dark. All the lamps in the room go out. This time it isn't the utter darkness of my nightmare. It's Demon.

Zain releases me at once, and Mr Monair's grip around my throat slackens. "Why has the light gone out?"

"He is here," Zain explains to his father.

"Wonderful. Then we'll finish her off in front of him."

An unholy, mocking laugh cuts through the darkness. "There are much bigger monsters lurking in the dark than the ones you consider yourselves to be. No one touches my wife unless they have a death wish."

Mr Monair is about to laugh in turn, when I feel a draft pass by me and hear his laughter turn into a gurgling wheeze. *What has Demon done? Where, is he, where?*

"What's happened?" Zain asks. "Dad? Where are you? Say something."

"Something," Demon jokes mockingly from the darkness. Then I hear a tortured cry from Zain. Panicking, I turn my face to the right, holding my sore neck, and trying to make anything out in the blackness. But I'm still dizzy from being choked and tiny lights are flashing across my field of vision. I gasp and attempt to breathe more evenly as I hear footsteps, then the sound of something falling.

"Get out! GET OUT, whoever you are!" Zain cries in panic. "Dad?"

"I'm not done with you yet. Your paedo father can't help you anymore. He's got to think of himself right now because he's bleeding out on the floor. What do you want to say goodbye to first? Your eyes or your fingers?"

I hold my neck, gasping, and feel around myself with my left hand. *Where are they?* "Demon."

"Just a moment, my rose. This has been a long time coming."

And before I can reply I hear a loud cry. The noise Zain makes seems to last forever and brings tears to my eyes. I put my hands over my ears as I am turned around and immediately pressed to a warm chest.

"Don't listen." It's Cameron's voice, which I had not been expecting to hear in this place. I hear a crack, followed by something or someone falling over with a crash. Demon is continuing his reckoning and toying with Zain, just as he said he would. God, what is he capable of?

"Wylder. That's enough." Cameron attempts to calm him.

"It's nowhere near enough!" Demon growls.

"Please, stop," Zain whimpers, before there's another crash and a strangled gasp.

"Why should I, you worm? You're just like your father. A monster who hurts other people. You've forfeited your right to life."

"My father hurt me too."

"But even that didn't make you turn out differently! I've seen those children. And when I looked into their eyes, I swore they wouldn't have to look their abusers in the face ever again!" There is a tortured cry. "You!"

Another crack.

"Are!"

The curtain is pulled down from the window with a jolt as Zain tries to cling onto it.

"Scum!"

Zain is kneeling before Demon at the window. And then I see a movement. One that happens so quickly and seems so insignificant and yet simultaneously ends a life. A blade draws across Zain's throat, and he desperately clutches his blood-covered neck. The last thing I hear of him is the rattling sound before he chokes on his own blood.

The whole thing is barbaric. Merciless. Inhuman. And Demon can read all these thoughts in my face as I watch, my mouth gaping wide in shock, as Zain's dead body slumps over slackly.

"What have you... done?" I whisper. "What have you..." The last word sticks in my throat.

Demon flicks the blood off his knife, then comes towards me.

At that moment, Mr Monair stirs on my left. Holding his bleeding chest, he spits a mouthful of blood and makes a strained gurgling sound.

When Demon realises he is still alive, he takes out his gun and, the next second, shoots him in the face. I cry out internally. Cry, because I can't bear so much brutality. A hand moves over my eyes, but it is too late, I've seen it all, and wish, I so fucking wish I hadn't.

Distraught, I pull the hand away from my face, because I simply can't believe what has just happened. A few minutes ago I was standing with Zain in his room, embracing him and thinking he needed consoling, until he revealed himself to be a monster. Now he and his father are lying there dead, in huge lakes of blood.

Demon comes towards me. "You're safe now," he says, and reaches for my face with a blood-covered hand.

I recoil from him in horror, shaking my head, although I don't go very far, as Cameron is still standing behind me.

"You killed them," I say in shock.

"They had to die. There was no other option."

"There was no other option?" I repeat, horrified. "Of course there was. They could have gone to jail and stood before a court, they didn't have to be executed by you!"

He lets his hand fall slowly as I move away from him, and the right corner of his mouth twitches. My fingers are itching to pull down his hood so I can see his whole face for once, just once.

"And then? What if they got out of prison in five, or fifteen years, say, to abuse more children? Hurt other people? No, the moment those sick bastards laid a hand on the first innocent child, they lost the right to live. When they left people to die within the walls of this building. Do you think people who've done that should live?"

Unexpectedly he holds up his phone, which shows a photo of a dark room with stone walls with children inside. Pale, dirty faces stare into the camera, with so much emptiness and fear in their eyes.

I recognise the face of a little girl and it suddenly dawns on me. It's the child I saw in the garden the day I arrived. I didn't imagine her. The poor child must have run away, but probably couldn't get over the fence.

He swipes to the right to the next picture, of a hunched figure in the corner.

"Do these arseholes deserve another chance? Should these pigs carry on living and destroy more lives? I might be wrong, but I always thought you had a sense of justice. What else have these men earned, if not death? A fulfilling life?!"

"I didn't say that. But..." I take the phone from him to look more closely at the picture.

I look for a long time at the dark-haired person in the corner of the room and am overcome with a dark sense of foreboding. "Who is that?"

"The Monairs' daughter," Demon says. No. *No, please, no.* But it has to be. "Mrs Warner is involved in it too, like the rest of the family."

When I alerted Mrs Warner to the fact that there was a

child in the garden, they must have realised straightaway that a child was missing. Fuck!

I swipe to the next photo, but it's not another image of the imprisoned children or the dead woman that I see, it's me. Just me: getting changed, going to bed, reading Ranja's diary, making a sandwich in the kitchen, jumping on the trampoline with Hailey...

Demon quickly takes his phone off me.

"Time to go," he announces. "Get the diary, Cam. The police will deal with the rest." I pull back as Cameron grips my shoulder tightly and Demon tenderly strokes my cheek towards my bruised jaw.

"No," I reply determinedly.

"No?" he asks. "No what?"

"No. I'm not coming."

"Hmm. Unfortunately I'm not giving you the choice, my rose."

"You can't make me, Demon. When I say no, I mean no. Tonight I'm going to..."

He looks up expectantly. "Stay here?" I hate it when he mocks me. "You messaged me an hour ago asking me to come and pick you up."

"Yes, no. I've changed my mind, I'm going to look for a hotel to spend the night in."

"All the hotels are fully booked," he says.

"Lies."

"Have you forgotten? I know everything. It's not up for discussion. You're coming with me." And before I can raise any further objections, he lifts me up. Angry and upset, I writhe in his arms, beat my hands against his chest, and try to slide out of his grip. But he just laughs.

"So violent, my queen."

"You're violent! A fucking monster!"

"I never disputed that fact. You don't call me Demon for nothing." I continue to struggle until I manage to slip out of his hold, only for him to pull me towards him by the hand. "Not so fast."

"Let go!"

Cameron follows us, his arms folded. "Do these power games turn you on, or do you have to tear each other to shreds every time you disagree?"

"Disagree?" I ask, appalled. "These aren't simple differences of opinion, they're fundamentally different attitudes to life. Your boss is a murderer!"

"Now that's a surprise," Cameron laughs. He's not taking me seriously, either. With the same move he has used twice before, Demon pulls me to his chest then lifts me by the waist and puts me over his shoulder.

"Put me down, you arsehole."

"Get down on your knees in front of me." Definitely not!

"Fuck you!"

"Say that again when I fuck you."

Cameron sighs theatrically as Demon carries me out of the room and I lift my head.

"If there's one thing you need to get your head around," Cameron says, "it's that my boss never changes his mind. Never."

I snort in frustration. *Just you wait. I'll get away, somehow.*

Although I'm really not sure I want to.

But Demon is a murderer! A killer. I can't ignore what I've seen. What else is he capable of?

CHAPTER 28

Nuria

Can a rose survive without water?
Is love alone enough
to keep it alive?

I watch from the back seat as Cameron opens a laptop. At least twelve different camera feeds are visible, leaving me momentarily speechless.

"The police will be there any minute," he says, clicking on the external camera, which is trained on the open front door.

For the first time I appreciate the extent of Demon's surveillance operation. He has tapped all the Monairs' cameras and has been monitoring my every step as well as the whole family's movements.

Demon drives the black SUV, periodically glancing at the images on the laptop screen. Just as Cameron predicted, three police cars arrive at the entrance to the estate and park in front of the house. Things are getting exciting now.

"Don't worry, the door's open," Demon answers the question I'd been asking in my head. I meet his gaze in the rearview mirror and then quickly look away. Instead, I watch the scene that is currently playing out inside the house. Four armed police officers enter the expansive foyer. They split up shortly afterwards. Cameron switches to the cameras on the first, then the second floor.

"Very good, keep going, you'll soon find them," he murmurs, concentrating.

Immediately afterwards a police officer opens the door to

Zain's room. His torch sweeps the room before coming to rest on Mr Monair's lifeless body. The officer reaches for the radio on his collar and gives an instruction. The sharp black and white recording captures both dead bodies. Mr Monair is lying directly in front of the camera, Zain is motionless on the right next to the bed, although only half his body is visible.

The sight gives me goosebumps. Everything that happened in the last hour still feels like a dream.

A few moments later, there are more than four police officers in the room, checking whether the people lying on the floor are still alive, and searching the room for anyone else.

I think of the twins, who are soon going to be torn from their sleep without me being able to explain what has happened to them. Without me being able to calm them and comfort them. It breaks my heart not to be with them.

Mrs Warner is standing on the staircase on the first floor in a bathrobe and is escorted to the foyer with the children by two police officers. She turns repeatedly to the officers, apparently talking to them about something or trying to explain something. Maily and Hailey seem dazed and frightened. A nasty guilty sensation settles in my stomach.

"Come on, why's it taking you so long to search the whole property?" I hear Cameron say.

"They can't have missed the secret passage. They'll find them," Demon remarks, driving the SUV rapidly along the coast road. He seeks out my gaze again. And again, I avoid his eyes. I can't look at him. Not now I've seen what he's capable of.

I knew Demon was no innocent, but I had no idea that he could mutate into such a monster. Although I have to admit he wasn't murdering innocent people, they were people who deserved to die.

A few minutes later, two more police officers – a woman with a ponytail and a tall man – lead several children down the steps.

My God! There are so many children.

They walk fearfully down the steps. Meanwhile, more police cars and two ambulances have arrived on the driveway.

"Mission accomplished, I'd say," announces Cameron with a triumphant smile. "That family can't do any more harm, and the children are free. Hopefully they'll soon be returned to their families."

Although help has come too late for Ranja.

Rest in peace. You did nothing to deserve this horrible death and this sad life, full of pain. I hope things are better for you now, wherever you are. I offer up a silent prayer.

My eyes fill with tears as I think of Ranja's diary entries, and the twins, who had warmed to me so much in recent weeks. I'm going to miss them, a lot.

I lose myself in my thoughts for a while, fighting back tears, and don't notice that Demon has already stopped outside his house. I quickly wipe my eyes.

"How are you doing?" Demon asks, turning around in his seat. I avoid his gaze and stare doggedly out of the side window. He groans in irritation then gets out of the car. Cameron shuts the laptop and follows him out.

I stay where I am.

I only leave the SUV when Demon opens my door.

"What are you unhappy about, *corazón mío?"* Demon asks, as he takes me into the sinister house where he and his friends live, in the middle of the night.

I can still taste the bile on my tongue, and feel miserable and nauseous from what I experienced a few moments ago.

"Don't act like you didn't want to see me tonight." He takes hold of my chin.

I roll my eyes. "Not like this." I can't forget the awful images from the house, Zain's cries, and all the blood.

He sighs.

"If it's any consolation, I also thought this evening would go differently. I thought we'd already be on round three."

"Round three?" I ask, exhausted, and allow him to touch me gently. On the one hand, I want to be close to him and feel safe after the horrors of the evening. On the other, I want nothing to do with the monster I saw in him today. He strokes my throat, which is still burning from the choking.

"Round three, fucking you in all the positions I've been thinking about all day."

I push him away with both hands. "The only thing you're going to fuck today is your hand."

I turn away from him proudly as Cameron holds open the door to the dimly lit hallway. "Welcome back, little queen."

He can't hold back a mischievous smirk as I enter the spacious entrance hall, with its antique walnut furniture, pendulum clock, dusty chandelier, and macabre paintings of animals on the walls.

I look around curiously, but I have barely taken four steps when Demon grabs me by the arm.

"My rooms are on the first floor."

"How nice for you," I reply curtly.

"For you too."

"No, I'd rather sleep on a couch than with you, you sick killer."

Cameron laughs. "You want to sleep with me? I haven't killed anyone this evening," he suggests. I turn towards him and see Demon pushing him backwards.

"Don't even think of it, Cam!"

I love his jealousy, and even more than that, his urge to protect me. But his instinct is more worrying when people's throats get cut. I rub my bare upper arms. I'm still only wearing an oversized T-shirt and panties.

"I get the message, calm down."

"If you're bored, Cam, go and sleep, or relieve Quest."

Relieve him from what? It's only now I notice that the big shots Lexton and Quest aren't here. Where are they?

Before I can ask, Demon lifts me up, plucking a white rose from a vase as he passes. Standing on dressers in the foyer are two large vases with arrangements of snow-white roses.

"Think you can win me over with a rose?" I smile. Because although I'd never admit it, I do find it flattering.

"I don't have to win you over, you already belong to me."

He carries me to the upper floor via an imposing staircase made of dark wood. The stairs creak dreadfully with each step, until we arrive at the first-floor gallery and Demon sets me down. This is my chance to get away from him, although he's pretty good at carrying me around all over the place like his prey, holding me captive, and hunting me down.

As though he had anticipated I would attempt to flee back to the ground floor, he holds out both his hands. "Do you really still want to play?" What I really want to do is to hit him in the face with the rose he's just used to make me smile. I try to get past his tall frame, first to the left, then to the right.

"Demon."

He's wearing a mask again, but this one only covers his eyes, so I can see the lower half of his face. He reminds me of a bandit, a masked avenger who ignores every law.

"Or we could start round one here. Cam will definitely be up for seeing how obedient you can be second time around."

"Forget it," I hiss, sticking my chin in the air and clinging on to his jumper, under which I can feel his hard muscles. I give him a dark look.

He lifts up my T-shirt unexpectedly, instead of forcing me to my knees. "Leave it," I complain, getting tangled up in my T-shirt as I try to stop him pulling it over my arms. Cameron's going to have a great view of my bare stomach and breasts from down there.

Then I hear the rip of fabric. "Shit, you haven't...!" My T-shirt is cut from my body and the shreds of material fall to the floor. "Are you kidding me?" I protest. I immediately fold my arms over my breasts. Demon takes a step towards me.

"If you don't want the same thing to happen to your panties, take them off yourself."

My eyes get bigger as his smile gets broader. Casually, he rotates the black and silver military blade between his fingers. "Three!"

I shake my head. The thought of the blade moving between my legs, perhaps nicking me... somewhere sensitive, gives me an icy shiver.

I step backwards on the old red carpet. Behind me lies a dark-panelled hallway, with several doors leading off it.

"Listen to him, little one," Cameron calls out. *I'm not taking orders from a madman.*

"Two!"

Instead, I turn and run. Flee into the hallway and frantically try every door handle. Every single door is locked. Why?

Only the last door at the end opens, leading directly to a living area with a heavy, dark-coloured Chesterfield suite, a stone fireplace, and a bed with dark wooden posts. *Shit!*

I've blundered into a trap.

"One," Demon breathes behind me, like a ghost.

I squeal in terror, not having realised he was there. His hand curves around my stomach, moves higher to my right breast, which he massages firmly. Then he pushes me further into the room, where to my right a wall lamp now flickers on, bathing the room in a warm, orange glow.

Before I can free myself he takes me not to the bed, but around a corner to the right where, out of the corner of my eye, I catch sight of a dark terrarium.

There is no time for me to look inside the huge glass tank, as the next moment I find myself in a bathroom.

Demon's fingers twist my left nipple so tightly that it makes me gasp breathlessly, then he licks my neck, and his teeth seek out my right earlobe. His left hand pushes possessively under my panties before his fingers slide into my pussy.

"Come on," I whimper.

I tilt my head back as he touches my clit and then rubs it. It still feels tender from last night but, although I try to resist it, I can't fight the overwhelming sensation he triggers inside of me.

"That's good. Fuck, I missed your little pussy," he moans into my ear as, for just a moment, just one tiny moment, I decide to enjoy how he's making me feel. I feel like I'm about to burst any second, to come, and I can no longer hold back my moans of pleasure. Although I wanted to resist.

The bathroom has a glass shower, a toilet, and a washbasin with a circular mirror. Unlike in the living area, he doesn't switch the light on here. A pleasant, masculine scent pervades the room.

"What is this?" I ask.

"What does it look like?" He releases me for a moment and shuts the door behind him, locking me in the darkness with him. I step backwards over the cool tiles, my feet bare, feeling blindly for the washbasin, as a hand on my hips pulls me towards him.

"Undress me."

"A please would be nice."

"Really? You're right." Suddenly he disappears, only to kneel down in front of me. Cool metal brushes over my right thigh, and before I realise that it's his knife, my panties slip off my right hip. Immediately, the black strip on the other side is cut and my left foot is lifted. I cling onto his hair so as not to lose my balance and then...

"God!" I gasp, as his tongue glides between my legs and pushes inside me without warning. I steady myself on the edge of the washbasin with my left hand, holding onto his thick, silky hair with my other hand. He licks me so hard and hungrily that my clit starts throbbing and I cry out as his finger drives inside me.

"This is... bribery..."

"I love bribes," he replies in his rough, husky voice.

He fucks me with his fingers, stretching me out, as he licks my pearl more and more firmly, holding onto my bum with his other hand.

"Demon," I whimper, as my nipples tingle, my pelvis throbs and I am about to explode into orgasm. My right leg is shaking so much, I'm worried it might give way at any moment, which would make me fall backwards and crack my head on the floor.

"Demon, please... I can't... anymore..." And then I am overwhelmed by a powerful orgasmic wave as he fucks me even deeper with his fingers and briefly bites my clit, so that I am completely beside myself. I writhe as he holds me, groaning loudly, grabbing hold of his hair, and throwing back my head. My knees give way slightly, and Demon moves me over to the bathtub so that I can sit on the edge. But without moving his fingers or tongue off me for even a second. I grab onto the opposite edge of the bath behind me just in time, as he lifts both my feet over his shoulders. And all I want is to feel his cock inside me.

The first climax has barely subsided when a second one follows. He spreads my legs wider, buries his face between my thighs, making me come a second time so deeply and for so long that I'm gasping for air. "Fuck. God, please...," I whimper. "Please stop... or... or fuck me."

He slowly licks my slit, then I can just feel his fingers inside me, but not his tongue on my clit.

"I love it when you beg. Will you undress me now, as I ordered you to?"

Shit. He's managed to get me where he wanted me all along. The bastard.

"Son of a bitch."

He growls menacingly. "You can swear while you do it, it turns me on even more."

Taking his fingers out of me, he lifts me off the edge of the bath with a jolt, and pulls my hands onto his body. "In case you don't know where I'm standing. Right in front of you."

"Stop taking the piss," I reply, gasping, and quickly pull his jumper over his head with my shaking hands, before undoing his belt and letting him push me down onto my knees in front of him. It's more than fair, given he's been kneeling in front of me for the last few minutes. As I undo his trousers he pushes the fingers that were just inside me into my mouth. I taste myself, taste him and then, as he takes his fingers out of my mouth, he shoves his hard cock between my lips. Don't forget to keep undressing me."

I can imagine his grin as he reminds me. With my right hand I take hold of his huge erection, which I can't even close my fingers around. I take him in deeper and more hungrily and suck his cock so firmly and moistly that I immediately hear his deep-throated groans.

"You're driving me wild, little rose." He grabs my hair so that he can push even deeper into me, down my throat, while I pull down his trousers with one hand. He tastes so sinfully good.

Breathing heavily and choking slightly, I take his cock deeper, letting myself be directed by him and aware of him stepping out of his trousers.

Then, just when I think he's going to completely surrender himself to the blow job, he pushes my head back. "As much as I'd like to let you finish the job, there's one thing I want even more."

With these words he lifts me up and carries me to another corner of the room. Only when cold water trickles onto my hair and shoulders do I realise we're standing in the shower.

"Shit, that's cold."

"You'll soon get warm," he growls. Without warning, he handcuffs me.

"What? Why are you tying me up?"

"So you don't fall down," he replies, with the superiority in his voice that turns me on so much. Once he's positioned my wrists above my head, he lifts me up, pushing me against the tiled wall and thrusting into me. He's so unrestrained and impatient that I cry out with lust. He pushes deeper and deeper into me with hard, possessive thrusts, and I wrap my legs around his waist, which is my only support. Teeth bite my nipples, fingers hold my lower jaw, and a thumb inserts itself between my lips. Demon's tongue licks the tingling spot between my breasts, making him moan, then he carries on taking me. He is so hellishly big, so dominant and possessed, that it makes me dizzy. I bite him hard on the thumb, before his lips seek out mine and I return his eager kiss. He carries on fucking me the whole time in the water, which is getting warmer by the second.

I ball my fingers into fists in the handcuffs as he puts his hand firmly around my throat. So firmly that I know he could choke me if he wanted to. This thrilling line between danger and sex just makes me even more uninhibited. I make a gasping sound, about to come at any second. My life is in his hands, and I know what he is prepared to do. That he could end my life with just a few grips or movements. Although he never would.

"Come for me, my queen. And then tell me who you want to feel inside you for the rest of your life."

Groaning, I screw up my eyes under the running water, as he increases his speed, touching a sensitive spot inside me that makes me cry out straightaway.

"Yes! Fuck, yes, I only... want you...!" Blind and completely at his mercy, I bite into his shoulder, overcome with pleasure. Until I taste blood. His blood.

"Fuck, I love it when you leave marks on me, *corazón mío!*" he gasps. I whimper, and my pussy contracts. It closes tightly around his huge cock, which almost tears me as, after three hard thrusts, Demon comes at the same time as me.

Something I've never experienced before. Half-groaning and half-growling, he drives into me one last time, then his cock pulses and he gushes inside me, while I cling tightly to the handcuffs to avoid dislocating my shoulders. I scream his name during the overpowering orgasm, which is so deep, so intense. It goes on and on, until he takes hold of my wrists and frees me from the handcuffs. As they release, I move my hands to his face to kiss him and be *one* with him again, to feel him with every fibre of my being.

Our tongues encircle one another greedily while he's still inside me, I can't get enough of him. At the same time the fingertips of my left hand glide over the irregular contours of his face. It feels like a mesh of scars, like a second layer over his skin.

Gasping, he releases himself from my lips, bites my lower lip again, and slowly sets me down. My fingers slide down his body, glide over his muscular chest, and I cover it with kisses as he holds me upright by my waist. "Fuck, I love you so fucking much, I don't regret for one second scaring you, stalking you, and spying on you."

What did he say? He loves me? The words get under my skin. I didn't expect to hear that. Not so soon, not now.

I take my lips from his chest, put the handcuffs around his neck, and stand on my tiptoes. He's so damn tall that he towers over me by at least a head; he could easily break every bone in my body with his bare hands. He holds my chin, kisses me again hungrily and insistently. "Come with me to Boston. Be my wife, be part of my life, my empire, my family."

I frown, flustered by his unexpected request. "What did you say?"

"I could force you, which would definitely be entertaining, but..." He strokes my damp hair carefully. "It would mean a lot to me if you chose me of your own free will."

Overwhelmed by his words, I struggle for air. I am not sure I have understood him properly. He wants me to go to Boston with him? To marry him?

"Nuria? Say something." It's the first time he's sounded unsure. As though he regrets having spoken his request out loud.

"Give me time," I reply.

"Your answer is no?" There is a disappointed and mistrustful edge to his voice.

"No, it's not a no. But..."

He gives a tortured groan.

"Let me finish."

"It was a mistake to have asked."

"No, it wasn't," I reply. "It was the first step in proving to me that you'll involve me in your decisions, that you won't patronise me or make decisions over my head."

"And this proof of trust still isn't enough to get a straight yes from you."

"Demon," I begin, seeking his shoulders with my hands. "I don't know who you are. I know next to nothing about you.

Moving to a foreign country, a foreign city, it's... it's just too much."

An oppressive and somehow threatening silence settles over the rushing sound of the water. He killed two people just a short while ago, and now he's asking me to go to Boston with him? I am not gullible or stupid, and I will not be driven to a hasty, disastrous decision by sex and this attraction between us. If I go to Boston, it won't be so easy to leave again. I don't know a soul there.

"Give me some time to think about it."

"Do you love me?" he asks suddenly, pushing me back against the tiled wall and blocking me in with his massive body. A hand cups my face. "Do you love me, Nuria, or not? I want an answer."

I can't give him one. It would be a lie if I said no because I feel this attraction towards him, this tingling on my neck, this fluttering between my ribs, this nervousness when he's around me. And I think about him constantly, about the nights, his words, his body, his voice. God, this voice and the way he smells.

Yes, I feel drawn to him like I've never felt drawn to anyone; I'm just not sure whether it's love. And, to be honest, I'm scared of loving him. Loving a man who can be so unpredictable and dangerous makes me afraid. Is this attraction enough to follow him blindly to Boston?

"Nuria," he says, demanding an answer. I breathe deeply in and out, and even though it breaks my heart, I shake my head.

"No, no... I don't love you."

It feels as though the water temperature changes abruptly with the half-lie, if that's what you can call it. From warm to ice-cold.

He snarls, then pulls away from me. "That doesn't mean I don't like you." I try to salvage the situation.

He snorts, as if these words are the last straw. "You like me. The way you liked Mrs Warner, who took the imprisoned children their food at night?" *What?*

"Or the way you liked Zain, who almost got to fuck you, with his hypocrisy?"

"What? No!" I reply. "I would never have slept with him."

"Oh, come on," he growls angrily. "I know what I saw at the window. You hugged him, you kissed him, you let yourself be so taken in by him that I'm not even sure you *like* me." He stresses the word "like", as though it's the worst word he's ever heard.

"Demon." I try to interrupt him and stretch my hands out in the shower, searching for him. But I can't feel him. Where is he?

"Tell me I don't mean anything to you. That will make the decisions I need to make easier."

"Do they finish with you just taking what you want?"

A bitter laugh cuts through the darkness as I find the tap and turn off the water. Demon has obviously left the shower.

"Seems to be the best way for us."

"No! Forget it. If you don't respect me and just treat me like I'm your prey, I'll never come with you to Boston."

"You talk about respect, but you're the one who throws yourself at other men – first Anston, then Zain. Be careful what you say!"

"We're not together, Demon!" I tell it how it is, although things clearly look different in his mind. "I. Am. Not. Your. Property!"

"You belong to me."

"No. Not when I haven't decided I want to belong to you."

"How ridiculous."

"You think that's ridiculous?" I say, and leave the shower, but not without banging my shoulder on the stupid wall. "Shit," I curse, and he approaches me and strokes my shoulder.

"Did you hurt yourself?"

"It's ok. Where was I…"

"In the process of telling me that you belong to me," he replies.

I snort with anger. "I didn't say that."

"Fine, then you don't belong to me, and from now on you're on your own. I'll come by for a fuck, and if someone threatens you with a weapon again or tries to steal your phone, I'll just watch. No problem."

The whole thing sounds really off when he says it like that. "I'm not just fucking you."

"Apparently you are. Nice to know I'm good enough for your bed, princess."

"You're way off! I'm not one of those women who just shags a man without feeling anything."

"Hmm." He is very close to my face. "That begs the question of what you're currently feeling. Do you sleep with everyone you *like*?"

God, he's so good at twisting everything I say.

"Do you know what, fuck you! I'm not talking about this crap with you." I dodge away from him, to the right, as a hand towel is thrown at my head. "You can dry yourself for sure, because fuck buddies don't do that."

"You can be really unpleasant."

"You're only noticing that now?" he says mockingly, before tearing open the bathroom door and going into the illuminated living area. With just a hand towel around his hips, I can see his muscular back, including my scratches from last night and his snake tattoo. His dark, wet hair is slicked back. My moment. He's not wearing a mask.

I quickly let the towel drop, then run towards him stark naked. At the same moment I am grabbed by the neck. "Where are you going so fast?" Cameron asks. Was he listening to us? How long has he been here?

"Pack her things, Cam, my flower is coming with us tomorrow."

"No!" I reply. "I haven't decided yet."

Demon walks over to his bed and then disappears into the adjoining room on the right.

"Why are you doing this to him?" Cameron asks, turning to me.

"I'm not doing anything to him," I whisper. "He needs to give me time."

"Time?" Cameron raises his dark brows. "Time for what? You love him, you are just as obsessed with him as he is with you. Why do you need time?"

"Because I don't know anything about him."

"Must you know? Isn't love enough?" I wasn't expecting this question from him, of all people. "What do we know about you? Not a great deal, either, but he still wants to bring you into his empire, offer you his protection, his loyalty and love. Isn't that a fair deal, in exchange for coming to Boston?"

It sounds as though I'm permanently in danger and in need of protection. Although...

Because I know when you're lying, my darling.

The man who has spoken these words in my nightmares is dangerous, and I know he is looking for me.

I lower my eyes thoughtfully. "It's not that easy."

"Then I'll make it easy for you," Demon says suddenly, from behind me. Fuck, how does he do that every time, move through the room so silently that I never know where he is?

"You come to Boston and be my wife." Is he mad? As I look over my shoulder, horrified, I see him wearing a fresh black mask which only covers half his face. "Tell Quest and the others in Boston. I want a big reception."

"What's the matter with you, Demon, or rather Wylder? I'm not coming with you voluntarily."

"But you will."

"No!" Without signaling my intention, I slap him. And this time he doesn't see it coming. His face flies to the side, his mouth open in astonishment. "I'm not coming with you if you don't give me any time. I certainly won't be your wife if you make the decision without consulting me." Doesn't he understand?! Do I have to express myself more clearly so that he finally understands that he doesn't get to decide what happens in my life!

Cameron inhales sharply. I'm expecting Demon to fly at

me at any moment, to grab me by the throat and shove me against the wall. But his lips form a nonchalant grin. "Hit me, curse me, hate me if you like, my rose, my decision won't change. And there's one thing you'll never get from me," he says ominously, his face lowered, "I'll never hit a woman. That's exactly what I saw in your eyes, the fear that I might ram my fist into your face."

I wasn't expecting this. "Time for bed. Today's going to be a tough one."

Without any warning, he and Cameron lift me up and carry me over to the bed, my hair wet, naked and squirming. "Boys, this is..."

"Tie her tightly to the bed. I have a suspicion she's either going to drive a knife into my heart or try to escape."

"You're absolutely right there," I growl, writhing like mad on the bed and hitting Cameron's hands as they put handcuffs on my wrists. Demon helps him secure me on the bed and I cry out angrily. "Our first night sharing a bed, my rose. This is exactly how I imagined it," he mocks as he looks down at me, standing next to Cameron. I immediately draw my knees together so that they can't glimpse between my thighs.

"You pigs."

"I'm starting to understand what it is you love about her," Cameron remarks, looking at me lasciviously. "She's got a lot of bite."

My eyes wander briefly to the place where I sank my teeth into Demon's shoulder.

"Indeed. Her little teeth are not without charm," Demon agrees.

CHAPTER 29

Nuria

Behind every mask
hides a secret.
So many people never take off their masks
and play a role their whole lives.

Demon turns to me, also naked, to stroke my face. Cameron has gone, and I am frantically trying to work out how to get out of the handcuffs.

"You won't have nightmares tonight," Demon assures me.

"Because now I don't need to shut my eyes to have a nightmare?" I provoke him.

He huffs, then rolls over to me, making me bend my legs so his hips can slide between my thighs.

"I am fairly sure there's someone out there you're even more afraid of than me. Tell me his name and I'll take care of it."

I swallow hard. In the meantime, he switches off the light, filling the room with pale moonlight.

"Tell me the name of the person you're so afraid of."

"It's... it's not that easy," I tell him.

He pushes his pelvis slowly back and forth between my legs. "Why not?"

"Because I don't know who he is." He lowers his face, irritated by my answer. "He's a shadow in my memory, intangible and non-existent at the same time." I'm not even sure whether the person I dream about really exists. Or whether they're a figment of my imagination.

"You don't know who the person is?"

Sighing, I shake my head. "I woke up from a coma about a year ago. It was a terrible time, because..." Lost in thought, I lick my lips. "Because I didn't even know who I am, what my name is, where I come from."

Demon's face comes closer to me, and I feel his cock getting bigger. "Where were you for the three years before that?"

"No idea. I've asked myself so often and done thousands of things to try and make myself remember. I've tried hypnosis, conversations with my family and friends, with a therapist. Even my family don't know where I was, because I... because I ran away from home when I was seventeen, after a big argument. I was planning to go to my grandma and... after that all I can remember is the hospital room in Mexico where I woke up, and the doctors explaining to me that I'd been in a coma for six months. Some tourists found me lying on the beach, badly injured."

Perhaps that's why I dream about the cliff, because I fell from one. Demon's lips open and then close again.

"You had an accident that caused amnesia. Is that what you're telling me?"

"Yes. That's all I know. No one who was interviewed on the shore where I was found unconscious saw what happened. The police put out a call for witnesses but no one came forward. After weeks of searching through the missing persons reports, the police came across my parents. They contacted my family, who flew to Mexico to pick me up."

Demon looks kind of sceptical, as though he doesn't believe what I'm telling him, as though I'm lying to him. He looks into my eyes for a long time, moves his thumb over my lower lip, and straightens up over me.

"You have no idea what happened in the three years prior to your amnesia?"

"I told you. No. But..."

"But what?"

Should I really tell him about it?

"But the dark figure in my dreams is slowly taking on a face. It sounds crazy, but I saw it earlier when Mr Monair attacked me."

"What does it look like?" he asks.

"A man with dark blond hair, and dark eyes, such dark black eyes that look creepy, evil. And he was wearing a dark shirt and a white suit."

I bend my fingers inside the handcuffs until they brush the lever and I realise the cuffs haven't been locked.

So that Demon doesn't notice his mistake, I move towards him, lifting my pelvis. "I'll know more soon, I feel it. More and more memories are coming back." Admittedly only in fragments, but the blockage in my head is beginning to break down, even if I'm not sure I really want to know what is going to be revealed.

I brush my lips sensuously against the right corner of Demon's mouth, and he reacts immediately to my gentle kiss, tenderly taking my lower lip between his teeth. "We'll find out who's stalking you at night."

"We will," I agree, rubbing myself against his erection. Our tongues circle one another hungrily, the speed of the kiss increases rapidly, becoming more and more unrestrained, wilder and more passionate. God, he's such a good kisser. He supports himself above me on his muscular arms until he can feel that I'm ready for him. And then he enters me, sucks my right nipple and pushes deep inside me. After three thrusts he's completely inside me, and this time the sex isn't brutal, rough and demanding, it's passionate and intense.

I gaze into his shaded eyes the whole time, while he takes me, kisses me, then straightens up between my legs to feel me even more deeply. He looks down at himself, watching his erection enter me faster and faster. Meanwhile, my mind goes crazy. Because even if I hate it, every new touch, every kiss, every night together, breaks down the barriers I have put up to stop myself falling in love with this man.

Panting and moaning, I writhe with desire underneath him as he moistens his thumb and rubs my aroused clit. He circles my pearl more and more firmly as he thrusts into me. Shaking and moaning, I climax, as he increases the pace, his erection pulses, and he pours into me with a hot, dark murmur. Only to cloud my mind with kisses afterwards.

I act as though I'm completely exhausted, which isn't difficult, until he lies down beside me and pulls me onto his chest. After a quarter of an hour his fingers, which had been stroking my back, slide off me, and his breathing becomes even.

I wait patiently for another twenty minutes, carefully tapping his watch to read the time on it.

Although I feel really bad for pulling this stunt, I free myself from the handcuffs and carefully stand up next to the bed. Demon is lying on his back, the sheet barely over his hips, breathing through parted lips, which are visible in spite of the mask. He looks so good in the dark. So perfect. Presumably, like me, he has barely slept in the last two days.

I retreat from the room. I slip quietly through the unlocked door and run naked along the hallway. It's completely dark downstairs, no sign of Cameron. I hope Quest and Lexton aren't here to ambush me and drag me to their boss. The punishment would certainly be anything but gentle.

Luckily for me there is a black bomber jacket hanging on the coat rack downstairs. It's so big it just about covers my bottom. I find a pair of white Adidas trainers which are over four sizes too big for me. Still, any shoes are better than no shoes. Then I search through the remaining jackets and the chest of drawers looking for keys. I can't get away from here on foot. My pulse is racing like crazy as I envisage Demon appearing at the railing on the balcony at any moment.

I can hardly believe my luck when I find the key to Demon's Kawasaki. I head to the kitchen, as the front door is bound to be alarmed and under video surveillance. I may already be being filmed now, although I don't seem to have set off any alarm. Arriving in the kitchen, where I already know my way around, I open the window, get up onto the table where I sat with Quest only this morning, and climb out.

There's a drop of around 1.5 metres and I let myself fall, losing my right shoe in the process and staggering to my feet. *Fuck.* I hurriedly collect the shoe from the lawn, slip it on, and retie the laces. Then I look around, run around the building, and find the black racing bike next to the Escalade.

My plan is to go back to the Monairs' estate, pack my passport, phone and clothes, and then ride to Anston. He flies in around three hours. And if there's still a ticket to Barcelona, I'll book it. There's nothing keeping me in Australia anymore. Nothing at all.

An electrifying vibration passes through my body as I sit on the black racer, put the key in the ignition and start the engine. It's been a hell of a long time since I rode a motorbike.

I might not have a helmet, but the Monairs' property is less than ten miles away. I pull the jacket over my backside so it doesn't ride up, then pull away and accelerate.

In the left side-mirror I see someone looking out of the window on the first floor. *Demon.* He's awake. Fuck! If he catches me, I'm finished!

I immediately open the throttle and race along the drive of the old country house and down to the coast road. I don't want to imagine how much Demon is seething with anger right now.

Okay, I can't go to the Monairs' property. Demon will find me there straight away. Besides which, it will presumably be crawling with police, and I won't be able to get away. I only have a slight head start, and the option of going directly to the airport and hoping Anston will help me.

He has to help me get my passport, otherwise I won't be able to leave Australia any time soon.

That's why I decide to change course and ride along the road to Brisbane, towards the airport. My heart is pounding so fast with nerves that I feel as though I'm going to pass out any second. The wind blasts my face cruelly, making tears well up in my eyes. I'm probably breaking at least ten rules right now. Driving without a licence, without a helmet, without a seatbelt.

I couldn't care less! I have to get to the airport. It's so early that there are hardly any cars on the road, although things are somewhat busier at the airport. I park the black motorbike securely in a car park, jump off the seat and shove the keys in the pocket of the bomber jacket, which I keep tugging down to make sure no one can see my backside.

Sniffing, unkempt, and looking a complete state, I enter the glass building, looking for the departure boards. I see the flight to Barcelona via Shanghai, which boards at 6:20 a.m. at gate 48.

It's 4:40 a.m. That means Anston should be arriving at the airport any minute now. I wait by the luggage counters, hoping to see him among the other travellers. *Please, please, please, don't have gone through security yet. I can't have missed you.*

Anson isn't normally someone who arrives early for anything. On the contrary, he leaves everything until the last minute, so hopefully he'll do that today too.

I pace up and down restlessly in front of the counters, drawing suspicious looks from other passengers and airline employees. A woman marching through the airport hall with bare legs, oversized shoes, and a bomber jacket must be a rare sight.

Then a taxi finally arrives and a man with dark blonde hair gets out, someone who looks very like Anston. *Finally!*

I chew my lower lip nervously and wait for him to enter the airport building. But strangely, more men get out of the dark minivan, as the taxi driver opens the boot to unload the luggage.

There are at least two more people who look around briefly before entering the glass hall. In the same moment I am suddenly grabbed on both sides by two guys I didn't see coming.

"Hey!" I exclaim, looking at the men, who are wearing

suits and headsets and who are leading me towards the exit. "What's going on?" Has Demon found me this quickly?

But they don't answer, and drag me over to Anston and the other men. *Damn it! What the hell is going on here?*

"Leave me alone," I complain, kicking my legs and losing the blasted shoes. Other passengers look on but don't get involved. Presumably because they think I am being removed by airport security. But why? I haven't done anything.

The two giants stop when they reach the revolving electric door. I carry on pulling at their hands, squirming wildly, and cursing, until a man in a white suit appears in front of me, with Anston and another man standing behind him, all in their early thirties.

"Hello, Rinora. I'm very pleased to have found you at last."

My stomach turns as I look at Anston, who is regarding me indifferently, then at the man in the white suit. No. It can't be. Impossible.

It's him. The man from my nightmares. He has the dark eyes, dark blonde slicked-back hair, and eyebrows with two stripes shaved out of them.

I still can't think of his name. He looks into my eyes and the corners of his mouth twitch. "You have no idea who's standing in front of you, right?" he mocks. "Don't worry, it'll soon come back to you, my darling."

I swallow hard. "Anston, what's going on?"

"Anston?" The dark blonde man turns to Ans. "Does she mean you?" *Is that not his name?*

Anston shrugs his shoulders, bored. "I couldn't think of a crappier name."

The blonde man and the other man behind him, his dark hair tied back, laugh.

"Well, good. We've got what we want. Where do the private jets fly from in this airport?"

What?

"Out front there", says the man to my right. A baggage trolley holding the striking turquoise suitcase belonging to

Anston – or whatever his name is – is being rolled through the revolving door.

Before I realise they intend to take me with them, I am being carried through the airport. "Forget it. No way. I'm not flying."

"No one asked you," says the dark-haired man, who is now walking alongside the monkeys as they manoeuvre me through the glass hall like a piece of furniture.

"Hel..." I start to scream, but that moment my mouth is covered.

"Shut your mouth and don't make a scene, unless you want me to fly you back trussed up like a parcel." *What does back mean? Where is he flying to?*

I bite the fingers over my mouth, trying to fight my way out, kicking, screaming and tearing at their arms. Someone will help me, someone has to help me! "Help! Help!" I scream.

Then I feel a scratch in my right upper arm. I don't actually see it happen, but I am injected with the contents of a syringe that very quickly makes my tongue feel numb and heavy and makes it a struggle to keep my eyes open.

Please no... No. I regret not having stayed in bed with Demon. I want to go back. Back to him.

The last thing I see is the zip of the bomber jacket being pulled down. Then someone exclaiming: "He's carved the Dykats symbol into her!"

"What's the problem? You can just tattoo her or mark her with the Zetos sign in another, much more important spot."

Zetos...

Then everything goes black, and I am torn out of the darkness and into my worst dreams.

And in conclusion...

huge thanks to every reader who has taken an interest in Nuria and Demon's story. I hope the first volume thrilled you? In the sequel, you'll find out more about Nuria's and Demon's past. Some parts will be even more exciting and sensual than this first volume.

I am especially excited, as this is my first dark romance title to appear with the brilliant everlove publishing house. This is a milestone for me and a great honour. It would never have been possible without my wonderful agent, Carsten Polzin.

Thank you, Carsten, for believing in my dark stories, even before the trend took off.

My next thank-you goes to my wonderful editor, Anica Müller. Thank you for your amazing suggestions, your patience, and your support. I'm already looking forward to getting stuck in to the next volume.

Last but not least, I would like to thank my test readers, Jule and Gaby. Nothing escapes your eagle eyes. It's always so important to me, knowing you've been by my side for so many years. You are indispensable to me.

Stay vigilant. Even shadows have eyes.

Yours, D.C. Odesza

CONTENT NOTE

This book contains scenes and descriptions that may trigger traumatic memories in some people.

Please decide for yourself whether you wish to deal with the following topics emotionally:

Stalking, snake phobia, physical and psychological violence, murder, abuse, domestic abuse, torture, kidnapping, weapons, manipulation, alcohol and drug use, trauma, bondage, blackmail, ambiguity about consent, paraphilia, death.

Please read this book only if you feel emotionally prepared to engage with its content.

If you are currently facing these or other challenges, remember that free and confidential support is available at any time. Helplines exist in every country, and reaching out for help is a sign of strength. Please don't hesitate to seek support if you need it.

Your *everlove*-Team

What awaits you in the second volume of the dark romance series by bestselling author D.C. Odesza ...

cover images reserved

D.C. Odesza

Beloved Villain – You can't stay away from me (English Edition)

novel

Translated by S. Marshall
everlove, 316 pages
ISBN 978-3-492-06604-4

Nuria wants to continue to live out her passion for the mysterious stalker who has followed her to Australia and appears in her room at night. His nocturnal visits become a beloved taboo full of temptation for Nuria. But then a dark figure from her past reappears and wants to win Nuria over. She is torn between the two men, one more dangerous than the other and both enemies to the core. Nuria must decide who she will give herself to and trust.

everlove by PIPER

Reading samples, e-books and more www.everlove-verlag.de